Take the Shot

BY:

C. M. CONNEY

Published by
Ace Lyon Books
August 2017

Ace Lyon

Published by
Ace Lyon Books
Acelyonbooks.com
First Edition
Cover Design by S. M. Savoy
C. M. Conney Take the Shot
ISBN 978-1-947122-32-1

Dedication

TO my son, Cody, thank you for my beautiful new daughter. I hope you and Lauren always take the shot and follow your dreams.

CONTENTS

Take the Shot

ONE

◆

RONNY

Ronny placed his hands on his knees and breathed hard for a moment before straightening to admire the view.

Covered with scrub brush and scraggly pines, the steep hillside he'd just run up led to a darkly forested swath of ground that separated the city from Balboa Park. Behind him, the roof of the San Diego Nature Museum peeked from a stand of fir trees. In the distance, the harbor reflected sunlight in a glittering display. The city sprawled to either side, bustling with activity.

One of his favorite places to run, Balboa Park offered a variety of terrain and serene surroundings with great vistas. Mostly, he ignored the trails, running straight across country. Sometimes, he carried a full pack, but not today. Today, he ran for the joy of it, wearing sneakers and shorts instead of combat boots and pants.

After taking another moment to admire the spectacular view, he turned and jogged down the path. Hikers nodded greetings, and he passed two other joggers both wearing designer jogging gear with mp3 players on their shoulders, running in their own worlds. He slowed before he reached the main trail and stepped off the path to stretch.

A smile lit his face as a girl appeared. Dressed exactly like him down to the brand of sneakers, gray shorts, and white, sweat-stained T-shirt, sweat trickled across her tan face. She ran full speed up the steep hill, cutting through the low underbrush with blithe disregard for scratches, jumping obstacles in her path. When she reached the top, she paused and placed her hands on her knees, the posture so like his, it made Ronny chuckle.

The girl peered at him from startlingly blue eyes. Her gaze traveled him, and she smiled, blushing slightly when she met his eyes.

His smile widened.

Without a word, she ran her hands through her short, black, sweat-soaked hair and ran down the path.

Ronny sighed as he stared after her. "I should go see Dawn," he muttered, then frowned.

His wife was getting serious with his teammate Tom, and he felt like a shit for even contemplating sleeping with her. An ironic smile crossed his face that he felt guilty for considering having sex with his wife. Dawn wouldn't turn him down, but she wouldn't be happy about it either. A woman of her word, she took their bargain seriously. He did too, but her friendship meant more to him than a quick lay.

Aggravated, he gazed after the runner, but long tanned legs had taken her from sight quickly.

"Damn."

For another moment, he stared at the bend in the path, contemplating chasing her before glancing at his watch and regretfully turning away. He needed to find a new girlfriend. Maybe it was time for he and Dawn to divorce. Friends with benefits was great for a while, but he wanted something more; a real relationship like JT and Charlene had.

Thoughts of his boss had him quickening his step. If he wanted to beat rush-hour traffic, he had to leave now.

Traffic over the bridge to Coronado could be a nightmare, and if he timed it wrong, he'd be late for the meeting at JT's house.

He paused in the parking lot where he'd left the truck he'd borrowed from his roommate. Parked two cars away from him, June Reeves struggled with a large picnic basket. Dressed in casual clothes, Ronny almost hadn't recognized her so used to seeing her in formal wear on the admiral's arm. In jeans and a pink blouse with her graying blond hair curling loosely around her face, she appeared years younger.

"Ma'am." Ronny glanced at his watch and grimaced, then approached the older woman with a smile and gestured to the large basket she was trying to withdraw from her trunk. "Could I give you a hand?"

He could rush his shower and skimp his refresher on the maps.

The woman turned and smiled, her gaze traveling Ronny as she stepped back. "Thank you."

Ronny freed the basket from the trunk. Glass

clinked softly, and he winced, hoping he hadn't broken anything. "I'd be happy to bring this to the picnic area for you."

"No need but thank you." She reached out a manicured hand to take the basket. "It isn't heavy, just awkward to maneuver."

Ronny handed her the picnic basket and inclined his head. "It's a lovely day for a picnic. I just came from the upper trail and the bluebells are in bloom. If you walk to the top, you can see the harbor today. Maybe even catch sight of your husband as he sees the *Theodore Roosevelt* off."

June paled and took a step back. "I'm sorry; do we know each other?"

"Pardon me, Ma'am. No, we don't. I work for your husband."

"My husband?" June said faintly.

"Indirectly. Petty Officer Ronald Mitland at your service. I've seen you on base with him. I didn't intend to be forward." Ronny bit back a sigh and stopped himself from glancing again at his watch. He'd meant to be helpful and instead he'd frightened her. She probably thought he was some kind of stalker dude now.

"Oh." She tittered and clasped the basket with both hands. "I didn't realize you were a sailor. Though I suppose the haircut should've given you away."

Ronny ran a hand over his crew cut brown hair and smiled.

"Well, thanks for the help." She scurried away, peering over her shoulder once before disappearing around the curve of the path.

Ronny stared after her a moment before jumping in

the truck. Thoughts of the dark-haired girl distracted him all the way back to base. Tanned muscled limbs and bright blue eyes, he wanted to see up close and personal, ran through his mind all the way home. He hoped he bumped into her again while running.

His roommates Tom and Lee didn't glance up from the papers spread on the table when Ronny entered the apartment and dropped the truck keys into the bowl on the table. Lee had taken Dan's old room, moving in at the same time as Ronny. On base housing was always in demand and Ronny was grateful they'd let him take Juan's room, although he sometimes felt bad about replacing Juan so completely, first taking his position as Dan's spotter on the team, then his bedroom.

Four men shared the living space. Each had their own bedrooms and split two baths. A couch and two matching recliners sat before a large screen television off-center in the living room to make room for their weight set and a treadmill. A large picture window let late afternoon sunlight illuminate the dining table.

Located on the fourth floor, their apartment had a great view of the base and Fiddler's Cove Marina.

"Thanks for letting me borrow the truck. Are those the new maps?" He peered over Tom's shoulder.

Tom nodded absently and slid a closed folder to the side, tapping it with one finger. "Got the newest reports right here." He glanced at Ronny, a troubled frown on his face. "This has me nervous. Two teams lost so far with no sign or word from either."

Tom leafed through the reports and handed a page to Ronny. "Darmin wants us to get ready. He thinks we'll be sent in, and soon, to find them. Make yourself familiar with the missing personnel. Concentrate on distinguishing features. JT is getting us a few DNA kits. The heat there will make physical IDs impossible."

"You think they're dead, then?"

"I think the chances are really good they are," Tom said unhappily.

He leaned back in the chair and stretched. Muscles rippled under his ebony skin. Two inches taller than Ronny at six-foot-three, Tom outweighed him by a good fifty pounds of pure muscle.

Ronny grabbed the files and leafed through them. Most of the information was familiar to him. New maps covered the table. Their roommate Squirrel joined them a few minutes later. His long, messy, brown hair was caught in a quick ponytail and his cheeks were unshaven, giving him a heavy five o'clock shadow. He rubbed his eyes and yawned as he flopped into the seat beside Lee.

"Why didn't you wake me?" Without waiting for a reply, he grabbed the folder and glanced through it. "Shit, no new intel. I was hoping they'd have a lead by now."

Ronny slid the new map to Squirrel. "Narrowed it down a bit, but that's some rough country. The natives are unfriendly and obviously prepared for us. Granted, the first two teams weren't SEALs, but still..."

Squirrel nodded, his gaze intent on the picture. A tanned finger stabbed the map. "Here's where I'd look. The closest source of water and the densest population. I'm letting my beard grow out. We'll need to get in there and observe."

"No one is getting in there unnoticed. Population

three hundred or so. Those fuckers all know each other. A new face will be noticed," Ronny said

Squirrel snorted. "I'm not walking in and ringing the doorbell, dumbass."

Tom laughed as Ronny frowned.

"Look, kid, sorry." Squirrel stood and slapped Ronny on the back. "By all means, tell us if you think we're screwing up. New doesn't mean stupid. Stay with Dan and do your job. Don't pull any dumb shit, no heroics, listen to Dan. He's been out country and knows what he's doing."

Squirrel pointed to the map. "I go in wearing a robe and headscarf like theirs but stay way back. The goal is to run into no one, but if I'm seen, a beard makes me blend, and a real one is easier to manage than a fake. The fakes itch and sweat makes the glue fail. Dan will have my back, and you'll have his."

Ronny nodded. The idea of a mission excited him. Two years of training to get here and he was ready.

———————◆———————

"Oh boy," Ronny murmured when he spied Commander Darmin's SUV parked before JT's house.

Tom snickered as Ronny opened the folder and scanned the pages.

"Relax, this is informal, not a test. Darmin shows up once in a while. He remembers being one of us. Treat him like anyone else."

Ronny hid a grimace and nodded. Being the new guy sucked. Not only replacing Juan, who the guys spoke of with great affection, but the constant corrections and criticism rankled. He wasn't completely green; he'd served two years before going for SEAL training. Although to be fair, his teammates meant well and were nice about it.

JT's wife, Charlene, greeted him with a hug which he returned, being careful to keep it brief, resisting the urge to savor the experience. Delightfully voluptuous, Charlene was a treat to hug.

The team's sniper, Dan, greeted him with a raised beer can. Ronny grabbed a beer from the refrigerator and sat beside him on the couch in Charlene's immaculate living room. A small, fluffy, orange kitten jumped into Dan's lap, narrowing golden eyes at Ronny.

"Talked Charlene into taking one of the little demons off your hands?" Ronny tentatively rubbed the cat's head. The kitten tilted its chin and began to purr. Reassured by its purr, he petted the kitten more aggressively. "Or has your wife tamed them all?"

Dan snorted and ran a finger down the length of the small cat's back. The purr deepened.

"No, she hasn't. Angie gave Charlene the sweetest one. We still have two left. I admit, they're cute little buggers, but the remaining two take after their father. I pity whoever gets them."

Ronny laughed. "You better hope the baby takes after the mother if you think kittens are trouble."

Dan beamed. "Two more months and we can't wait."

Ronny punched his shoulder and grinned.

Their teammate Lee flopped to the floor beside Keith and grabbed the bowl of potato chips. "How's Ang taking the new training?"

"Fine," Dan said as he reached for the chips. "Man, these are good. Chips are banned from our house, too much salt." He ate a big handful before continuing. "Angie's okay with me deploying. Agent Wisniewski keeps us informed on gossip in Chicago. We're being careful, but none of Vincent's guys are left." Dan shrugged and grabbed another handful of chips. "Ang knows we'll likely be called out soon to handle this, and while I wouldn't say she's happy about my traveling to Pakistan, she isn't freaking out either."

"Good," JT said and plucked the kitten from Dan's lap. His hand dwarfed the small cat as he cradled it against his shoulder. "Char promises to keep an eye on your wife and report if she thinks there's a problem. The men on base will be keeping an eye out too; she'll be well protected." His brown eyes scrutinized his men. "When we go, keep your head in the game. Leave home worries here. If you can't commit, stay behind."

"Aye, aye, sir," they mumbled.

JT nodded, sat in the brown leather recliner, and kicked his feet up. The kitten stretched across his chest. Commander Darmin entered from the kitchen followed by Charlene. She made sure everyone had a drink and placed a tray of sandwiches on the coffee table. After kissing her husband's cheek, she headed back to the kitchen.

Darmin took a sandwich and gestured with the hand holding the beer can to a map tacked on the wall behind him. Used for informal meetings all the time, JT stored a corkboard behind his large screen television.

Darmin began speaking between bites. "Two five-men teams have been lost in this area." He pointed with his sandwich to a red circle on the map of northwestern Pakistan. "Because of the sudden and permanent nature of the disappearances, we believe the occurrences are manmade. The first group was sent in to determine if Alfarsi was there. The second group was sent to find the first. While not SEALs, both groups were well trained and informed of the dangers in the area."

Darmin's mustard stained finger traced the terrain. "The Sulaiman Mountains and Obasta Tsukai are sparsely populated. The chances of just running into someone able to take them out is so small as to be nonexistent. Our men were supposed to go cross country and observe from a distance. The worry now is Al-Jadr have some sort of alarm system in those hills. Somehow, they knew where the men were."

"We're sure it wasn't a leak on our end?" JT asked.

"Possible, but unlikely. Only Admiral Reeves knew where he was sending them. The helicopter that dropped them off received sealed orders in the air. It's much more likely they were apprehended at the village. One group disappearing could be explained as bad judgment, carelessness, or even bad luck, but two... no, the second group entered in a different area knowing the first disappeared and would've been alert for unforeseen dangers. That both disappeared without a word... at first, we thought comms were down in the area, now... we don't know."

Darmin paused and finished his beer. "Diplomatic means are still being pursued, but I expect to send a team in. Finish the com classes and brush up on anti-surveillance techniques. If they do have something new, we not only want to spot it before it spots us, but we want a full report on it."

Darmin ran a hand through his short, gray hair. "That's our priority. Get us intel. Yes, we'll retrieve our men, but find out how they're doing it. The original mission is a class one priority. Locating Alfarsi is vital for the safety of the United States. The man is dangerous. Under his guidance, Al-Jadr has grown much more aggressive. Too many attacks have been planned. And while we've stopped them, the chance is too great we miss one. The CIA will be working with us on this. So far two of their operatives have gone missing. Operatives they thought firmly entrenched. One of which reported a new cipher before disappearing."

"Just a new code or— "

Darmin cut JT off. "A new code and the name of the man who invented it. Doctor Joshua Greer, MIT graduate. Brilliant, but unstable with two arrests. One for breaking and entering and destruction of property. The other for illegal wire taping. He's disappeared. The CIA think he's working with Komar Alfarsi, the leader of Al-Jadr. Greer is a sexist, anti-government nut. Al-Jadr's rhetoric would be easy for the doctor to swallow.

"The doctor is convinced women in the workforce get special treatment and are holding him back. Before he disappeared, he posted a long rant on the inequality and danger of, as he calls it, the injustice of women taking credit for men's work. The CIA is sure both arrests were inspired by Alfarsi. So, we have a home-grown terrorist to deal with. A man with knowledge, potentially devising communications for the enemy."

Ronny sighed in disgust. Why would anyone help men who cut the heads off people who disagreed with them and strapped bombs to themselves to blow up innocent civilians?

JT headed into the kitchen, returning with

Charlene and more beer as the men talked over their ideas and plans.

JT pulled Ronny aside as the group began to break up for the night. "Commander Darmin asked me to deliver this to Reeves." He handed Ronny a small, wrapped box. "Drop it off on the way to class tomorrow. Don't forget. If Darmin's birthday gift is late to the admiral, we'll never hear the end of it."

Ronny tucked the small box in his pocket, gave JT a two-fingered salute, thanked Charlene again, and jumped in the passenger seat of Tom's truck.

As the new guy, all such chores fell to him. He didn't mind, they were all the new guy once. Besides, it wasn't out of his way at all. Traffic over the bridge from Coronado to San Diego Base could be slow, but he had to go there anyway for his classes.

When he'd dreamed of becoming a Navy SEAL, he'd never envisioned the amount of classwork and study needed. The team never stopped learning something new or reviewing what they'd already learned. He swore he could disarm any bomb with his eyes closed and distinguish different landmines by the clicks and whirs of activation. Still, study never hurt.

Tom snorted as Ronny used the flashlight on his cell phone to examine the small map again.

TWO

---◆---

PRACTICE

A sharp blat woke him. Rain hissed against the window in his dark bedroom. The pager on his nightstand vibrated against the glass top. Ronny snatched it as he fumbled for the light switch. Before he checked the number, he realized it would be Dan.

As Dan's spotter, it was Ronny's job to warn of changes that could affect the shot. Weather was a big part of that. The two men practiced in every condition they could find or manufacture.

Ronny had thought he was a good shot until he'd seen Dan shoot. Hand-eye coordination coupled with muscle memory let Dan fire as the call left Ronny's lips. If Ronny called the shot correctly, Dan never missed, and he was fast, the best sniper Ronny had ever seen.

The first time he saw Dan shoot he thought his job was superfluous, but with Ronny watching for misses, and picking the next target, Dan improved his speed dramatically.

Ronny threw on his uniform and stamped his feet into boots as he grabbed his bag. He scribbled a note and grabbed Tom's truck keys from the bowl. Tom wouldn't mind. The forecast had called for rain and Tom knew they'd planned to practice. Dan's skill kept everyone alive, and the entire team helped set up practices for them.

He promised himself to car hunt soon. Dawn had taken his clunker when her car shit the bed. Before he bought a new car, he needed to make sure she had a safer one. Tom had offered Dawn his truck, but she preferred to drive a car. A grimace crossed his face. He kept putting off the car search because of the awkwardness of the conversation with Tom. He should talk to him about his plans before doing anything with or for Dawn, but they both found those conversations awkward.

———◆———

At the range, Ronny greeted Dan with a grin. Mostly deserted, only a few early birds, or maybe night owls, took shots in the distance on the end of the line.

"We have this entire side for two hours," Dan said, gesturing to their left. "I want to practice some separated shots. Get to the left about halfway between me and my targets." He handed Ronny a regulation headset.

Ronny took the headset, pulled his ghillie suit from the bag, and put it on. Meant to hide him in the brush, fake leaves and strips of fabric covered the back and sides of the green, camouflaged suit. He slung his M151 spotting scope and FN SCAR rifle over his shoulder and headed out. While the suit wasn't necessary for stealth on the range, it helped to wear it to accustom himself to the odd flutters the dangling scraps of fabric made in his peripheral vision.

The scope wasn't heavy but holding anything up to eye level for hours could be tiring. A tripod attached to the scope with a simple connection, but they often practiced without it.

Ronny called out shots, switching randomly on the marked targets. Usually, he lay two feet behind Dan on his right and watched the vapor trail of Dan's shots from there.

At two hundred yards away, and off to the side, it was much harder to track the path of the bullet. Not that Dan needed much tracking. Ninety percent of his shots hit where he intended. The last ten percent were always near misses. It was Ronny's job to inform Dan on where the misses hit and call the corrections.

The farthest targets sat at two thousand feet. Two were of a man standing, one a man crouching. Bands of color lined the target for ease of marking where shots hit, Ronny could call for a 'colored' shot. A total of twenty-five targets lined the hillside, the closest twenty feet from Dan's position.

Light wind gusted rain across the night vision adapter screwed onto the front of Ronny's scope despite the gloved hand he angled over it. Cool water trickled down his neck, making him shrug irritably. The small gesture annoyed him even more. In the field, remaining motionless could be the difference between life and death.

In as soft a voice as he could manage he began calling out targets. Neither he nor Dan needed sniper cards to keep track of windage and elevation, both could do the math in their heads.

For 'realism' he added detail on the assailant. "Man with a rifle at two o'clock. Wind at three miles per hour, five MOA. Two clicks up, one point four mils."

The roar of Dan's fifty-caliber answered him less than three seconds later. A hole now covered the heart of the target in Ronny's sights.

"Man with a hostage. Eight o'clock, four clicks up, twelve degrees south, hostage at center of mass."

Another shot echoed across the hillside and the target's head disintegrated. Ronny grinned and called out further targets in a long string.

The rain softened as the sun rose. Ronny placed the night vision attachment on the ground beside him as sunrise lit the sky a soft gray that changed to bright orange with startling suddenness. A glance at his watch showed only a few minutes remained before this course opened to others. The rain turned to mist. A light fog, barely more than wisps of cloud, rose from the ground.

Night vision tinted the world green, shrouding the edges in darkness, but the mist and fog gave the illusion of movement and distracted the eye.

"Orange, one thousand five hundred yards, ten MOA, wind west, northwest, five miles per hour." Before he finished speaking, the gun roared and the targets orange hand disintegrated. Ronny laughed and stood, removing the wet ghillie suit before walking out. More people lined the outer edge of the course, and he didn't want to get shot accidentally.

He ran to the edge of the course closest to him and jogged back to Dan. "Amazing shooting, man," he said happily.

Dan glanced up from the gun in his hands and smiled before resuming cleaning. He nodded toward the line.

"Let's see what you've got."

Ronny swung his rifle to the front and lifted it, peering through the sight. The two men continued shooting, trading rifles and sidearms. Ronny used a SIG Saur P226 MK25 while Dan preferred a Heckler and Koch because it had a safety, which made his wife happier. The sun shone overhead, drying Ronny's clothes and clearing the mist.

"I'll go get us more ammo," Ronny offered and tucked his bag beneath the table his rifle rested on.

Dan busily broke down the pistol in his hand, ensuring the heavy fire hadn't damaged it.

On his way back, Ronny halted and stared. The girl from the park stood on the end of the line, firing a forty-five. Sunglasses held unruly black hair from her face. Beside her, an M-14 rifle lay chambered open on the table beside a box of unused cartridges.

She was a petty officer, the same rank as him. Other men eyed her covertly. Ronny wasn't sure if it was for being an attractive woman or being a good shot. The target before her held tightly grouped shots in a clear pattern.

While he stared, she finished the pattern and holstered her gun, turning to peer up the lane. One hand rose to shade her eyes as she reached for binoculars lying beside the rifle. Ronny followed her gaze and grinned. She was watching Dan. Taking her interest as an omen, he boldly approached.

"Want to meet him?"

She spun to face him, lowering the binoculars. From this close he noticed a line of faint freckles crossing her nose. Inky, black lashes framed her amazing blue eyes.

"Who," she said, sounding confused.

"Dan Barstow. He's my partner and could give you some pointers if you like. That was his first gun too. May I?" Ronny gestured at the gun lying beside a shooting log.

"Sure," she said and grinned, revealing straight white teeth.

Ronny loaded the rifle and took a shot. "Smooth. Nicely sighted. Want to meet him?"

Her gaze narrowed.

Ronny laughed. "No, he didn't send me; I saw you admiring his work. Dan's happily married."

She laughed and held out her hand. "Cameron Howard."

"Ronald Mitland."

Her hand in his sent a tingle through his entire body. He didn't want to release it.

"I'd love to meet him. I admire his shooting very much."

"Don't we all," Ronny said as he cracked the rifle and picked up the box of bullets.

She grabbed her bag and followed him.

"Are you taking the sharpshooter course?" Ronny asked.

"In two months. I'm basically a translator, but I want to keep my options open. Besides, I'm occasionally stationed in dangerous parts of the world."

"Knowledge is never wasted. Neither is skill. And

you have skill. That was some nice shooting." Ronny slowed as they approached Dan and lowered his voice. "If he offers you a kitten, say no."

"What?" She sounded confused and suspicious.

"I warned you," he muttered as he set the bullets on the table beside his rifle. "Dan, this is Cameron, and she'd love some pointers. I saw her shoot, and it was real tight."

Dan didn't let him down. He smiled and shook her hand, acting like Ronny brought people by all the time.

Dan's eyes lit on her rifle, and he grinned. "Sweet, I haven't shot one of those in a while. May I?"

"Sure." Cameron handed him her a gun.

"Three hundred yards," Dan said as he brought the rifle to his shoulder. A hole appeared in the target. Dan lowered the rifle and reloaded.

"Five hundred," Ronny said and brought his binoculars to his eyes.

Beside him, Cameron did the same.

Dan shot.

Cameron let the binoculars dangle from their strap as she clapped. "Impressive, especially for an unfamiliar gun."

"Want to try mine?" Dan gestured to the SR-25 sniper rifle laying on the table.

Cameron's eyes lit, and Dan laughed.

Ronny called out targets for them.

A grin on his face, Dan handed him Cameron's rifle. "Take the shot," he said and winked.

Ronny knelt beside Cameron and lifted her gun. Dan called out shots he knew Ronny could make. Ronny glanced at Dan, thanking him with his eyes. Dan could easily make him look bad, calling shots beyond his skill. Instead, he was trying his best to make him look good, and Ronny was grateful.

A small crowd of spectators gathered as the rifles rang out simultaneously. Ronny found it hard to concentrate, kneeling beside Cameron so close the heat from her body penetrated his damp clothing; he wanted to pull her even closer. Her perfume was light; *maybe not perfume but soap*, he thought and leaned closer.

They shot an entire box of ammunition before Ronny regretfully rose. Dan took his place, making minute adjustments to Cameron's hand and stance the same way he'd done for Ronny when he'd joined the team. Spotter scope held to his eyes, Dan crouched behind Cameron and offered advice in a low voice.

Cameron nodded seriously, her entire attention on Dan.

For another hour, they shot.

Finally, Dan rose and brushed off his pants. "We have class. It was nice meeting you." A thoughtful expression crossed his face. "You wouldn't be interested in a kitten, would you?"

Cameron grinned, turning slightly to wink at Ronny. "Actually, my mom is looking for a kitten."

"Your mom," Dan said sounding disappointed but looking thoughtful.

Ronny laughed at Cameron's confused expression. "Your mom wouldn't happen to be a CIA agent or a lion tamer or something, would she?"

Head tilted to the side, Cameron regarded him quizzically.

Ronny's laugh deepened. "He's considering it and feeling guilty because he knows what kind of hell his demon cat can cause."

She laughed and turned bright eyes on Dan. "My mom has a way with animals. No promises, but if you let her meet them..."

Dan grinned and then winced. "I really do want to take advantage here. But Ronny's correct, the kittens are part demon. I'm sure your mother is as nice as you are... Although, the kittens are half angel too... hmmm."

"He's talking himself into it," Ronny whispered in a loud aside.

Dan snorted and gave Cameron an apologetic smile. "Tell your mom we think they might be possessed and if she's still interested, give me a call. My wife really needs a break from them."

THREE

---◆---

C. HOWARD

"Demon kittens?" Cameron asked dubiously as she tucked her cell phone into her bag after adding Dan's number.

Dan had left, leaving them alone. Ronny gathered the last of the spent shells and straightened.

"Cute little buggers but sired by the evilest cat you ever met. Angie probably does need a break." He glanced at Cameron. "His wife is seven months pregnant, and they have a four-year-old. A cute kid, but he's a four-year-old..."

Cameron laughed. "You don't like kids?"

"I like them fine. In moderation. Dan and Angie might be a bit, um— enthusiastic about them."

"Two kids aren't a lot..."

"They've only been married a year and a half."

Cameron rose an elegant black brow.

"Sam is adopted. It's a long story." Ronny took a deep breath and plastered on his best smile. "One I'd love to tell you over drinks?" he added hopefully.

A delicate flush tinted Cameron's cheeks. "Sure, sounds good. When and where?"

"Tomorrow? I know a great Irish pub near Balboa Park."

Recognition lit her eyes, and the flush darkened. "See ya then."

"If I get called out, I'll text, but I think we have a few days."

"Work takes precedence," she agreed. "My schedule is pretty steady at the moment, but if I can't make it, I'll call."

Ronny grinned as she walked away, long, athletic strides taking her from sight quickly. Usually, he preferred short, curvy women like his wife, Dawn, but something about Cameron riveted his attention.

Ronny smacked himself in the forehead. *Dawn!* He needed to call her. She graduated in May, and their deal would be up for renegotiation. He was sure now he wanted a divorce. Number ten speed-dial connected him to Dawn.

"Hey, sunshine," he said when she answered.

"Hey yourself, handsome, what's up? Is something wrong?"

"No, just thinking of you."

"Oh..."

Ronny winced and smacked himself again. Of course, an early call would alarm her. Now she thought this was a booty call and didn't want to do it or say no. "No, not like that. I was thinking we should divorce."

She laughed. "Tom worrying you?"

"A bit."

The laugh changed to a snicker. "Aww, you met a girl. What's she like? Who is she?"

"Just met her. We haven't even gone out yet."

Dawn was silent a minute. "Wow, I'm kind of hurt."

"Dawn, you know I love you, but we were never in love." Ronny closed his eyes and rubbed them. The rifle case banged painfully into his elbow. "You'll always be my best friend— "

"You too, don't worry about it. But she must be amazing if you take one look and want to divorce me."

"Not just her, there's Tom too."

"Tom."

The dreamy way she said his name made Ronny snigger.

"Yep, it's definitely time to divorce."

"Fine," she agreed cheerfully. "Um," a catch in her voice she continued hesitantly, "I always thought we'd have one last wild night, but..."

"No worries. I understand. Besides, I have plenty of memories. My favorite is the night we made our pact, remember the ottoman— "

"Stop," she yelled, making Ronny chortle again. "Never mention that to Tom! Never!"

"I got your back, and your front, and if I remember correctly, your feet— "

"Stop," she yelled again, this time laughing. "I really do love you, Ron."

"I love you too, sunshine."

Ronny awkwardly put the phone back in his bag with one hand, and humming happily, headed home to change.

24

He left for class forty minutes early. Located on Thirty-second street base, Rear Admiral Reeves office was on the top floor of a three-story building. In the first-floor hallway, Ronny met a man he went through basic with and stopped to chat a moment.

"Todd." Ronny held out a hand, and the two men shook.

"I heard you were stationed overseas," Todd said in surprise. His eyes widened, and he grinned, tapping the trident on Ronny's left shoulder. "Congratulations, man, I hadn't heard. What are you doing here?"

"Dropping off a gift to the old man from my commander. Our team is taking classes next door. What have you been up to?"

Todd's grin widened. "Got married two years ago, and we just had a baby girl."

"Congratulations to you too."

"You and Dawn still married?"

"Yeah."

"Any kids yet?"

"No, and we don't plan on having any." Ronny debated telling him they were divorcing and decided not to. Todd had no idea he and Dawn were never that serious, and he didn't want to explain or accept false sympathy. Ronny glanced at his watch. "We should meet for drinks or something, but I gotta run if I'm going to make my class. Good seeing ya, man."

Two at a time Ronny took the stairs, pausing before the closed door of the admiral's office to smooth his uniform and perform a quick check to make sure his shirt was tucked in and shoes clean before knocking once and opening the door.

A man glanced up from the desk, he half rose and

leaned forward before sitting down again. "Can I help you?" he asked as he slid a blue folder closed and tucked it into the top drawer.

"I have a birthday gift to drop off from my commander."

The man rose and extended his hand. "The admiral isn't in right now; leave it with me."

Ronny's bit back his laugh as he handed the man the small box. His nametag read C. Howard. It was as if the universe aligned to put Cameron in his thoughts.

"Thank you." Ronny handed Howard the gift. He couldn't wait for his date that night.

Howard escorted him to the door, locking it behind him.

In the classroom in the building next door the instructor showed them how to rewire a security camera to insert a prerecorded loop. Perched on the corner of his desk the instructor observed them practicing for a few minutes.

"If nothing else is handy, and you just have to cross a monitored space, a flashlight pointed directly at the camera might temporarily blind it and be taken for lens flare. Of course, a string of cameras 'flaring' will be extremely suspicious, and you need to get really close, but it can be done."

He demonstrated the effect. "It's likely to bring a security guard to check but might not trigger an alarm. Use care. Let's go over window and door sensors again." He pointed at a doorway set up in the center of the room. "Old school surveillance and alarm techniques can be trickier to dodge or fool than the newer types. See if you can avoid my powdered floors and bells on a string."

Ronny glanced at his watch for the fifth time in ten minutes. Cameron was late. While he didn't know her well enough to be sure, it seemed very out of character. Absently, he rose his hand and motioned for another drink.

The bartender snickered as he wiped the countertop. "Girl stand you up?"

Ronny peered up startled. A sheepish grin crossed his face. "That obvious?"

"New jeans, clean shirt, and I bet if I looked your boots are shined. Yeah, pal, it's obvious."

"Ten minutes isn't that late..." Ronny heaved a heavy sigh and gulped his beer. "I offered to pick her up, and she said she was taking her bike."

The bartender handed him another bottle. "On me."

Ronny nodded his thanks and accepted the offered beer.

Damn, he'd been so sure she'd come. Dan had told him earlier he'd heard from her mother and she was coming to see the kittens this weekend. He stared discontentedly at his undrunk beer.

Maybe she had a good excuse, he told himself and checked his messages again.

Another ten minutes passed with him checking his phone and turning the beer bottle before him.

The bartender lifted an inquisitive eyebrow as he passed.

"Twenty more minutes," Ronny said, as he checked his messages again. "If she isn't here by then— "

The bar quieted, and Ronny glanced at the door to see what had drawn everyone's eye.

Cameron swayed in the doorway. Blood streaked

the side of her face, and she cradled an arm across her chest. Blood had also stained her white, lacy shirt and short blue skirt.

"Jesus," Ronny exclaimed as he jumped to his feet and rushed to the door. "I got this," he said to the two men who rose to follow.

"I need your phone," she gasped as he reached her.

A long gash across her thigh ended at a swollen, heavily abraded knee. Red shading to deep purple discolored the entire left side of her leg. Sweat trickled down the side of her face, and she swayed slightly.

"What happened?"

"Phone," she repeated, sounding desperate.

He handed her his phone and reached for a chair as she dialed. The patrons at the bar spoke in low, hushed tones over the music that still played. Some turned back to their conversations although most kept an eye on them. Two more customers offered help, which he waved away.

Cameron smiled and thanked them as she brushed her hair off her forehead, wincing as her hand came away bloody. Bits of dirt and grass stuck in her hair making a once carefully arrange hairdo a matted mess.

"Do you need an ambulance?"

She sat as she waved a hand at him. He ran back to the bar and leaned over the counter, grabbing a towel. The bartender handed him a glass filled with ice.

"Should I call for an ambulance? Or the police?"

"Don't know; let me see. Man, that's a great excuse..." Ronny exchanged rueful grimaces with the bartender and hurried back to Cameron.

"No, I'm sure it wasn't an accident, sir," she was

saying into the phone as he approached. "Yes, I'm safe here. I need a medic, but I'll be fine. If this is about that file I translated, you could be in danger too." She took a deep breath and winced. "Sir, I hate to suggest this, but the only other person who knew I saw that file was Gregor. Yes, I can get myself to the hospital. There's a SEAL at the bar. Yes, sir, hold on." She handed the phone to Ronny. "My boss, Rear Admiral Reeves, wants to speak to you,"

"Sir," Ronny said hesitantly as he took the phone, handing Cameron the ice and cloth.

"Whiskey?" She motioned to the bartender with one hand while dabbing at the blood on the side of her face with the towel clenched in the other.

"Name, rank, commander," a man barked.

Ronny recognized the admiral's voice and swallowed heavily. "Petty Officer Third Class Ronald Mitland. I report to Commander Darmin."

"Yes, good man Darmin. I want you to see Petty Officer Howard to the base hospital. Don't leave her side until an escort arrives for her. An attempt has been made on her life. Use extreme caution. Am I clear, sailor?"

"Yes, sir."

"Dismissed."

Dial tone buzzed in Ronny's ear. He crouched before Cameron, taking the cloth from her, and wiping the blood dripping down her chin. "Somebody tried to kill you?"

"Yeah, we need to go."

The bartender approached, holding a wet towel and a shot glass of whiskey.

Ronny fished in his pocket, removed his wallet, and

handed the man three twenties. "Sorry about the mess. I'll take her to the hospital."

The bartender nodded and handed Ronny the towel and her the glass. She knocked back the drink and handed the glass back to the bartender.

Ronny poured the ice in the towel and wrapped it around her knee.

She stifled a gasping moan behind clenched teeth and a grimace.

"Where else are you hurt?" Ronny asked as he examined her quickly.

The pulse under his fingertips beat fast but steady. He used the flashlight app on his phone to check her eyes. Both pupils dilated normally.

"Just what you see, I think. Let's get out of here; I feel like a sitting duck."

Ronny helped her stand. "I could carry you to my truck, but with that knee..."

A grimace on her face, she began to hobble out the door. He took her arm and placed it around his neck, holding her up with an arm around her waist. "Not quite how I pictured this," he muttered, and she laughed, the laugh changing to a drawn-out hiss.

"Let me try carrying you," Ronny said as she bit back another moan.

Gingerly, he lifted her, trying to be as careful as he could of her knee and arm. She clutched his shirt with both hands and buried her face in his chest.

He strode as quickly as he could to the truck, fumbling for the keys in his front pocket as he clutched her awkwardly with one hand. It took him a moment to unlock the door one handed and ease her into the seat. After buckling her in, he ran to the driver's side and started the truck while hitting speed dial with the other hand.

"Meet me at the base hospital with my sidearm and a clean shirt. Come armed. Tell you there. Hurry."

He hung up and reached to check her pulse again. Finding it steady, he pulled onto the road. "What happened?"

"I took my bike to meet you, and someone ran me off the road along the only stretch at all dangerous."

"Could it have been accidental?"

"No. I was up near the museum. I went the long way to admire the view. No one was around. The car passed me and turned, gunning the engine. I glanced back in time to turn down the hill, but he clipped the back of my bike. If I'd had my mountain bike, I would've been fine, but the ten speed... I flipped, then tumbled down the mountain. If he hadn't gunned it, I might not have glanced back."

"Did you see the driver?"

"No, not really. I'm not even sure it was a man. I didn't notice a passenger. The car was a dark-blue Dodge Durango, the new model. Probably not a scratch on it."

"License plate?"

"California plate, but it was too dark to make out numbers. His lights were off, and I didn't look the first time he passed." She dabbed at the blood still trickling down her cheek and scowled.

"How the hell did you get to the bar?"

She winced and rubbed her right temple. "Rolled down the damn hill and practically landed in the road. It wasn't that far of a hobble. My cell was smashed to shit, and I figured I was better off going there than a stranger's house in case he tries again. A crowd might deter him." She shivered and rubbed her leg, biting her bottom lip. "I wish I'd been armed though. I kept expecting him to show and I couldn't run."

Ronny took her good hand in his. Finding it cold and clammy, he released it to feel for her pulse. She lifted a shaking hand to dab at the blood on her face again.

"Head wounds bleed a lot. The knee worries me more. How are the ribs?"

"Might be broken. It hurts to breathe," she admitted.

"Almost there," he said reassuringly.

Squirrel met him outside the exam room and slipped him his sidearm. Dressed in loose jeans and an old flannel shirt with a baseball cap on backward over his unruly brown hair Squirrel appeared anything except military. His brown eyes narrowed as he examined Ronny's bloody shirt.

"Not my blood. Someone ran my date off the road, and I've been ordered by Reeves to guard her until security arrives for her."

"Never a dull moment with you guys," Squirrel said cheerfully as he slapped Ronny on the back. "The admiral thinks she's in danger? Or was it a lone nut."

"Something to do with whatever they were working on today." A frown crossed his face, and he took his cell phone from his pocket. One finger held indicating he needed a second, he scrolled a moment, then made a call.

"Sir, this is Petty Officer Ronald Mitland. Yes, sir, we're at the hospital now. Earlier today I dropped off a gift— No, sir, this isn't about the gift, it's about the man who accepted on your behalf. His name tag said C. Howard, and he sat at the desk right outside your room. Yes, I'm sure he was a man. About six feet, one seventy, brown hair and eyes. He was looking at a blue folder when I entered and locked the door behind me when I left. No, sir, no distinguishing marks. Well, one, he wasn't tan. I will, sir, thank you."

Ronny hung up and turned to Squirrel who watched with raised eyebrows.

"Darmin's going to be pissed if you mislaid his gift," Squirrel said.

"Darmin's gift might be the clue that catches the spy. Reeves and Cameron never said what they were working on, but we know information is leaking somehow. If that man is pretending to be his secretary while no one is in the office..."

"Is Cameron his secretary?"

"Don't know. Maybe. She said she worked for Admiral Reeves as a translator. I noticed the man's name tag but didn't think anything of it. Howard is a common last name."

"A sibling?" Squirrel suggested.

"No, this guy was more European. Cameron screams Irish. I'm betting if she has siblings they all do. Besides, the admiral's questions prove that Howard was a fake."

"What do we do now?"

"I stay with her until relieved."

"Not without backup you don't. I'll call JT, fill him in, and arrange backup. Keep me informed on where you'll be." Squirrel sauntered off, headed to the other end of the hallway. He made a call, then leaned against the wall, pretending to use his phone.

The gun in his waistband made Ronny much happier than the knife in his pocket. He replaced the knife in the ankle sheath and resumed standing before the door.

The doctor ordered x-rays and blood work. Ronny followed Cameron and waited outside the x-ray room and stood beside her as the nurses took blood and cleaned and wrapped the injuries. Four hours later, the doctor discharged her. The knee was wrapped in ace bandages with an air cast. More ace bandages secured her wrist. A large square of white gauze was taped to her forehead covering the one-inch laceration. Butterfly tape crisscrossed her leg, holding the cut there closed.

Taking slow, careful steps on crutches, she hobbled from the hospital. Ronny carried her prescriptions and helped her into the cab of the truck. From the corner of his eye, he spied Squirrel getting on his motorcycle.

"One of my teammates is following us and will remain outside. If you're hungry, he can stop for food."

"No thanks. Sorry to be such a bother. All I want is a shower and bed."

Ronny's pulse leaped, and he cleared his throat before speaking. "Shower tomorrow. Don't waste all that wrapping. Let the ace bandages do their work. Ice the knee and get some sleep."

A soft sigh escaped her as she lightly massaged her knee. "This wasn't what I had in mind for a first date."

"Well, can't say you were boring." He grinned and smoothed her matted hair back.

The nurse had helped her rinse it, but nothing short of multiple rounds of shampoo would make it clean.

34

To his pleased surprise, she took his hand and kept it for the remainder of the ride.

He helped her inside her small one-bedroom efficiency. A dirt bike leaned against the wall beside the front door. Above it, a snowboard hung on hooks beside skis. Balls of all sorts filled a wire basket beside the kitchen counter with a hockey stick jammed in the center.

Ronny paused in her living room and whistled softly. Beside the small television, a wooden rack held an assortment of swords.

"These must have cost a fortune." He traced the elegant swirl on a silver sword, being careful not to touch.

"My dad began the collection. I inherited it two years ago. That one" – she pointed at the sword he was admiring— "I bought last year." She removed a sheathed sword from the top and drew it. "This one I practice with." She lightly touched his chest with the small ball on the end of the sword.

"It's prettier than any fencing sword I ever saw," Ronny said with real appreciation.

"My mother gave it to me for my thirteenth birthday." A grin lit her eyes. "Maybe, someday, I'll show you the gun collection in my bedroom."

"I look forward to it," Ronny's voice deepened as he stepped forward and traced the unmarked side of her face with two fingers.

Pink stained her cheeks.

He stepped back and smiled. "You need ice, Tylenol, and rest."

"There's ice packs in my freezer."

Ronny handed her two ice packs. She nodded her

thanks and hobbled awkwardly to the bedroom door.

"I should check it first. I wanted to wait to be invited, but safety..."

She laughed and gestured him to enter.

The light switch by the door revealed a simple room with one small dresser across from a neatly made bed. Two nightstands, one on either side of the double bed, held chrome reading lamps. His gaze traveled the room, landing on a padlocked door.

"Yep, my gun closet. And my closet, closet, but it was easier to lock my guns in there than buy and move a heavy safe."

"I can't wait to see them."

She grinned and sat on the bed, plumping the pillows behind her head and leaning back with a relieved sigh. Ronny checked under the bed and in the small bathroom before kneeling in front of her to remove her sneakers.

"Need help changing?" he asked hopefully.

She winked. "Nope, I sleep naked."

"Stop, you're killing me." He laughed as he stood and waved his hands at her in a no more gesture. "I'll bring you a glass of water."

"Can you grab me the Tylenol?"

He returned with the prescription strength Tylenol and a glass of water. She swallowed the pills and leaned back again. Ronny grabbed the blanket from her couch and covered her. He hesitated a second, then kissed her lips gently. Her hand rose to pull him closer, and she deepened the kiss. They were both breathing harder when she pulled away.

"Get some rest." His voice cracked, and he cleared his throat. "I'm right outside if you need anything."

Two fingers resting on her lips, she smiled.

His heart pounded. More than anything he wanted to kiss her again. She tasted of whiskey and dreams.

FOUR

———◆———

INTRUDER

A soft click woke Ronny from the light doze he'd fallen into, jerking him upright from the wall in the softly lit corner of Cameron's living room. Not trusting himself to stay awake on her overstuffed couch, he'd chosen to stand guard in the corner of the room.

The front door opened slowly.

When they'd arrived, the hallway had been dimly lit, now it was pitch black. A gloved hand appeared on the edge of the door. Ronny drew his sidearm, pressed send on his cell, and then dropped it on the couch.

As quietly as he could, he eased to the side of the door. Dim light from the kitchen glinted on black combat boots. Before the door could open further, Ronny grabbed the man's wrist and yanked hard while twisting. A curse erupted from the intruder's mouth as his knees hit the floor. Ronny kicked him in the back and stomped on the hand holding the gun. The intruder uttered a short scream.

In the bedroom, Cameron called for him.

"Intruder," he yelled. "Don't move," he said in a normal voice as he kicked the gun away.

Both hands pressed to the floor, the intruder attempted to push himself up. Ronny kicked him again. The light came on in the living room. Cameron stood in the doorway, a Colt forty-five held in both hands.

A shot rang out in the hallway followed by another.

"Go, I got this," Cameron said.

Ronny hesitated. Another two shots rang out, echoing against each other. He kicked the man on the floor one more time, knocking the intruder flat and making him swear, and ducked low, peering around the doorframe.

Three doors down, the light from the living room revealed Squirrel pressing his back against a door by the head of the stairs. As Ronny glanced at him, Squirrel lifted his gun and fired three times. Ronny turned in time to see the gunman duck around the corner.

He followed. The man ahead of him slammed through a metal fire door and raced up the stairs. A loud clatter of boots on metal stairs drowned out Ronny's pursuit.

At the top of the steps, he hesitated, then peeked around the doorway, sticking his head up as far it could go. A full moon lit the night. The quick glance showed C. Howard running toward the edge of the roof. Ronny ran after him and was only two steps behind when the man jumped.

Without hesitation, Ronny followed. A gunshot

whistled past his face as he collided with Howard on the next roof. Both men went down in a tangle of arms and legs. Lights sprang on in nearby apartment buildings.

Ronny used the hand holding his gun to smack his assailant's head hard. Howard gasped and reeled back. Ronny dropped his gun and grappled for the one in Howard's hand. A loud 'oof' and a hissing moan followed Ronny's knee to the groin.

Ronny took advantage of the man's involuntary reflex to curl and grab himself, and hit him with a quick uppercut and two short jabs to the kidney. He grabbed the wrist above the gun and squeezed while twisting. The gun clattered to the roof top.

"Mother fucker," Howard gasped as he lunged for the gun.

Ronny leaped to his feet and kicked him in the side, flipping him over. He followed it up with a kick at the grasping hand. A sharp crack made Howard scream. He began yelling obscenities as Ronny snatched his gun up, tucking it in his waistband

Ronny stepped back, letting Howard sit. His gaze traveled to Ronny's gun four feet away.

"I dare you," Ronny said and stepped further back.

Howard glared, cradling his hand to his chest.

Ronny snatched his gun from the rooftop and pointed it at Howard.

"You got this?" Squirrel hollered from the other roof.

"Yeah, get to Cameron." Ronny gestured Howard to rise and nudged him to the roof doorway at gunpoint. A broken padlock dangled from the doorframe.

"Hands behind your back." Ronny grabbed both wrists, ignoring the man's shriek as he twisted the broken arm.

Sirens in the distance came closer as Ronny prodded his captive down the stairs.

A group of men had gathered by the entrance to the stairs. Two held bats. One a knife. Three carried no weapons. Ronny bet if he frisked them there would be pistols on them somewhere.

"What's going on?" one of the weaponless men asked.

"Caught an intruder."

Up and down the hallway more doors opened, and half-dressed men appeared. By the time he reached the main floor, a small parade followed him. Two MPs greeted him with drawn guns.

"Inform Admiral Reeves," Ronny said as he handed over his captive.

The MP winced. "Haven't you heard? Someone shot the admiral."

Ronny gasped. "Killed him?"

"No, but he'll be out of commission for a while. A few days at least."

"Shit, did he arrange security for Petty Officer Howard?"

"I wouldn't know. Is he involved with this?" The MP jut his chin at the man being pushed into the back of his jeep.

"Petty Officer Cameron Howard works with the admiral, and someone tried to kill her tonight. Twice. Admiral Reeves ordered me to stay with her until security arrived." He quirked a half-smile at the MP. "I think we can safely assume she's involved."

The MP sighed hard. "Bring her down to the station with you, then. You both need to give statements anyway."

"She was injured and will need assistance getting there."

The MP nudged the radio on his shoulder with his chin and called in his position as he followed Ronny to Cameron's apartment. Another group of men had gathered by the doorway of Cameron's apartment. The man Ronny had subdued lay on the floor bound with a telephone cord. Two MPs spoke with Cameron and Squirrel inside the apartment while two more picked up the bound man and carried him downstairs.

Ronny and his escort joined Squirrel and Cameron right as she began to hobble to her bedroom.

Ronny laid a hand on her arm. "Need help?"

"If I do, I'll holler. Thanks, Ron, you saved my life."

"Meh, you could've handled him. All I did was wake you."

She gave him a sad smile and continued to her room.

Ten minutes later, she emerged dressed in her uniform. Instead of pants, she wore a black skirt. A shoulder holster contained a SIG Saur p226 and Ronny was willing to bet a knife was sheathed to her good thigh. The thought of her thigh made him flush.

"Can you grab me a coat from the closet please?" Cameron asked.

Ronny grabbed her the regulation coat for service dress and helped her put it on, covering the shoulder holster. The MPs exchanged glances, but neither tried to take her gun.

Without asking, Ronny swung her into his arms and carried her to the waiting jeep. The effort to resist kissing her left him breathless. A soft smile tilted her full bottom lip. Two fingers rose and rested on her lips a moment as her blue eyes peered into his. Her soft breath of laughter met his stifled groan.

At the police station, they wrote statements and gave reports, answered a million questions, and were finally released. Dan waited for them outside the station.

"I brought my wife's van, figured it would be easier to get into. You're coming to my house. My security is state of the art. Do you need help getting to the car?"

Ronny picked her up before she could answer. She placed an arm around his neck, massaging it lightly with two fingers. He tightened his hold on her.

"My apartment is fine," she said.

Dan shrugged. "Darmin's orders. Until the admiral orders differently, SEAL Team Nine is guarding you, and the best place to do that is my house. We can stop at your apartment and pack a bag though if you like."

Lee waited in the van. Squirrel sat on his motorcycle behind it.

"Tom and Keith are back at my house with Angie, supposedly checking the perimeter, but more likely playing with Sam," Dan said as he sat in the driver's seat.

Ronny placed Cameron on the seat and climbed in, sliding the door closed behind him.

Set back from the road hidden from sight by a dense planting of trees, an electric gate blocked access to the Barstow residence. Cameras swiveled as Dan punched a code into the keypad. With a soft whir and thunk, metal spikes dropped into the ground as the gate swung open. The curving drive led to a Victorian style home including a round turret and gingerbread trim. A porch wrapped around the three-story edifice. Someone had begun to paint the trim a bright blue. A black man, holding a small child about ten shades lighter than himself tucked under his arm, opened the door.

"Excuse the mess inside; we're still remodeling." Dan parked before the door and took the child, swinging him into the air and catching him. The boy shrieked with laughter.

"Daddy, Tom says I have to be extra good because your friend has a boo-boo and needs to rest."

Dan settled the boy on his waist and turned to Cameron. "Cameron, this is my son, Sam. Sam, say hello to my friend Cameron."

"Hi." Sam glanced at Cameron then turned to Ronny, gray eyes alight with excitement. "Mommy says we're having a sleepover tonight and we can make popcorn and cook dinner on the fireplace."

Tom reached out, shook Cameron's hand, and mumbled, "Nice to meet you."

Ronny reached for Sam who came to him willingly. He tossed him in the air, then set him on his feet. "Cameron is my good friend. Can you help bring in her bags?"

"Sure, Mommy says I'm a terrific helper." Sam grasped the handle of a small carryon bag with two hands and staggered towards the stairs.

Cameron bit back a laugh.

Ronny picked her up.

Lee grabbed her suitcase, grunting under the weight. "What's in this thing?"

"Bullets," Cameron said.

Lee's eyes lit.

Ronny frowned. "Back off; I saw her first."

Lee rolled his eyes and laughed. Cameron snickered and leaned her head on Ronny's shoulder. Angie greeted them at the door. Blue paint marred her cheek and the tip of her blond ponytail. More blue smudges decorated the loose white shirt she wore over a yellow sundress that fell in loose folds around her very pregnant stomach.

"What did I say about painting?" Dan said sternly, placing his hands on his hips.

Tears clouded Sam's eyes. "Is Mommy in trouble?"

He dropped the bag and ran to Angie. She reached down to him as he hugged her knees.

"Yes. Mommy shouldn't be climbing ladders. No ladders for anyone except me, am I clear?"

Sam nodded his head. Gray, tear-filled eyes stared worriedly between Dan and Angie.

Angie heaved a sigh and nodded her head too, then leaned down to kiss Sam on the cheek, smoothing the tight, short curls on his head. "Daddy's right; no ladders. I won't do it again. Let's go get the cookies and milk." Sam's hand in hers, she turned to Cameron.

"Welcome. Excuse our mess. We have a room on the first floor with its own bath mostly finished. If you go outside, use code, four-three-nine-zero on the keypad to exit and enter. Ronny, bring her to the living room; I'll bring food and drink." Angie led Sam away.

"And cookies, right, Mommy,"

Angie's bright laugh drifted back to them. Dan gazed after them with a smile on his face.

"You have a lovely family," Cameron said as Ronny placed her on a chair and slid an ottoman under her feet.

"I'm the luckiest man alive," Dan said as he sat in a leather chair before a large, stone fireplace.

Toys were scattered around the room and worn furnishings gave the room a comfortable lived-in look. Ronny loved this room. He never worried about messing it up like he did Charlene's house.

A trail of cheerios led to the toy box in the corner. A stack of two-by-fours and a pile of sheetrock sat alongside it. Beside the chair Dan sat in, a half-eaten, browning apple laid on a side table. The sight reminded Ronny of his childhood in a home in Texas very like this one. A little blond girl playing with the boy would complete the picture in his mind.

Dawn had been his companion and friend his entire life. As if thoughts of his wife conjured him, Tom entered and sat on the couch, putting his feet on the coffee table.

A low growl built to a savage snarl. Tom sighed and stood, pulling the cushions from the couch. A look of distaste on his face, he lifted a dead mouse by the tail and stalked from the room, holding it at arm's length. The snarl followed him.

Ronny gestured at Tom with his chin. Cameron stared after Tom.

"Behind the couch— he'll pounce any second." Ronny laughed as Demon bounded after Tom, swatting at the mouse dangling in the air.

Since the last time he'd seen him, the cat had gotten another notch in his remaining ear and gained three pounds. No longer long and lean, he waddled a bit.

Keith entered the room, giving Demon a wide berth.

The smallest man on the team, Keith was the same height as Cameron but had broader shoulders. He'd begun growing out his blond hair, copying Squirrel's messy do. In poor light with makeup and a sari he could pass for a woman. Right now, with his five o'clock shadow, Keith looked all too manly for Ronny's comfort as he approached Cameron with a hand extended and a welcoming smile.

Ronny glared, hastily forcing his expression to neutral politeness at Cameron's worried frown.

Keith smirked and shook Cameron's hand before taking a seat on the couch.

"We got him fixed, hoping that would help; instead we made him fat," Dan said as the cat trailed Tom from the room, swatting at the mouse, his growl a snarl again. "No matter what we do, he hides his prey everywhere. Seraphim has the decency to leave hers by the back door."

Two balls of orange fur raced into the room following Sam. "Careful, son, keep your laces tied, or they'll trip you.

Sam knelt on the floor, a frown of concentration on his face, and tied his sneaker. The kittens attacked his foot as he stood. Small growls became hisses as they stopped fighting the laces and began fighting each other.

Ronny pulled Sam into his lap and retied the sneaker. The kittens rolled under the coffee table and began grooming each other.

Cameron chuckled and leaned down, snapping her fingers and making kissy noises, trying to attract the kittens.

Ronny grinned. "They'll pounce on anything

dangling or sparkly. If Dan could train them to attack gun-carrying men, he could sell his security system."

"It's an impressive system." Cameron nodded to the cameras in the corners of the room.

Fingers laced across his chest, Dan gazed complacently about the room. "Should be— we paid a fortune for it. Beside every doorway, there's a panic switch. The closet in the guest room, the pantry in the kitchen, and every bedroom closet on the second floor is a safe room."

"We have to go the safe room if the alarm sounds," Sam piped up.

"That's right, son. And when can you come out?"

"When you or Mommy say so, or my uncles."

"Or," Dan prompted.

"Or if the red-light flashes. Can I have the apple?"

Dan picked it up and examined it before tossing it to Ronny. "The red light is a fire alert. The house has a sprinkler system. The fire alarm won't trigger inside the room unless the blaze is severe. The house fire alarm will trigger for burnt toast..."

"Daddy burns the toast a lot," Sam said through a mouthful of apple.

Angie entered with a tray of sandwiches. Tom followed, carrying a tray of drinks with a brown jar tucked under his arm.

"Darmin and JT are on their way over. The two men you apprehended aren't talking, but fingerprints tell their own story." Tom set the drinks on the coffee table and then the jar, which he opened to remove a cookie. He handed the cookie to Sam as he sat back on the couch.

Angie passed out sandwiches and drinks and sat

on the arm of Dan's chair.

"C. Howard is really Mitchell Kurt. Another MIT graduate and a classmate of Greer's. The feds are all over him. Petty Officer Gregor has disappeared, and a nationwide alert has been placed. Admiral Reeves is awake and fingered him as the shooter. Your warning saved the admiral's life, Cameron. Gregor got a shot off as he was running for his life. The admiral thinks he nicked him if not a real solid hit. All hospitals have been alerted, but he won't go to one. My guess is he'll show up dead."

"Heh hmm." Angie loudly cleared her throat, glancing at Sam.

Tom winced and mouthed 'sorry.' "All Gregor's friends and movements are being investigated."

"He didn't have access to the schedule though," Cameron said.

"Mitchell is the man they believe responsible for stealing the intel. Gregor could've informed him when the office was empty –"

"It's not that easy." Cameron set her glass on the side table beside her chair. "The office is locked and the files are protected by password locks. The computers require a thirteen-digit login key. If you enter it incorrectly, security arrives, and you have to show ID. Even the admiral's desk is locked with a digital keypad."

"We could break that security," Ronny said thoughtfully.

"Without leaving traces?" Cameron rose a questioning brow, then winced and held a hand to her face.

The left side of her face had darkened into a blue

bruise.

Angie rose and headed into the kitchen.

"No, you're right, we'd leave traces." Ronny handed Sam to Dan and opened the carryon bag, emerging with the Tylenol.

"Unless we had the codes," Dan said thoughtfully as he tucked the boy against his chest and offered him a bite of his sandwich.

"So, they had the codes," Tom said.

"Seems likely." Dan took a bite from the sandwich in Sam's hand, making him giggle.

"Not necessarily," Cameron put in. "Greer is a computer genius. Maybe he's devised a way to crack the system without leaving traces."

Angie returned with an ice pack that she handed to Cameron.

"Either way. The entire department is being investigated," Tom said.

"And don't forget our missing men," Ronny added. "Any word on when we go?"

"We went last night. Darmin sent Schrowder's group. JT is pissed," Tom said.

"Damn."

"Cameron glanced from Tom to Ronny and winced. "Sorry."

"Not your fault," Ronny said quickly.

"I'm not sorry; I like my husband home." Angie kissed the top of Dan's head

He smiled and pulled her close. Sam grinned at them.

"I really need a shower." Cameron lifted a hand to her dirty hair and grimaced.

"I can help." Angie offered Cameron a hand to

stand.

"Is there somewhere I can lock my gun?" Cameron gave Sam a meaningful glance.

"Yep, in your room. I'll show you."

Ronny handed Cameron the crutches, and the two women left the room, talking quietly together. As soon as they disappeared, Dan spread the blueprints of his home over the coffee table.

"Two Marines are on duty beside my back gate." Dan ran a finger over the map. "If we keep a man here and here, we'll have the exterior angles covered..."

A frown of concentration on his face, Ronny listen carefully as Dan put security in place for Cameron. He was sure the terrorists wouldn't stop at two attempts if they were willing to kill an admiral.

FIVE

---◆---

Duty Calls

Ronny sat on the back step of Dan's porch with a beer in his hand and watched Angie and Cameron teach Sam to play croquet. A half-acre of green lawn separated the house from the trees in the backyard. The boy's bright laughter carried easily to where Ronny sat.

"Warms your heart, doesn't it," Dan said as he sat beside him and popped open his beer.

"It really does. When I think of how quiet and withdrawn he was..."

"Angie really worked a miracle. That woman truly is an angel. Sam and I are both blessed to have her in our lives. He hasn't had a nightmare in months. We want to adopt another after Juan is born."

"It's a boy, then?"

Dan grinned and toasted Ronny. "Found out yesterday."

"Congratulations; we better repaint the room before Angie decides too."

Dan laughed. "The doctor calls it a nesting instinct and says the paint won't hurt her if I can keep her off ladders. I took all my power tools to JT's house." He grinned at Ronny. "Cameron keeps her occupied. And Sam of course."

A pensive frown crossed Dan's face. "It's funny how tragedy can bring a blessing into your life. Juan's death gave me Angie, and the death of Sam's mother gave me Sam. I sometimes feel guilty about that."

"Don't, I guarantee Sam's mother would be happy her boy is safe and loved. Neither death was your fault."

"True." Dan brightened and placed his beer can on the railing. "Bet you one mouse patrol I can beat you in croquet."

Ronny laughed and placed his beer beside Dan's. A sharp crack of wood-on-wood was followed by Sam's squeal of laughter. Ronny rose to peer into the yard in time to see Demon grab the ball and roll onto his back with all four paws wrapped around it.

"No fair. Your cat's cheating," Cameron called, making Sam laugh again.

Ronny's smile grew as the cat raced after Angie's ball. "You must be getting sick of us; we've been here two weeks now. Any word on when Cameron can return home?"

"Pfft." Dan made a disparaging noise and grinned mockingly at Ronny. "You mean you're sick of us chaperoning you."

Ronny laughed. "I won't lie; I'm looking forward to real privacy with her."

Dan snickered. "Our bedroom is soundproofed."

"Not really," Ronny mumbled.

Dan blushed to the roots of his blond hair.

Ronny laughed and slapped him on the shoulder. "Sometimes you leave the windows open."

The blush on Dan's cheeks darkened.

Still laughing, Ronny grabbed a croquet mallet.

———————◆———————

Three days later, Ronny escorted Cameron back to her apartment.

"I'm sort of sad to end this duty. I really enjoyed spending time with you." He laid her suitcase on the kitchen counter.

"Me too, your friends are really nice."

"Your friends too now. Angie will miss your company."

Cameron laid her purse beside the suitcase and stepped closer to him. "My mom and I are taking her shopping tomorrow. And before you say it, I'll be careful and stay alert."

Ronny placed his hands on her hips and kissed her. "How about we go for dinner tomorrow night?"

She wound her arms around his neck and really kissed him. Only a few inches shorter than him, her body fit perfectly against his. Ronny moved his hands to the small of her back, under her shirt. One hand rose higher, his thumb brushing her nipple under her bra, making her moan softly.

His breath caught as her hands dropped to his belt. He used both hands to unclip her bra and pull her T-shirt over her head while she fumbled with his belt. A light pink nipple pebbled under his tongue as he bent her backward, sucking lightly on her small, firm breast. Her hands left his belt and pressed him closer, fingers running through his short hair.

The pager on his belt beeped. Ronny groaned and straightened, releasing her reluctantly.

"Sorry," he mumbled as he grabbed his cell phone.

She snatched her T-shirt from the floor and held it before her as he made the call.

"We go in thirty," JT said.

"On my way." He kissed Cameron quickly. "Sorry, gotta run."

"Duty calls," she said, sounding disappointed.

He groaned and kissed her again. The shirt fell unheeded to the floor as she kissed him back.

"Damn it, I really got to go."

She laughed and pushed him away.

He ran out the door.

———————◆———————

The rappelling rope slipped smoothly through Ronny's hands as he exited the helicopter. Rotors disturbed the loose sand and shale on top of the deserted hillside, blowing up a cloud of dust. As soon as Tom's feet hit the ground, the helicopter peeled off. A blacker spec in the black night it was soon lost from sight. The radio Lee carried crackled.

Lee crouched, pulled the antenna up, and spoke quietly, reporting their safe arrival as the rest of the team slipped night-vision goggles on.

With the helicopter gone silence descended on the barren Pakistan hills. The target lay thirty-eight miles to the north. From now on they'd maintain radio silence as they still weren't sure how the other teams had been located.

Ronny used the scope he carried to examine the

steep mountain below them. Low shrubs dotted the mountainside interspersed with a few scraggly pines. Only small glows of animals met his searching gaze, and those were distant.

Beside him, Lee held infrared goggles to his eyes and scanned three hundred and sixty degrees around them while the team waited for his all clear.

Tom whistled and gestured when Ronny glanced at him. The seven men began climbing down the side of the mountain, moving fast over the loose rocks and shale. By sunrise, they were at the bottom twenty miles from where they'd started.

In the lee of a giant boulder, they crouched and ate a quick meal of prepackaged energy bars before resuming their trek. A long, low valley spread before them covered with dense, wiry grass and prickly bushes. Light puffs of dark-gray smoke rose in the distance. Pine trees and a rock outcropping blocked the cause of the smoke from sight.

At a fast walk, they headed to it, keeping low and using the scrub as cover. Three hours later, the source of the smoke came into sight. A dirt road curved before a low line of homes built along the edge of a steep mountainside. Three goats wandered the road chased by a small boy wearing a dark robe with a white scarf around his neck.

Dan signaled he'd pause to search with his scope. JT acknowledged Dan with a hand wave and led his men forward. Dan and Ronny hunkered into the scrub brush. Both held scopes to their eyes. Fifty yards away, JT halted.

Ronny used a laser to target the tree before JT.

JT held a thumb up indicating he understood and

continued forward.

"Two men to the left of the third building," Dan said softly. Ronny marked the rock JT crouched behind and received a thumbs up.

"Ah, there he is," Dan said in satisfaction. "Five hundred yards off the left corner of the farthest building to the west."

Ronny signaled JT. Two quick flicks of laser light then the code that gave position. JT held a thumb up.

Squirrel eased forward away from the group. Twenty yards from his target, he crouched behind a pine and whistled three warbling bird calls.

Ronny grinned when their target turned and answered. "Contact," he murmured.

Dan nodded, not taking his gaze from the scene before him. Ronny resumed sweeping the road and forested hill behind them with his scope.

Fifteen minutes later, their target crouched beside Dan and Ronny.

"Benson, good to see ya still kicking," Dan said as he shook the man's hand.

Benson grinned, crooked teeth showing briefly in his swarthy face. "Nice of Darmin to send you along to admire my work."

JT cleared his throat, and Benson straightened.

"Schwartzy is around the bend, keeping our quarry in sight," Benson said. "Greer is here along with twelve armed men and thirty-two civilians, including eight women, and twelve children, but no sign of Alfarsi, just two of his sons."

"Does Shrowder have a plan?" JT asked.

Benson opened his map, spreading it on the ground between them. A dirty finger traveled a line of penciled in shapes. "A rough assortment of 'homes' lie around the corner. Some adobe, but the majority are tents with a few crude stick huts thrown in. So far, we've seen no sign of any high-tech surveillance at all. Guards with dogs patrol. Everyone suspiciously avoids the road branching to the left, whether that means it's mined or the natives were told to keep their distance from the head honchos is anyone's guess.

Benson tapped the top of the mountain on the map. "Our sniper and spotter are up there and have reported sighting our man entering this house here." He tapped a square drawn in on the map. Benson turned to Dan. "A good spot for you to set up is on the hillside to our left. Between the two of you, we'll have every angle covered."

JT sat back on his haunches. "When we engage, feel free to use the radios, but maintain radio silence until then. Ronny, watch your backs. These men have primitive gear but are sneaky sons of bitches. Don't get caught with your pants down."

Ronny saluted and stood, shouldering his pack and making sure his scope was securely attached to the strap on his waist.

Dan bumped fists with his teammates and headed back into the hills. Ronny followed. The two men darted from tree-to-tree, pausing to examine the terrain before moving on each time. Sweat trickled down Ronny's back and ran into his eyes. A hundred degrees outside, the ghillie suit he wore felt like a sauna.

Three hours later, they reached a spot Dan deemed a good position and settled in beneath a tall pine. A homemade camouflage net covered Dan's gun, leaving only the tip of the barrel showing. Ronny lay beside Dan on the dry, rocky ground. Both men removed small rocks and other debris from beneath them.

Ronny scanned the mountaintop before them and spotted the other sniper team, but only because the man signaled.

"They saw us get into place," Ronny said, keeping his voice low, but not whispering.

A whisper traveled farther than a soft, low voice. Dan nodded acknowledgment, not stopping his examination of the scene before him. Both SEAL teams spread out, guiding each other closer with hand signs.

Directly overhead, midday sun blazed down on them. The men in their gray and brown camouflage blended into the hillsides and sides of the buildings.

Beside him, Dan tensed. "Shit, two women approaching Tom's position."

Ronny swung his scope to Tom and risked a laser light on the wall beside him. Tom didn't turn his head, continuing to peer around the corner, giving Ronny no angle to his eyes.

Ronny fingered his headset.

"No," Dan said. "Maintain radio silence." He reached to his ankle and removed the twenty-two holstered there. "This little thing shouldn't make a noise big enough to be heard that far away." He sighted carefully and pulled the trigger.

Tom jerked his head around as a piece of the building four feet away crumbled. Ronny flicked the laser on and off quickly. Tom gave him a thumbs up and eased around the corner of the building just as the two women rounded the corner.

Ronny glanced at the laser sight and grinned. "Nine

hundred yards. Nice shooting."

Dan snorted. "I was aiming for his fat head."

Ronny laughed.

An hour later, he watched tensely as two men from Schrowder's team entered the target building. Too far to hear gunshots inside a closed structure, Ronny had no idea what was happening inside the building. Lee and Tom entered the building, and still no one spoke on the radio.

"They haven't engaged yet," Dan murmured.

"Back check," Ronny said and swiveled, scanning the hill behind them. Every few minutes he checked the area surrounding them to ensure it remained clear.

"Goats, eight hundred yards left." Ronny peered at the five goats through his scope and spotted the shepherd sitting at the base of a tree with his eyes closed. "Civilian, male teen, currently no threat."

"Roger that."

Ronny scanned around them again, then the village below them. His gaze traveled to the goat herder, but the boy hadn't moved.

Ten minutes later, two men exited the building with bound and gagged men thrown over their shoulders.

"Movement," Dan warned.

Ronny swung his scope around and took in the scene, then rechecked behind them.

Seven men exited the building. Five wore stained, dirty, camouflage pants and bare feet. One wore a filthy white shirt. The others had used their shirts as bandages. Shredded white cloth was tied around arms and legs. Tom paused outside the door and held his hand up. Ronny flashed the laser on the wall beside his hand. Tom began signing.

"The other five are dead," Ronny said sadly as he acknowledged receipt of the message.

Dan nodded, his face grim, covering his team's retreat. When the last man rounded the bend, he and Ronny ran back to the rendezvous, this time not checking their path, trusting it remained free of booby-traps since they'd came in. What had taken them three hours that morning took twenty minutes to traverse that afternoon. Ronny was slightly disappointed they hadn't engaged and appeared to have gotten away clean.

When they rejoined their team, Ronny removed his ghillie suit and drew his knife, cutting the front of the suit into strips. The thick padding would make makeshift shoes for the barefoot men. Dan crouched on the hillside, guarding their backtrail as the rest of the team offered first-aid and meal bars and tied the lengths of the suit to the rescued men's feet.

The captured men glared behind their gags.

JT handed out candy bars and passed his canteen around.

Benson crouched beside Dan. "Our snipers should be arriving any minute. We've called for extraction."

"We leaving our dead?" Ronny asked.

"For now. We know where they are, and we'll retrieve them for burial, but let's get the live ones home and our captives debriefed." JT turned to peer back the way they'd come. "We'll be back."

SIX

---◆---

DIDN'T WANT TO WASTE A MINUTE

Ronny called Cameron on his way home. "We'll be home in thirteen hours, and I get forty-eight hours off. How about we go away for the weekend? Maybe a hotel on a beach somewhere?"

"Sounds perfect. I'll make arrangements and you can meet me there. I'd ask how it went, but I assume it's confidential."

"It is. Sorry, Cam. Everyone is fine though and headed home."

"See ya in fifteen hours. And, Ron, I really missed you."

Ronny grinned from ear-to-ear as he hung up. Her voice held a world of promise. The rest of the ride home tested his patience. He finally fell asleep and slept deeply, not waking until their plane landed in Coronado. She'd emailed him the address of the hotel and said a key would be waiting at the front desk. The place she'd picked was less than an hour from the base, which suited him perfectly. A long drive would kill him.

He dumped his duffel in the closet and grabbed a suitcase. In five minutes, he was out the door showered, shaved, and packed and headed to Kona Kai Resort.

———— ◆ ————

His suitcase bounced against the firm mattress, mussing the crisply made bed. Light-blue curtains framed the view of the harbor from the private patio. Open to the late afternoon sun, the curtains wafted in the gentle breeze that smelled of ocean.

Ronny stepped to the doors and breathed deeply. He started in surprise and whirled when a hand touched his shoulder. He hadn't heard Cameron enter the room.

"No more crutches?"

Barefooted, she pressed against him. "Don't need them." She ran her fingers through his hair. "I don't plan on going anywhere except the bed."

"Is that an invitation?" Ronny asked huskily.

For answer she kissed him, dropping her hands from his hair to the buttons on his shirt. The blood rushed from his head, leaving him lightheaded.

"Birth control?" he murmured between kisses.

She drew back and began undoing the clasp of her skirt. "I'm on the pill."

Filled with heat, which her excited gaze flamed, he reached out and ripped her shirt off. Buttons scattered across the carpeted floor.

"I'll buy you a new one."

She laughed and pushed him back with one hand

as she removed her bra with the other. His pants hit the floor before her bra. One hand on either side of her waist, he slid the skirt down, trailing kisses across her body. She giggled when he picked her up, laid her on the bed, and knelt between her knees on the edge of the mattress.

Lithe and tan, she lay before him, her breasts a startling white against the coppery brown of the rest of her skin. His heated gaze traveled the smooth muscles of her abdomen to another white triangle of skin.

He kissed the hands that reached for him, holding them to the side. "Let me look at you. You're so beautiful, Cam. More beautiful than I imagined, and I have a very good imagination." His voice deepened as he released her hands to run his palms over her breasts, making her gasp. "I want to kiss you everywhere."

"Yes, kiss me everywhere— afterward." Not taking later for an answer, she leaned up and grasped him with both hands, stroking his length and running her thumbs over the head of his cock, tugging him lightly towards her.

She wound her legs around his waist, urging him closer as he shifted forward. They both moaned when he slid inside her. Tight and wet, she welcomed him with up-thrust hips. The legs around his waist squeezed as he thrust, sliding easily despite the tightness. He'd wanted to make love to her slowly and savor every sound and sensation the first time, but his plans fled his mind; every fiber of his being concentrated on the delicious feel of her body around his.

He was so caught up he didn't realize she'd come

already till her legs released, and he paused in midmotion. Inner muscles clenched him as her hips bucked, making him groan loudly. One hand spread low on her stomach, he pressed lightly as she writhed against him. Sweat dripped from his brow. He had to remove his hand to wipe his face. She didn't seem to notice him sweating, her eyes were closed, and head tipped back, her hips still jerking spasmodically against him.

"Mmm," he said as she panted beneath him. He used both hands to push her legs back, giving himself a deeper angle and began thrusting again, making her moan.

He paused again. "Was that a good moan?"

"God, yes, don't stop."

"You feel amazing. So tight and wet." The aroused sound she made caused him to jerk his hips hard. She used both hands to pull him closer, surging with him, making a deep groaning noise.

"Harder," she moaned.

Ronny smiled and pushed harder. "Tell me to stop if I hurt you."

"Harder."

The slap of fles-on-flesh competed with the loud squishing noise he made on each thrust. Beneath him, she began to keen. The sounds of her arousal filled him with heat like never before in his life. Not even his very first time had he been so excited. He came hard, each thrust a glorious release. She screamed and bucked her hips as she came again, wetting his balls with her orgasm.

Laughing, she pulled him down for a long kiss. "That was amazing," she said when they broke from the kiss. "I've never done that before. You think that was a one-time thing because we were so frustrated?"

"Give me twenty minutes, and we'll find out."

She laughed again and ran her hands over his arms and chest. He smiled and gathered her close, rolling her from the wet spot. He loved how uninhibited she was, how excited she became. A glance at his watch showed he had forty-four hours before he had to report for duty. He began kissing his way down her body, wanting to make every moment count.

A sleepy mumbled, 'See you tonight,' answered his morning kiss as she rolled over, pulling the blanket over her head.

He chuckled as he dressed from his untouched suitcase. They hadn't left the room at all. The room service bill would be astronomical, and he couldn't care less. It hadn't been a fluke. In fact, every time they made love it felt better. He didn't know how it was possible, but she got him hotter each time. He'd never had sex before with such an athletic woman. She'd ruined him for anyone else. The thought of large breasts and soft curves did nothing for him now. Just thinking of her smooth skin and small, firm breasts made him groan. He couldn't wait for tonight.

A grin on his face, he headed home to change before heading to the range.

SEVEN

——— ◆ ———

WRONG FLOOR

Ronny held the passenger-side van door for Angie, then helped Cameron into the back with her crutches. She didn't need help; he just liked to touch her.

She grinned her thanks and ran two fingers over her lips. Heat filled him, making his jeans uncomfortably tight. He knew she was thinking of last night. They'd spent every night together since he'd returned a month ago. The best month of his life. Her company made everything better. Hell, he was even willing to escort her and Angie shopping to spend time with her, something he'd never done for any woman in the past.

"Where to first?" He'd offered to drive, not liking the thought of Angie cramming herself behind the wheel.

"My doctor's office. I have an appointment, and it shouldn't take more than ten minutes for him to confirm I no longer need the crutches." Cameron's eyes met his in the rearview mirror, and her grin widened.

A hot blush scalded his cheeks, deepening when she snickered. She reached forward and rubbed his neck, her expression changing to one he recognized but had never seen outside the bedroom before. They were both looking forward to her being able to kneel. He wouldn't let her be on top, too worried she'd hurt her injured knee. Last night she'd tried to tease him into it and had almost succeeded.

He cleared his throat and turned hastily away before his body reacted anymore to her.

———◆———

When Cameron exited her doctor's office, she carried the crutches under her arm.

"Good as new." Cameron winked at him.

Angie rose awkwardly from the waiting room chair and stretched.

"You sure you're up for shopping?" Ronny asked doubtfully, eyeing Angie's bulk. She looked ready to pop to him.

"Yes, just one stop to buy material for the baby's bassinet. An hour tops."

Cameron took Angie's arm, grinning at him.

"Lead on," Ronny said and bowed them into the elevator with a flourish.

The elevator lowered and dinged. Ronny stepped out, then laughed. "Wrong floor, Ang. The car is above us."

"You sure?" Angie stepped forward and extended her arm.

In her hand she held the remote for her car. Instead of the beep-beep of a car alarm, an explosion above them rocked the building. A cement pillar beside

Ronny crashed to the ground, missing him by a hair. A wave of hot air and dust mixed with small bits of concrete rocked him back. Cameron grabbed his shoulder and yanked him into the elevator as dust and fragments of cement exploded past him.

She stabbed the down button. As the door closed, another grinding screech heralded the arrival of an enormous block of cement. Pieces broke off and slammed against the door of the elevator, denting it. The noise of the impacts was lost in the rumbling roar above them.

Angie screamed and clutched Ronny's arm. He automatically put an arm around her. The bulk of her belly against him filled him with horror. This parking garage was coming down. The lights in the elevator flickered and dimmed.

"Come on!" Cameron chanted and stabbed the down button repeatedly as she reached for the phone in her back pocket.

With a jerking groan, the elevator began to descend.

Cameron turned to him, her face white as the lights went out. The screeching crash above them picked up in volume, the noise so loud it rattled his bones. Angie screamed again and grabbed him harder. He put both arms around her, afraid she would faint and hurt the baby. Cameron grabbed him too. She seemed concerned for the baby as well, putting her body on the other side of Angie, both of them holding her up.

Outside of the elevator, a loud continuous roar was broken by explosions.

"Cars exploding," he said as Angie screamed again.

The elevator jerked to a stop, the floors and walls vibrating. Above them, the metal of the roof buckled.

Dim light lit the small space. Cameron had her cell phone out. He glanced at the display panel above the door, hoping it would read one or two but it too was dark. By his best estimate, they'd descended one floor before the elevator jerked to a halt.

Cameron yelled into her phone, "Car bomb. We're in the parking garage elevator, heading to the bottom floor of the River Medical Center. Hello? Hello? Fuck, I lost service. The admiral will know where I meant as soon as the news plays," Cameron said reassuringly and turned her phone off.

"My beeper." Angie released Ronny to fumble with her purse.

Outside, the sounds had become more muffled and slowed. Another loud crash above them made Angie moan. The elevator jerked twice and began to fall. Ronny grabbed Angie and pulled her to the floor on top of him.

"Oh God, the baby," she wailed.

He wanted to wail too. "We'll be okay, just hang in there." He meant to say more, but the elevator crashed into the floor, the impact jolting his entire body. Air left his lungs in a whoosh. Angie bit back a scream, this one different from the others— pain filled, not afraid.

A series of crashes was followed by a thunderous roar so loud he couldn't tell if the women with him screamed or not. The light from Cameron's phone appeared hazy when she stood and played it around the elevator.

"Dust, not smoke. It'll settle." Cameron took her metal crutch and braced it against the door. The other she placed upright in the corner before kneeling awkwardly beside Angie. "Are you okay?"

"I don't know." Angie sounded scared to death.

Ronny tightened his hold on her. "Don't move yet. Let's all be still while the building settles. Cam, try your phone again, then mine. It's in my back pocket."

Cameron tried her phone, then his, then Angie's; none got a signal.

The glow of her phone showed more dust filtering into the elevator. Angie began to cough. She moaned and grabbed her stomach, slipping to the floor beside Ronny to curl up.

Cameron glanced at her, then Ronny, her lips tightened, and she moved to put her back to the door, trying to use her body to stop the dust from entering the crack in the door.

"It's okay. Everyone, remain calm," Ronny said. "The dust will settle soon, and it's good we have air. Is all we have to do is wait for rescue."

He rolled onto his side to put his arms around Angie.

The smell of smoke came to him over the bitter scent of concrete dust. He peered over his shoulder at Cameron. Her bleak gaze met his.

"Keep trying the phones," he said.

Outside, the sounds died down to an occasional groan and creak.

Cameron switched off her phone and crammed it into her back pocket. "We might be stuck here awhile. I'm going to turn off Angie's and my phone and use yours. You had the lowest battery." Cameron placed her hands against the metal door and nodded reassuringly. "Cool to the touch still. I can smell smoke, but it doesn't seem to be traveling to us. Ang, did the fall hurt you?"

"My back hurts a lot, and I think I peed myself."

Cameron handed Ronny his phone and knelt beside Angie. "Did your water break?"

"I don't know. I've never done this before. Dan was supposed to be with me. I can't have a baby now—here!" her voice rose, becoming shrill.

"I agree, don't have the baby here," Ronny said.

Cameron snorted.

Angie laughed half-hysterically.

"I hope you peed yourself. You're not due for two more weeks." Ronny smoothed her hair and rubbed her back.

Angie moaned and curled tighter. "I need Dan."

"I'm sure he's coming as fast as he can. Try to relax," Cameron said as she sat beside Angie and stroked her hair. "I'm going to turn off the phone to save the battery. You aren't alone; we're here."

Ronny took Cameron's hand and rested their clasped hands on Angie's back. The three of them sat silently, listening to the building settle around them.

"I think it's over," Cameron said an hour later.

"Ang, how you doing?" Ronny straightened in alarm when she didn't reply.

The glow of his cell phone revealed her closed eyes and tear-streaked face.

"I think she fell asleep. Leave her alone," Cameron whispered.

"You sure?" Ronny leaned closer, trying to see if she breathed.

"Does it matter? What could we do to help her?" Cameron said, sounding grim and worried as she stood and took her phone from her pocket. She played the light over the ceilings and walls, then the ceiling again.

"There's a trap door in the ceiling but look how dented it is. I'm betting there's chunks of cement on it. If we open it, we could let an avalanche inside," Cameron said.

Ronny crawled to the door and pressed his eye against the narrow crack. "Still smells smoky, but not too bad. It looks to me like debris is right up against the door almost the entire way. Big, heavy chunks and broken rebar we won't be able to move. I don't think we should open this either."

He returned to Angie and examined her. Dust coated her face, sticking to the tears and dulling her blond hair.

"We should save the light," Cameron said.

Ronny nodded and turned off his phone. "They'll come for us."

"Will they? Won't they assume we're dead? Eventually, they'll dig us out when clearing the rubble, but will they hurry? We have no food or water and a very pregnant woman. And let's say others are trapped in this wreck. We'll they be careful to not crush us while digging to them?"

"Those are some cheerful thoughts, Cam."

"We need to contact someone and let them know we're in here."

"How?"

"I don't know."

They were both quiet. Ronny considered their predicament, and his thoughts made him really unhappy.

"Cam, how long do you think it will take to reach us, assuming they try? The parking garage was six stories, and it sounded like the entire thing collapsed."

"The elevator is on the edge— I'd say fifteen – twenty feet inside. The reinforced concrete probably saved our lives, but it'll be a bitch to cut through. The explosion likely knocked out the building support above us, so five stories of concrete and maybe a vehicle or two, but not many. The handicapped parking spot near us was empty and the lot itself less than half full, so likely fewer cars were on the top level. How many explosions did you count?"

"Six distinct ones, you?"

"Same. So, either all the cars didn't explode, we missed some, or a bunch of people already left."

"You think the cars were rigged like hers?"

"No. I think compression caused some to explode."

"So, the others could go at any time?" Ronny sighed when Cameron didn't answer. "It could've been worse. We could've gotten off on the right floor."

Cameron sounded congested when she spoke as if fighting back tears. "This might be worse. I don't look forward to starving to death with my pregnant friend. Lack of water will trigger labor." Her voice caught on a sob.

"We'll be okay. Dan won't give up. The admiral will realize we were in the elevator. Come over here beside me and get some rest."

The elevator creaked as Cameron crawled around Angie. She settled against his side, resting her head on his chest. He ran his fingers through her short hair, the silky strands soft despite the dust that coated them.

"I wish we were alone," he said.

A soft breath of a laugh met that.

"I wish Angie hadn't driven me or came along," Cameron said bitterly. "I wish I'd come here alone."

"Me too because I'd never stop trying to find you." Ronny lay back with his eyes closed, taking her with him.

From the relaxation of her body, he assumed Cameron slept. The sirens in the distance had faded leaving him in silence; silence broken by sharp cracks and pings as the building continued to settle. The distant sounds didn't bother him. The ones on the roof above them terrified him.

An indeterminate amount of time later Angie stirred.

"Ronny?" Her voice wavered, and her hands gripped him hard.

"I'm here, and we're okay, just resting."

"I have to pee."

"Go ahead. We can't see a thing. Do you need a light?"

"Um, yes, please. I want to make sure I'm not bleeding."

Cameron woke when he sat to hand his phone to Angie.

"We'll turn our backs."

"How long have we been here?" Cameron asked.

"Six hours," Angie said.

She returned and handed Ronny his phone.

"You okay?"

"Just a few spots of blood. My back still really hurts, and I'm thirsty. I'm always thirsty, and I pee constantly." The sound of fumbling in the dark followed. "I brought a water bottle, and it didn't break. And I have two granola bars we can share."

"Cam and I did some figuring, and we'll be here a day or two, so go easy on the water," Ronny said.

"Will they look for us?"

Ronny reached for her in the dark and slid closer until he could put an arm around her. "You know Dan will never give up."

She sighed and relaxed against his shoulder. "Was that bomb meant for me or Cameron do you think?"

"Hell, for all we know it was meant for me. Let's not worry about that now."

"Poor Sam." Tears laced Angie's voice.

"No crying; we need to conserve water," Cameron said. "And besides, Sam is fine. Char will take good care of him until you get back."

Angie said nothing, her warm breath on his neck stuttered as she bit back a sob.

Poor Sam is right, Ronny thought as he stroked Angie's hair. To lose another mother would be a big blow, one he wasn't sure the child could recover from. Sam had given his heart to Angie, trusting she would always love him; to lose her...

"So, who knows a good ghost story?" he said, trying to sound cheerful and upbeat.

Cameron made a thoughtful sound as if she were thinking.

"I know a good story, but it's real," Angie said.

To Ronny's relief, Angie sat straighter and sounded calmer.

"The story of how my grandparents met is hair-raising. He was a Marine in World War Two and got separated from his platoon after being shot and left for dead. When he woke, he was alone behind enemy lines. For a week he trailed his outfit, to slow to catch up. Every day he got sicker, infection had set in and he was feverish.

"A woman found him; she'd been out scavenging for food. Anyways, she brought him back to her hideout and nursed him to health. Bombs fell around them and men fought nearby, but Gramps was too weak to seek help. His radio no longer worked, a dead battery they had no way to charge. The woman, my future grandmother, had an idea. They could connect—"

"That's it," Cameron said, sounding excited and pulled out her cell phone.

"What's it?" Angie let Cameron take her purse.

Cameron rummaged through it and emerged triumphant, clutching the beeper.

"Give me your knife."

Ronny unsheathed the knife on his ankle and handed it to her.

"Ang, do you have hair clips? I need something to clamp these lines." While she spoke, Cameron pried open the back of the beeper. She laid it on the floor and used the knife to pry the door of the locked emergency panel open.

"There's no power," Ronny said as he knelt behind her to hold up the phone.

"I'm counting on that." Cameron used the knife to unscrew the cover over the buttons behind the door and let it fall to the floor. "We don't need power; we need an antenna. If any of these wires can reach the outside, we might be able to get a signal through. Hand me the beeper." She stripped the edges of a group of bundle wires with the knife and separated them.

Cameron attached the beeper to the black wire and

turned it over and began typing. "I'm calling Dan. We'll send this message for an hour, then I'll switch wires. We'll work from left to right. Ron, see if you can get the panel off the control switches; there'll be more wires there. Be careful though, we don't really know if there are any live wires."

Ronny took the knife she handed him and examined the cover over the call buttons. A row of eight large screws held it in place. "The knife is too thin to stick in the grooves."

"There's the security camera too," Angie said.

"Great idea! I'll try that one next. That might have a wireless receiver," Cameron said. "Maybe I can even power the receiver." She finished connecting the beeper and shone her light on the camera in the corner. "Can you give me a hand to reach it?"

"Maybe my keys will work better to unscrew the bolts." Angie opened her purse and searched for the keys. "Damn, I can't find them."

"Probably dropped them," Ronny said as he lifted Cameron towards the camera.

Angie rose and began examining the floor. "Ah ha," she said triumphantly and stooped for the keys. "Ahh!" she screamed and clutched her stomach, falling to her knees.

EIGHT

———— ◆ ————

CAMERON'S GOT THIS

Ronny dropped Cameron and raced to Angie. "What?"

"It hurts. Help me; it hurts." Rocking and moaning, Angie clutched her stomach.

He threw a panicked glance to Cameron who met his eyes with a worried squint. She knelt beside Angie.

"Take deep even breaths. Can you lay back?" Cameron asked calmly.

"Yes, it's better now." Angie's voice trembled. She stayed curled in a ball on the floor. "Oh, God, Cameron, the baby— the baby." Her voice trailed off to a moan.

"Okay, don't try to move." Ronny reached down and grabbed her wrist. Her pulse beat fast against his fingertips. Sweat beaded her brow, showing clearly in the dust that coated her face.

"I'm going to be sick," she moaned.

"What do we do?" he whispered to Cameron.

Cameron shrugged helplessly and gathered Angie's hair from her face. "Hand me her purse."

She removed an envelope and began fanning Angie. "Breathe nice and slow. That's it, nice easy breaths."

The pulse under his fingertips accelerated. He was ready when she sat and heaved. Both arms around her stomach, she continued to dry heave between moans. Ronny supported her weight and laid her gently on the floor when she was finished.

"The baby is coming," Cameron said calmly. "We can handle this. Juan will be fine. It might take a while, just relax as much as you can." She kissed Angie's brow and smiled crookedly at Ronny before rising and heading to the beeper. "I'm going to try a new line. I think waiting an hour is too long. I'll do them all for ten minutes, then an hour."

Ronny wished he could do something to ease Angie, but he couldn't even wipe her face with a damp towel. The limited water needed to be saved for drinking.

"There's antacids in my bag; can I have one please?"

The small, scared sound of Angie's voice nearly broke his heart.

"You're going to be just fine," he said forcefully as he grabbed her bag and rooted through it. He handed her two antacid tablets and the water bottle. Behind him, Cameron mumbled too low to make out, but he thought she was praying.

Ronny picked up the phone Angie had dropped and tried again to make a call, but still had no service. Cameron returned and sat beside him. He turned off his phone, leaving them in darkness. The dark seemed to magnify Angie's panting breath.

"Get the camera wire; I'm okay," Angie said.

The lie was clear in her voice. Ronny winced and kissed her temple. "We're right here."

Beside him, Cameron flicked on her phone and rose to examine the camera again. "I'll need something to tie my phone to my head so I can see what I'm doing."

"My bra has a ton of elastic in it, and underwire; maybe you could use that?" Angie offered.

"Give me the knife, and I'll cut it off. Don't try to move." Cameron held her hand out for the knife.

Angie laughed, then groaned as Cameron cut the bra off her.

Cameron held the empty bra before her and giggled. Ronny laughed, and grabbed it, then took the knife to cut the elastic out.

"I think I grew two sizes since becoming pregnant," Angie said defensively, causing Cameron to laugh again.

"We could make baby clothes with this." Cameron held up the discarded cup and stretched it out.

"Oh, don't make me laugh," Angie gasped, laughing as she grasped her stomach.

Cameron chuckled, tied the elastic around her head, and slipped her phone under it. "I feel ridiculous," she muttered as she grasped the knife in one hand, using the other to balance against the wall as Ronny lifted her. "I need both hands; can you hold the knife a sec?"

Ronny tightened his grip on her legs and took the knife she handed him. "Hold on, I'm going to change positions." He turned and leaned on the wall, bending one knee and bracing it against the wall, he shifted her until she stood on his knee. "How's that?"

"I can reach. Am I hurting you?"

"Nope," Ronny lied.

For a few minutes she fussed and tugged at the camera. The cell phone didn't give enough light to tell what she did or show Angie as more than a darker blob in the darkness. A shower of small debris cascaded onto him, making her swear.

"Okay, let me down to get the beeper. The camera won't do a spit of good. Its receiver is outside the elevator, and I can't reach it to attach to a phone. I'll try the beeper 'cause what could it hurt?"

Angie groaned.

"Contraction?" Cameron asked

"I don't know. I never had one before. It hurts though."

"We'll keep track. Still feel sick?"

"No."

"Great. We can do this. Just try to rest." While she spoke, Cameron disconnected the beeper and returned to Ronny who was massaging his leg. He let her stand on the other one this time. Connecting the beeper took much less time.

"What message are you sending?' Ronny asked.

"Stuck btm elev. The beeper can only send a short message. I can change it for the next round."

"No, that seems pretty good."

Cameron relocated the beeper twice more before Angie groaned again.

"Thirty-five minutes or so apart." Cameron knelt beside Angie and took her hand. "When they get closer we should remove your sweats. I'll deliver the baby."

Ronny heaved a relieved sigh, making both women laugh. "It's not that I don't want to help..."

"We got this. You can sit behind her and support her upper body. The delivery should be easier if she's more upright. And you can hold the light. Do you have matches or a lighter?"

"No, sorry."

"Me either," Angie said.

"Okay, we don't need it. We will need your T-shirt though for the baby. Not yet." Cameron laid a hand on his arm and squeezed when he began unbuttoning his shirt. "This will take a while, and the floor is dirtier than you are."

"I'll put it in her purse." Ronny removed his lightweight, long-sleeve, button down shirt and white T-shirt. He shook them out, then folded both and placed them in Angie's purse.

"Get the knife as clean as we can." Cameron squeezed his arm again hard.

Ronny realized she was worried about how dirty this elevator was but didn't want Angie to worry.

"I'll wipe it good, but it should be pretty clean. I just cleaned it a few days ago and only used it here." The hand on his arm loosened. He grabbed it and kissed it before setting it back.

"Good," Cameron said, sounding relieved.

"There's a small package of baby wipes in my bag I use on Sam's face," Angie said. "I'm sorry to be so much trouble."

"You aren't." Ronny felt in the darkness for her hand and held it. "Cameron has this all under control. She knows what to do. You relax."

Cameron sighed sadly in his ear. He released Angie to pat her cheek. "Cameron's got this," he repeated for Cameron's benefit.

"Three minutes apart now." Sweat beaded on Cameron's forehead. The sickly blue glow of the cell phone illuminated her face briefly before she turned it off. "Take another sip of water, Ang. Soon you're going to be too busy."

"Dear God, make it soon," Ronny mumbled under his breath.

For thirty-two hours now they'd been cooped up in the elevator. Thirty-two hours of progressively worse pain coming more frequently. Angie was so exhausted she dozed between contractions, waking with a cry that changed to hard pants as she tried not to cry out.

"Will the baby be okay?" he asked as Angie relaxed her grip on his hand and dozed.

"No idea. God, I hope so. I'm not sure if we should keep her laying or have her walk. Walking will bring the pains closer, but it hurts her when she stretches out. I'm afraid the fall injured her."

"Let her stay on the floor."

Angie shrieked and gripped his hand.

"Much closer now, Ang. It's almost over." He tried to infuse his voice with confidence. "What was that, one minute, Cam?"

"Yep. Nice deep breaths." Cameron knelt between Angie's knees and breathed with her.

Angie sobbed as her water broke and squeezed his hand hard. He squeezed back. "Juan wants out. We're almost there."

"Push with the next contraction, Ang," Cameron said calmly.

Ronny had never been so grateful for Cameron's presence in his life. Her quiet directions calmed him.

Cool and competent she guided the birth of Angie's son.

"I see his head. You're doing great.

Angie screamed and fell back against his chest.

"I've got him."

Angie began crying. "Is he—"

A baby's wail cut her off.

"Give me a hand here," Cameron said.

Ronny slid Angie to the floor and took the small bundle wrapped in his T-shirt.

Too dark to examine him, he brushed his fingertips over the delicate skull to the pulse in his neck that beat fast, but steady.

"Just a few more, and these will be easier," Cameron said.

"Can I see him?" Angie reached for the baby, grabbing his arm.

Ronny laid Juan on her breast and closed her arms around him, keeping one hand on the baby's back.

"Thank you, both of you. You saved his life and mine." She groaned and panted.

Cameron swore, stopping abruptly. The light wavered crazily as she pulled off her shirt.

"Tell Dan his name is Juan Ronald."

Ronny inhaled sharply as Angie's arms fell to her side.

"Cam?"

"She's bleeding quite a bit. Ang? Have the contractions stopped?"

"I'm so tired," Angie murmured.

Cameron sobbed and called her name again.

"I'm okay, just tired."

"Okay, rest. We'll take care of Juan Ron." Cameron

laughed semi-hysterically. "I love that name; he's going to grow up to be a real ladies man.

"Juan Ron," Angie murmured and giggled. "I love you."

"Sleep, we've got your son." Tears burned his eyes. The cell phone revealed Cameron's distress, and blood covered hands. She'd used her shirt to try to staunch the bleeding. Ronny gathered the baby who squirmed a moment before settling. He felt for the pulse in Angie's neck. It beat slow, but it beat.

"Great job, Cam." He crawled to her, carrying the baby, and kissed her lips. "How can I help?"

She shook her head and lifted tear-filled eyes to his.

"You rest too; I'll watch them both. When Angie wakes, we'll give her the rest of the water."

Cameron nodded dully and stretched out beside Angie. Ronny sat beside them, holding the baby to his chest. Four hours passed. He gradually became aware of noise in the distance. He wondered how long the noise had been there before he noticed. He felt dull-witted. Exhaustion and stress had taken their toll, making his reactions slow. The baby in his arms stirred.

"Hungry, little man?"

He nudged Angie who murmured sleepily. Her skin felt cold and clammy.

"Cam?" He had to shake her to wake her. " I think the baby is hungry, and do you hear that?"

She took the baby from him and got to her feet. "Yes, sounds like machinery. Is Ang—"

"Alive, but weak. I don't think she's strong enough to feed the baby."

"I'll help her. Sit her up a bit."

Ronny sat and pulled Angie into his lap.

"Is the baby okay?" she asked.

"He's fine. Don't try to sit, Cam and I will help."

Cameron knelt beside Angie and unbuttoned her shirt, holding the baby to the breast she revealed. Ronny held Angie's arm around the baby. Small mews of discontent changed to sucking sounds and they all relaxed.

"Can you hold him?" Cameron asked.

"I got him," Ronny said.

Cameron rose and removed the beeper. She fiddled with it a moment before replacing it. "I wish I knew if the messages are getting through."

"I think he's full," Angie said.

Cameron removed the baby, handing him to Ronny and closed Angie's shirt.

Ronny patted Juan's back gently.

"I changed the message. Another son. Dan will come," Cameron said.

"Yes. Soon I hope. I don't think I'll produce milk for long."

Reminded, Ronny handed her the water bottle. "Finish it. We can hear them outside; it won't be long now."

Angie drank the water and fell asleep again.

"Let me take the baby, and you sleep," Ronny said as he peered through the dark at Cameron.

She held the baby to her shoulder, a tender smile on her face. The sight faded too black as she turned the cell phone off. He wanted that smile for himself. He wanted a family with her. Her strength was more than physical, it was mental. Solid and dependable, a woman to count on, one that could cradle a baby or rifle with equal ease. With all his soul, he wanted her. He drifted to sleep with daydreams of a life with Cameron dancing in his head.

When he woke, Cameron slept beside him, the baby between them still wrapped in his shirt placed on Angie's sweatpants. Dust coated Ronny. The dry, desiccated state of his mouth and throat convinced him he'd breathed in a fair amount. He'd kill for a sip of water.

His cell phone had long since died. Soon they'd be completely in the dark. Only Angie's phone still held a charge and that one small. A muffled crash was followed by a closer sharper bang. Both women woke.

"Use the light to feed and check the baby." Ronny shuffled on his knees to Angie, carrying the baby, and handed Juan to Cameron. She helped Angie feed him then unwrapped him. Everyone stared at him. The dim glow of the cell phone turned his skin a sickly blue. Smeared with blood and flaking white patches it was hard to judge his condition.

"The shirts only a little damp. We can still use it," Cameron rewrapped him as she spoke. "The light won't last much longer. Nobody moves when they wake until they're sure the baby is safe. We don't want to step on him in the dark."

Another sharp clang interrupted her. Above them, the ceiling groaned. Ronny leaned over Angie, blocking a rain of pebbles from her with his body.

"Can I hold him?" Angie's hand trembled against his arm.

"Let's move her to the wall first," Cameron suggested.

Ronny nodded and picked Angie up. Her slight

weight was easy to move. No longer cold and clammy, she felt hot as if she had a fever. He placed her against the wall and put her sweatpants in the crook of her arm. Cameron placed the baby there.

He and Cameron sat beside her. The cell phone died, leaving them in darkness.

Angie spoke to Juan in a quiet voice, telling her son how much she loved him. Tears filled Ronny's eyes, she wouldn't last much longer without medical care. It had been over two days now and hours since she'd had even a sip of water. He'd never been so thirsty in his life. A headache throbbed behind his right eye.

Another loud series of bangs rattled the roof of the elevator. A muffled beep followed by a distant crash ended in silence.

"Sounded like a truck backing up. They must be close," Cameron said.

"Cam, grab the crutches. We'll lean them on the wall over Ang and Juan."

In a few seconds, the crutches were in place. Ronny and Cameron sat before them ready to use their bodies to block debris falling from the ceiling.

"I think they're trying to come down the elevator shaft," Cameron said an hour or so later.

Angie had stopped speaking and dozed off. At least Ronny hoped she'd dozed off. Her pulse fluttered under his fingertips. He wasn't sure if she slept or was unconscious.

"Jesus, this must be horrifying for her."

Cameron took his hand and kissed it before speaking. "She's been so brave. I don't think I could be that brave."

Ronny snorted. "You're the bravest woman I know.

Braver than me anyway. I couldn't have delivered a baby like that. How'd you even know what to do?"

"I didn't; I was making it up as I went along."

"Well, you're amazing. I—"

A loud squeal interrupted him. The roof buckled with an ominous sound. Small chunks of debris rained down. Light flickered and grew into a steady beam. Somewhere, an engine hummed, and men hollered.

"We're down here!" Cameron yelled.

Ronny glanced at Angie, the dim light revealed her dust coated face, but she didn't move.

Cameron continued to yell. The light disappeared. Another long metallic screech ended in a rain of bigger debris. Light returned. A hole gaped in the ceiling where the hatch had been torn out. Cameron laughed and hugged him. She quieted when a man called on a bullhorn.

"We're lowering a harness. The sides are very unstable so try not to contact them. Let the winch pull you out."

"You go first with the baby." Ronny picked up Juan and kissed his cheek. The baby mewed and swung a tiny fist. Cameron bit her lip and nodded. She took the baby and tucked him close to her chest. Ronny removed the radio attached to the rope and helped her step into the harness.

"Tell them Angie will be unconscious. See if they can send down more straps so I can tie her." He kissed Cameron and stepped back, giving the rope a sharp tug and flicked on the radio.

"This is Ronald Mitland, Cameron Howard is in the harness and ready to ascend; she has a baby with her."

"Oh thank, God. Is Angie okay?' Dan sounded sick.

"No. She's alive but very sick. Have medical standing by. Juan seems to be doing well."

"Ron..."

"I'll get her out." Ronny knelt beside Angie and replaced her filthy sweatpants. The blood-soaked shirt between her legs made him grimace. "So much blood," he murmured as he picked her up. Debris rained down, knocked loose by Cameron's passage. Ronny blocked the bulk with his body, but small pieces bounced off him onto her. Angie didn't wake.

The harness returned. A water bottle and extra straps accompanied it.

Ronny smiled as he chugged it. Cameron's idea he was sure.

"How much can this winch hold?"

"Five hundred pounds."

He laid Angie beside his feet, stepped into the harness and tightened it. Her limp weight was awkward to handle. He curled her against his chest and used the straps to hold her to him.

"Pull us up."

Hunched over Angie's head, he blocked the rocks from her face with his body. Sharp, jagged edges of metal and cement lined the narrow hole cleared in the elevator shaft. A boom hung out over the hole from which the harness dangled.

Floodlights lit the night sky, blindingly bright after days of darkness. One side of the shaft appeared to tumble away, the other towered above him, three stories of teetering concrete. Rough concrete scrapped his back as the boom swung him away. Fire trucks and police cars surrounded a cleared area where three ambulances waited with lights flashing.

Dan reached him first, guiding his body to the ground. Pale and haggard his dirty face broke into a grim smile. "Thanks, man." He unclipped his wife and turned to the ambulance.

"Ha, thank you."

Dan didn't acknowledge his thanks too busy with his unconscious wife.

Paramedics ran up and began connecting IV's. Dan placed her on a stretcher, and he and Ronny backed away to give the paramedics space to work.

"Go— we'll talk later." Ronny slapped Dan's back and pushed him after his wife.

Ronny headed to Cameron. Wrapped in a gray blanket, she sat in the back of an ambulance holding a water bottle. Squirrel sat beside her cradling a rifle.

"Ronny," JT called.

Ronny halted and turned to his boss. A deep sigh escaped him as he stopped and straightened. He wanted to go to Cameron and tell her he loved her.

JT gestured him to the third ambulance. "We can talk on the way to the hospital."

Ronny peered over his shoulder. Cameron held up a hand in farewell and said something to the paramedic with her. The paramedic closed the doors.

"She's safe," JT said and followed Ronny into the back of an ambulance.

Ronny let the paramedic give him an IV. He accepted the water bottle gratefully and drank it all. The paramedic handed him another and began cleaning the scrapes on his back.

"We have guards on Cameron and Angie. The explosives used makes us think this was Al-Jadr though. The amounts used was ridiculous. Either they have no idea what they're doing, or they were taking no chances it would miss. They blew the top floor right off the building. Chunks rained down in a half-mile radius. Luckily no one was killed by falling debris but the property damage is in the millions."

"Was anyone else caught in the explosion?"

"Two assumed dead. The attendant escaped as the top floor crashed down, and twelve people were hospitalized with minor injuries. Rescue efforts continue, but it's unlikely the other two are alive. We thought all three of you had been killed until Dan received the messages. Then the messages stopped, and we thought you'd run out of air or something.

"Our lights died, and Cam couldn't change the beeper anymore. I wonder which wire worked."

"What?"

"Cam connected Angie's beeper to different wires, hoping one would work as an antenna."

"Ah, that explains the timing of the messages. Dan got a new message about every hour and a half, then they slowed to one every six hours or so, then none. He was frantic. I don't blame him. I can't imagine how crazy I'd be if Char had our son under those conditions. How bad is Angie injured?"

"I'm not sure. The birth was rough, over thirty hours of labor, and she bled a lot. I think the elevator falling hurt her. But maybe it was the lack of food and water."

JT winced. "This is the third attempt on Cameron's life. The admiral has ordered Darmin to send a team to retrieve Alfarsi. You going to be up for it?'

"Hell, yes!" Ronny straightened and tried not look

as tired as he felt.

JT chuckled and slapped his shoulder. "If the doctor clears you, we go tomorrow."

"Hoorah!"

NINE

———◆———

Take Care of Our Family

Twelve hours later, Ronny entered Angie's hospital room. Pale and haggard, Dan rose from his seat beside her and grabbed him in a hard hug.

"Thank you."

"How is she?"

"She'll be okay. They're keeping her here until her blood count is normal, but they say it should happen fast with the transfusions. I thought she was dead— that you'd all been killed. When I got that message, I've never been so relieved and afraid in my life. She's taking years off my life. I've gone on a hundred missions, and she scares me more than anything I've ever faced."

"And Juan?" Ronny leaned down and kissed Angie's brow.

She stirred but didn't wake.

"Perfect. I can't thank you and Cameron enough. Sam is with Charlene visiting Juan now. Sam has no idea anything happened except Mommy had the baby and needs rest. They have Juan under lamps to clear his jaundice, but he's going to be just fine too." Dan cleared his throat and rubbed his stubbled cheeks hard. "Ronny, you just can't know... I can't thank you enough."

"I did nothing except be there, and frankly, I feel horrible for bringing danger to your lives. JT says the bomb was from Al-Jadr."

"Yeah, I knew that on day one. They sent a message. Komar signed it himself." Dan lowered his voice. "I get him in my sights, he's a dead man."

"You coming, then?"

"Yes. My family will be much safer with that man dead." Dan took his wife's limp hand and kissed it. "Lee is packing my kit and will pick me up. I won't miss it."

Ronny eyed Dan skeptically. A two-day growth of beard covered his cheeks, and dark circles ringed his eyes. Worse was the way his hands jittered. "Have you slept at all?"

"Not much. How could I? I can sleep on the way over." Dan flexed his fingers and shook his hands out as if he could cast off the jitters. "Too much coffee, but I'll be fine in a day."

"Tell your wife I stopped by. I'm going to go see Juan. See ya on the plane." Ronny slapped Dan's back and left the room, letting the door slid closed behind him.

A two-man Marine guard stood in the hallway outside Angie's door; another two stood before the door of the nursery. One checked Ronny's ID against a list before his partner let him enter.

Sam ran to him and grabbed his legs. Cameron glanced up from her seat beside the small crib and smiled.

"Hey, pal, how do you like your new brother?" He scooped the boy up and kissed his cheek.

"I love him. I'm going to be the best big brother ever. Come see him." Sam wiggled to be put down.

Ronny released him. Sam grabbed his hand and tugged him to the baby.

A nurse cleared her throat. "Please don't touch him unless you wash and put on a sterile robe.

Ronny laughed and tried to bite it back. Cameron's giggle made him laugh hard. He waved his hand apologetically at the nurse who looked offended. "Sorry, it's just he was born in a pile of rubble. He's a tough little guy.

The nurse smiled and peeked into the crib. He's a miracle, that's for sure." She ruffled Sam's hair and left them alone.

"How are you?" Ronny kissed Cameron's cheek, wanting to really kiss her, but Sam inhibited him.

"Fine, you?"

"Rested and ready to go. We ship out in a few hours."

"I know. The admiral stopped by to inform me. A bomb was found in his car too. My call saved his life. It's how they know the type and amount of explosives used. You be careful, you hear me?"

"Yes, Ma'am." Ronny ran a hand over her hair.

At his side, Sam danced with impatience, tugging on him.

"Come on!"

Ronny laughed and turned to Juan. "He looked

better in the dark."

Cameron giggled again.

"He'll fill out quick. He isn't undernourished or anything, all babies are wrinkly and red. The lights will get rid of the yellowish tone. He's a good baby, isn't he, Sam?"

"He's the best baby," Sam said loyally, glaring at Ronny.

"Yes, I can see that," Ronny said hastily. He bit back a laugh as Sam eyed him suspiciously before smiling.

Charlene entered dressed in scrubs and wearing a face mask. "I would hug you, but I'm all sterile to hold the baby. Cam, can you bring Sam to his parents? Tell Angie I'm feeding Juan, but she should be able to for the next feeding."

Cam rose and held a hand to Sam who took it readily.

Ronny knelt on one knee before Sam. "I'll be away a while; you take good care of Mommy, Juan, and Cameron."

"I will." Sam released Cameron and ran to him, throwing his arms around his neck. Ronny picked him up and kissed his cheek, then handed him to Cameron and kissed her lips. He traced his thumb over her bottom lip.

"I'll be waiting when you get back," she said.

Ronny smiled after her. Her body language and tone spoke to his soul like no other woman ever had. Simple words spoken quickly held such meaning for him, as if she'd promised to be his forever. He hoped she felt it too when he spoke to her.

Charlene had taken Cameron's seat. The nurse

handed her the baby and draped a light blanket over him.

"He really is okay?"

"Yes. Nothing a day or two of tanning won't fix," the nurse assured him.

"I'll take good care of everyone," Charlene said. "You take care of our family."

"I'll do my very best." Ronny saluted and left.

———— ◆ ————

Freshly shaven and showered, and wearing a clean uniform, Dan slept beside him in the cramped airline seat. The men around them kept their voices down, but Ronny thought Dan could sleep through a siren. He hadn't stirred since he sat down.

"He's going to be stiff as hell," Lee said, nodding at Dan.

Tom glanced at Dan too and shrugged. "As long as his hands stop shaking." His brown eyes turned to Ronny and narrowed. "Did you call Dawn?"

Ronny groaned. "No, I completely forgot about her."

"Too late now." Lee slapped his knee and grinned at him.

Tom's glare deepened.

Ronny sighed and stretched, wriggling his shoulders to ease the soreness. "I'll call her as soon as I get a chance. You told her I was okay, right?"

"Yes, but I'm sure she'd rather hear it from her husband." Tom bit off each word as if they tasted vile.

"Don't start. You know that isn't how it is."

Tom sighed, closed his eyes and leaned back in the chair. "Right, sorry, and none of my business anyway."

Ronny hesitated, then burst out, "Fuck, this is awkward as fucking hell. Did you two have a fight?"

Tom snorted.

Lee winced and looked away, pretending to read a newspaper. The pretense would've been better if he turned the paper right side up.

Ronny sighed hard. "Dawn is my best friend. That's it. I'm happy for her if she's happy with you." A flush covered Ronny's cheeks, and he lowered his voice. "Dawn and I haven't been together in years."

Tom grunted and closed his eyes.

Ronny sighed again and grabbed the paper from Lee. He turned it right side up before pretending to read it.

The next thing he knew they were landing. He didn't remember falling asleep.

Dan woke and groaned when he stretched. Ronny was happy to see Dan's hands were steady. They swung their gear on their backs and waited their turn to disembark. Hot air slapped them in the face as they exited the plane.

Bagram Airbase sat in an ocean of gray. Dust coated everything. No greenery shaded the barren countryside. *Even the personnel seemed gray*, Ronny thought as they hiked across the hot tarmac. Khaki clothing blended into the landscape. Tan, sweaty faces glanced at them then away as if the heat sucked the curiosity from them. They ate a quick meal inside the cafeteria before changing into their gear and climbing aboard a helicopter.

Dusk was beginning to fall as the helicopter lifted off. Pink light tinted the land, turning a fiery, orange-red as the sun sank beyond the horizon. The ground they traveled over appeared dark and deserted. The deep thwap of the helicopter blades made talking difficult. No one spoke for the three-hour ride. Ronny examined his map of Pakistan again with a pen light. Beside him, Dan dozed with his SR-25 rifle at his feet.

"Don't miss the bus back," the pilot warned as they approached their drop off. "It's a hell of a long, dusty walk outa here."

Clouds of dust rose as the helicopter hovered feet from the ground. His pack already on his back, Ronny jumped the three feet to the ground with his rifle clutched in his hands.

SEAL Team Nine jogged away as the helicopter lifted and turned, heading back the way it came. JT lead them through the night. At dawn, they stopped. Steep forested mountains rose to their left. Before them, the dusty plain changed to a grass covered field leading to rolling foothills.

"We'll sleep a few hours before resuming our trek," JT said and settled himself against a dusty boulder. Ronny examined the ground before stretching out. Beside him, the other members of his team settled down to sleep. Without being told, Squirrel sat with his back against the lone, scraggly tree with his rifle in hand. He'd wake Keith in two hours. Keith would wake Lee, and Lee would wake Ronny.

Or maybe not, Ronny mused as he closed his eyes. They guys might skip him in guard rotation due to the recent events. Either way was okay with him, six hours of sleep was plenty.

He groaned and shook his head when JT woke him five hours later. "We leave in ten."

Ronny rose and stretched. He gobbled a meal bar and changed into his ghillie suit. Sweat immediately formed on his brow. In minutes, his shirt was damp from sweat. He tied a bandanna across his forehead to keep the sweat from dripping into his eyes.

JT slapped him on the back and began jogging. Ronny followed. JT lead them further west. After the first mile, he slowed to a fast walk. Every hour he stopped for five minutes. Signs of civilization appeared. Fences and rutted tracks dotted the landscape. A thick, green, wiry grass grew underfoot, appearing deceptively soft. More trees showed on the horizon, and the air around them cooled.

In mid-afternoon, JT called a halt. Ronny wanted to fall to the ground and wheeze, but the others barely seemed winded. Sweat soaked him, making even his pants feel wet. He bit back his groan and squatted to take a meal bar from his pack.

JT spread a map out. "We should be running across people soon. A small brook runs through the mountain here and crosses this plain before us. We can refill our water bottles. One purification tablet outa do it. "

Dan reached for his water bottle and drank the entire thing. Ronny copied him. Images of cold beer filled his mind. He'd kill for a fresh, cold draft right now. He almost snickered, he was about to kill for free.

As if reading his mind, JT narrowed his eyes, his gaze raking Dan and Ronny. "No one fires until I fucking say so. We want his ass alive. We have permission to be here. We don't have permission to shoot up the neighborhood. Our orders are to catch him!"

"Yes, sir," Dan said cheerfully.

JT rolled his eyes. Squirrel snickered and changed it to a cough when JT glared at him.

"Let's, go." JT sighed hard and rose. He folded the

map and stuck it back in his pack. His gaze traveled them, and he shook his head. "Darmin should've sent Schrowder's team," he muttered.

Ronny pondered that as they hiked. The only reason he could think of why Schrowder's team hadn't been sent was that Darmin wanted Alfarsi dead. With two members of the team with a personal grudge, it seemed likely he'd get his wish.

They stopped at the stream to wash and refill their canteens. Ronny dropped in the purification tablet and shook his canteen hard before drinking all the water and refilling it.

"We should reach the outskirts in another hour. We're going to hole up until dark and find positions." JT stood and took the binoculars from his belt. He scanned the countryside a moment, then gestured them forward.

Twenty minutes later, they lay in a depression in the grass. A small copse of jand trees grew behind them. Before them, the land settled downward for about a mile before rising steeply to form low hills. Wind brought the scent of wood smoke to them. The smell of roasting meat made Ronny's stomach growl.

He took out another bar and ate it. No one could see them nestled in the grass unless they stepped on them. Squirrel returned to the trees. Ronny crawled up the low bank and scanned until he saw him lying on his stomach beside a tree, peering through binoculars, then he slithered back down and closed his eyes.

He'd barely fallen asleep before JT woke him again. Cool night air dried the sweat on his face, and his clothing had dried while he slept. This was usually his favorite part— the stalk. He and Dan headed out across the field headed toward the hill. JT would move the others up behind them.

Every sense alert, Ronny listened hard for changes in the hum of insects and the call of birds. He smelled the goats before he saw them.

A small herd climbed the hill about fifty yards away. Dan stopped when he did and clicked his mic twice. Ronny lifted his scope to his eyes and scanned the hillside slowly. The night vision attachment gave everything an eerie, green glow. When he was certain the goats were unattended he rose.

Dan clicked the mic twice, and they continued. Slinking slow and careful they crested the hill. Before them, a valley spread out dotted with buildings and fences. According to the CIA, Alfarsi hid somewhere in this village. Ronny counted quickly; thirty-six structures lay before them. Each would need to be checked.

"Fuck," he murmured.

Dan grunted. The two laid side-by-side and peered through their scopes.

"Let's get to the left more. We can see the doorways better." Dan clicked his mic three times and slithered backward down the hill. At a crouch, they ran along the edge of the hill. From this new position, a thick forest of trees became visible further to their left filling a narrow defile that led behind them. One side was sheer, the other steep and dotted with boulders and low scrub.

Dan clicked his mic five times. Ronny peered back the way they'd came. His team inched their way up the hillside. He turned back to the view before him.

"What do you think? The biggest house?" Ronny

asked.

Below them, one house stood out. Two stories tall, it towered over the other squat structures. A barn with a thatched roof sat beside it. Low stone walls surrounded it. To either side broad fenced pastures spread to the tree line.

Lights glimmered in the windows, but most telling was the man in the black robe who sat with his back against the wall beside the door. A rifle lay beside him.

"We wait and see."

Ronny peered over his shoulder again in time to see JT crest the hill. He sank down beside Dan.

"Nice spot," JT said.

Ronny had to agree, Dan had picked a nice vantage point. Only two trees grew on the steep hillside. Nothing else which should interest even a goat. There should be no reason anyone would approach them. As long as they didn't give themselves away, this was a great spot. If they were seen, the nearby trees offered concealment.

It would be possible to shake pursuers and escape— or kill them, Ronny thought with vicious satisfaction.

The mountain rose sharply at their back, lessening the chance someone would wander along below and see them. The spot where they lay was a shallow bowl that had once housed a boulder, which now lay cracked in half below them. From the amount of soil surrounding it, it had fallen quite a long time ago. Cultivated fields lay to the south. Smoke rose from house chimneys although the contour of the land hid the distant houses.

Dan pointed out the guard to JT.

"Watch for a day and see what's what. Squirrel, you, Lee, Tom, and Keith head to the trees and hunker down. I'll join you at daybreak. Dan and Ronny, get some sleep; it's going to be a long, hot day tomorrow.

Ronny handed his scope to JT and closed his eyes. He let his thoughts drift with memories of Cameron, trying to ignore the hard ground beneath him. Sunlight on his face woke him before JT did. Beside him, Dan still slept. Ronny took back his scope and waved JT away.

JT patted his shoulder and eased backward. Ronny waited until JT was out of sight before turning to his side and urinating. *One good thing about not eating for days,* he mused as he did up his fly, *was not having to shit.* He took out four meal bars and laid them in the dirt beside him, then lifted the scope to his eyes. He ate a bar as he scanned the buildings.

Dan woke and accepted a bar with a nod of thanks. His homemade net covered his gun that lay propped before him. He used the Nikon camera he carried to view the scene.

All day, Ronny and Dan observed the comings and goings below them. Sweat pooled beneath him as the sun crawled overhead. With slow, careful movements, Ronny unrolled a fly strip and placed it beside him. Sweat and urine attacked the flies. Too many could give them away.

The strip did its job, catching the flying pests. JT rejoined them an hour after the sun set.

"I counted six different guards, but didn't see Alfarsi," Dan said.

One of the guards was his son Mahir, or maybe Jahir, I can't tell them apart," Ronny added. "He's still inside unless there's another exit.

"Patterns?"

"Every four hours a new man sits on the porch. They head to the third house on the right when they're relieved. Two women came at noon and dinner carrying baskets. They stayed mere minutes. We might be able to use that. Both women were completely shrouded with only their eyes showing."

JT grunted. "Surveillance to the south showed just what you'd expect. Farmers going about their day. No sign of armed men or anything suspicious at all."

"The people here walk past with downcast eyes if they have to pass. Most go out of their way not to. I don't think he's too popular." Dan handed JT his camera and slithered backward. "Bathroom break."

JT nodded and took his spot. "How's he holding up?"

"Calm. Normal." Ronny shrugged.

"And you?"

"Fine."

JT snorted. "I know you want this asshole dead. We all want him dead, but we need him alive. It won't help Cameron if we can't question him."

"Uh huh. Um, yes, sir."

JT sighed.

Ronny eased down the hill when Dan returned.

When he rejoined them, his entire team had gathered.

"What's the plan?"

TEN

---◆---

THIS WAS THE PART RONNY HATED

Ronny's pulse pounded. Squirrel and Lee ran across the pasture beside the house. Invisible to his naked eye, they were glaring obvious in his scope. He tracked them while Dan watched the guard who so far showed no sign of alarm. When Squirrel and Lee reached the wall of the house, JT, Keith and Tom crossed.

This was the part Ronny hated, hanging back while his friends ran into danger.

"They got this," Dan whispered. "Stay still and watch their backs."

A flush climbed Ronny's cheeks as he realized he'd risen as if to run down the hill. He settled back to the ground. Dan now peered through the scope on his gun. The sight reassured Ronny.

He scanned the landscape using his scope. Only the guard by the front door and Ronny's team were visible. The five of them gathered. Tom boosted Lee to the window on the second floor. A minute later he disappeared. Ronny knew Lee would be removing a circle of glass to climb inside, then sliding the window up for the others after ensuring the window wasn't alarmed.

It always amazed him how graceful Lee was for big man. He could fit through a hole as wide as his shoulders without breaking the surrounding glass, and he made it look easy. Ronny couldn't do it. He'd tried numerous times and always broke the glass.

"They're in," he whispered to Dan three minutes later.

Tension built, and he cursed himself for not peeing earlier.

"Just pee already," Dan said, sounding as if he were trying not to laugh.

He did laugh when Ronny sighed in relief. Ronny was just doing his fly when Dan's gun sounded. Ronny snatched his scope and peered at the house in time to see Tom drop and roll off the porch.

A corpse lay on the porch floor with a rifle in his hand. Another armed man peeked from behind the doorway. Beside him, Dan fired again. The bullet traveled through the wall and the peeper disappeared, leaving just the tip of a gun in view in a growing pool of blood.

"Back left corner, Keith is in front," Ronny said, fighting the urge to stare at Tom and forcing himself to survey the area. Dawn would be heartbroken if Tom was dead and it would be Ronny's fault.

"Got it," Dan said.

Ronny tore his eyes away from the man fighting

with Keith and scanned the yard, then windows. His gaze wanted to travel to the corner of the building. It took willpower to not watch the fight and instead seek out threats. Relief made him sigh hard when he saw Tom up and crouching beside the corner of the house.

"Two houses to the right, a man with a shotgun, no threat currently, but approaching the house at a run, ETA— fifteen seconds.

The gun beside him sounded. Dan loaded anther bullet. Ronny glanced at the corner where he'd last seen Keith, then looked for the running man, both hostiles were dead.

"Lee is emerging from the front, top window left. JT is at the far-right corner; assailant attacking, but no angle." As Ronny watched, JT turned towards them and saluted before running to Lee's position.

"Watch far right corner, assailant imminent."

He'd barely spoken the words before a man ran around the corner. The gun beside him sounded again.

JT waved and signed, then pointed to the window above him.

"JT wants a shot in the center window top."

"Got it." A moment later Dan shot.

Glass twinkled to the ground, and JT gave a thumbs up.

"Man with a gun, but hanging back, third house to the left, second window, first floor, right. No threat at moment."

Ronny took a deep breath and let it out slowly. He wanted to look everywhere at once. He especially wanted to look where he knew the action was, but his team needed him to watch their backs. A distant ripple of gunfire tugged at his attention, but he remained focused, sweeping the terrain before him and checking the sides and back to ensure no one was sneaking up on them.

"Six men to the far left, on the edge of the field. I only see one gun. No threat at moment. I think they're villagers.

"Front of house, top-left-corner window, only saw him for a second; he has a sniper rifle."

"Got it."

Ronny scanned all the front windows, then the sides and checked to see if any of the armed men had moved before repeating the scan. Dirt kicked up against the hill they lay on as men fired at them blind from the house. No shots came close.

"Middle window, bottom-left-corner, same gun."

"Got it." This time Dan shot. "Got him."

Ronny's shoulder blades relaxed. He hated when he knew another sniper was out there. Dan always teased him, saying it was the ones you didn't know about that should make you worry.

"Keith and Lee are exiting the front door with a captive."

Beside him, Dan tensed.

"Alfarsi." Vicious anticipation filled Dan's voice.

Ronny glanced at him before resuming his sweep. He expected to hear a shot any second. He wanted to yell— take the shot. His soul cried out for Dan to take the shot. A tight smile crossed his face when he noted how far Lee and Keith stood from their captive. Neither wanted to get hit by blood or bullets.

A shot echoed from beside him.

Ronny drew in a deep breath and scanned the front of the house. Alfarsi still lived, peering over his shoulder at something behind him.

Lee and Keith both stared upwards behind them. Ronny tracked it and saw the dead man. He carried a rocket launcher and had apparently tumbled from the roof.

A flush climbed Ronny's cheeks. Dan had done his job for him while he contemplated murder.

Dan breathed hard beside him, then growled before relaxing. Ronny fingered his gun. He could shoot Komar and end the threat to Cameron. Except the threat was ended. Komar Alfarsi would be on his way to Gitmo with the full blessings of his own government. He relaxed as he made the decision that he wasn't a murderer.

"Far right corner."

"Got it."

Ron continued to call out positions of hostiles as his team retreated. None of the armed men he saw made any attempt to follow. Most hung back, giving Dan no shot. The six men beside the fence were joined by four more, but none approached. Ronny spotted three more men peering from their homes, but none exited. Dan left them all alone as they presented no threat.

"Front door," Ronny said forty minutes later.

"Got it. Damn missed," Dan said as the echo of his shot rolled off the hill.

"Truck, black, to the back-right-hand-corner, third house on the left."

"Got it."

Three sharp bursts of static filled Ronny's ear piece. "Time to go."

"Gimme one second."

Ronny swung his scope back to the truck in time to see Dan shoot it. He ejected and replaced bullets as fast as he could, shooting the hell out of the truck. Men ran behind the nearby building, but none returned fire.

Dan took a minute to gather his spent shells as Ronny scanned before them with his scope. Seeing no one new, he grabbed his night vision goggles from his pack and stuffed his scope in it.

The two men ran back down the hill.

"Snake," Dan warned and gave the sleeping reptile a wide birth.

"I figure we have thirty minutes before they get the nerve to try again," Ronny said as they jogged back the way they'd come.

"JT will have called for pickup. The helicopter is three hours out, keep running."

Ronny snorted a laugh. Now that Alfarsi was apprehended, and there was no need for stealth, he enjoyed the run. He wished he could take the ghillie suit off. Even in the cool night air, the suit was hot and stuffy. The night remained deceptively peaceful. It felt as if he and Dan were the only people for miles.

"Nice night for a run," Dan said.

Ronny laughed.

———◆———

They'd reached the rendezvous with no sign of pursuit. Tied hand and foot, Komar glared from behind the gag.

Ronny squatted in front of him. "Hi, thanks for the little vacation. That three-day break really did wonders for my girlfriend and I."

Komar's glare changed to a puzzled frown.

"You remember when you blew up that parking

garage and killed those innocent people? You thought my girlfriend was killed, but we were all snug and cozy together. I was getting tired of you ruining my sleep though." Ronny rose and grinned down at the bound man at his feet.

"I'll never lose another sleep over you." He turned his back as Komar jerked at his bonds. Lee laughed and slapped Ronny on the shoulder.

Two men in blue suits arrived for Komar as soon as they landed back at Bagram airbase. "Which one of you guys is Jeremy Rubinstein-Wong?

Lee stepped forward. The man handed him a letter. "From your brother. I'd say it was nice to meet you, but we never met."

Lee laughed and waved.

"I need a shower." Ronny stretched and removed his backpack.

"I need a phone," Dan said and headed to the main building at a jog.

"We've got a flight home in two days," JT called after him.

Dan rose a hand in acknowledgment. Still wearing his ghillie suit and clutching his rifle, people stopped and stared as he passed.

Ronny trailed slowly, Tom's glare following him. He should call his wife, but his heart wanted Cameron. He picked up his pace. Dawn could wait. Tom was sure to call Dawn anyway. *Besides, it was Tom's fault if she were worried.* He never called her to tell her he was going on a mission. *Sometimes they didn't speak for weeks.*

He spared an angry thought for Tom. Dawn was sure to be upset, and he really didn't want to deal with it. He wanted to hear Cameron's voice and make a date with her, then shower. Then he wanted food, lots of it. He hadn't had a real meal in days.

ELEVEN

─ ◆ ─

WHO'S THIS

Ronny pulled a chair out for Cameron. Quiet music played in the candlelit room. A waiter in a black suit poured water and disappeared after handing Ronny a wine list. Ronny let the wine list fall to the cloth tabletop to reach across the table. The blue dress she wore complemented her eyes perfectly and he couldn't wait to slip the thin straps from her shoulders. She held his hands in hers, not glancing at the menu.

"How's the knee?" he asked.

"All better. The wrist is completely healed, and my rib doesn't bother me at all. The leg will have a scar though."

"What a pity; you have such beautiful legs."

She smiled

He grinned and kissed her fingers.

Her eyes darkened as she licked her lips. Without meaning to, he tightened his grip.

She leaned towards him, her eyes a deep, dark-blue and full of lust. "Let's get dinner to go."

He laughed and rose. "We can order in."

Smiling into his eyes, she leaned into his side with an arm tight around his waist as he led her from the restaurant. In the car, she kissed him and began unbuttoning his dress shirt.

The warmth of her thigh under his hand filled his entire body with heat. One finger traced the edge of her lacy panties beneath the silk dress.

"Drive," she murmured, running her hand over the erection in his pants.

Reluctantly, he released her and started the car. "My house is closer and my roommates are gone until tomorrow."

"Perfect," she breathed and kissed his neck.

In the hallway of his apartment, she laughed and kissed him, pulling his shirt off while walking backward.

"I love you," he said as he swung open the door of his apartment.

She stilled and stepped back, searching his face, eyes bright and serious.

"Ron?"

Shocked, his gaze flew to Dawn who sat on the couch holding a textbook in her lap with her feet on the table. In thin shorts and tank top intended for sleeping, it was clear she was at home there.

"Dawn, what are you doing here?"

"I came to see you." Dawn's smile fled as her feet dropped to the floor. Her worried gaze flitted over Ronny, landing on Cameron.

"Who's this?" both women asked at the same time.

Ronny paused, tightening his grip on Cameron's hands.

Cameron pulled away, frowning.

"This isn't what it looks like," Ronny said hurriedly.

Dawn laughed. "You didn't tell her about me?"

"Not now, Dawn." Ronny glared at his wife, then turned to Cameron.

Dawn held up both hands and waved them. "Sorry."

"Who are you?" Cameron asked.

Dawn glanced at Ronny and bit her bottom lip.

"My wife," Ronny said through clenched teeth.

"Ronny's friend," Dawn said at the same time and rolled her eyes at Ronny.

"Your wife?" Cameron pulled away. Wide, blue eyes flitted from him to Dawn.

"Not for much longer." Dawn stood, placing her book on the table.

Cameron paled. "I had no idea." She turned a furious glower on Ronny. "How could you? Jesus, you're a scumbag." She pushed Ronny's reaching hand away and turned to Dawn. "I really didn't know. I realize that doesn't make it better, but I would've never..." she stopped speaking and huffed behind clenched teeth. "He was an unfaithful asshole."

"Cameron, wait," Ronny said as she brushed past him. The look on her face shriveled his heart.

"It's not like that," Dawn called after her.

Ronny chased Cameron down the hall and grabbed her arm as she reached the door.

"Look, it isn't what you think. I told Dawn— "

"Let go of me. You're such a liar, I'll never believe a word you say again. And your 'friends'! "Jesus. What's wrong with you people? Or don't they know you're married? Where has she been all this time?"

"School, but it isn't what you think. Let me explain. Please!"

Cameron slapped him and stormed from the building. The contempt on her face hurt more than the slap.

Dawn stood in the doorway, looking worried. "I'm so sorry, Ron."

"Not your fault," Ronny said tiredly as he flopped onto the couch. "I'll let her calm down and speak to her. I should've told her." He blew out a deep, shuddering breath. "Honestly, you slipped my mind. I wasn't hiding our marriage or anything."

Dawn snorted and sat beside him, taking his hand in hers.

"Why are you here anyways? Not that you aren't welcome, but Tom is away until tomorrow."

"I came to see you and give you these." She reached into a blue bookbag on the floor and drew out a manila folder. "Divorce papers. You sign and file them here, and we're officially divorced when the judge signs them."

"How long?"

"Six months or so." Dawn ran a hand over his head and rested her cheek against his. "I'm really sorry," she mumbled. "You've been so good to me. If I've ruined this for you..."

"You didn't. I ruined it for myself." Ronny hugged her, the comfort of her presence not easing his heartache at all.

Angie called him two hours later. "Cameron called me. She's really upset, and I think I made it worse."

"How." Ronny rubbed his eyes and flopped back on

his pillow.

"She asked if I knew you were married. It surprised me. I assumed she knew. I sort of blurted 'you didn't know,' and she slammed the phone down on me and now isn't answering my calls."

"Thanks for calling me, Ang. I'll handle this. Dawn completely slipped my mind."

"Dawn's here at our house. She feels really bad about this."

Ronny winced. "I know. I told her she doesn't need too, but..."

"She loves you," Angie said softly.

"I love her too. That will never change." Ronny sighed and sat. "I'll call her— both of them. This is way more complicated than I thought."

"Marriages are. Your welcome to stay here too if you want company."

"Thanks, Ang."

Ronny called Dawn who answered on the first ring. "Hey, sunshine."

To his dismay, Dawn burst into tears.

"Please, don't worry about this. I don't blame you at all."

"I blame me," she said in a voice thick with tears.

"Remember the time I broke Henry Wilson's nose playing football, and you cried because the prom committee overlooked you two for king and queen? Remember how bad I felt?"

She laughed. "Okay, I get it but..."

"Best friends for life, sunshine."

"I love you."

Ronny hung up and called Cameron again. The phone rang once and turned to dial tone. She was still blocking his calls.

The next day he called at six a.m. His calls were still being blocked. Dressed in his best uniform, with his hat tucked under his arm, he tapped on her door.

"Please, Cameron, let me explain."

No one answered his knock. Without meaning too, he found himself pounding on her door and yelling. Doors up and down the hall popped open.

"Dude, get a grip," the man next door said.

Ronny leaned his forehead on the door, breathing deeply. A red flush heated his cheeks, partly embarrassment, but mostly worry.

Dejected, he headed to the range. After work, he went to her office, but she'd already left for the day. He spent the night sitting by her front door, knocking lightly every hour, ignoring the pitying and amused stares of her neighbors. He didn't know if she were there or not. For a week she managed to avoid him. A week where every moment passed with glacial slowness, each breath a lead weight in his chest. Cameron's mother slammed the door on him but told him Cameron was in Mexico with the admiral.

Dawn returned to school. He traded her unhappy glances for Tom's angry ones.

Over dinner that evening Tom picked at the plate of food before him, finally shoving it away and stalking from the room.

"Don't be such a dick," Ronny called after him. "I already feel bad enough."

Tom stopped and turned back. "You're an asshole. Dawn is really hurt."

"Fuck! I didn't do it on purpose."

Tom cocked his head to the side and regarded him

a moment. "You don't even see it, do you?"

"See what?"

"How your *wife* is hurting since you discarded her. She cried when she told me you forgot about her."

Ronny rose and clenched his fists. "My wife and I are none of your business."

Tom's lips tightened, and he spun away.

Ronny sighed heavily. "Sorry. That was unfair. Dawn isn't upset over the divorce; I promise you that."

"Could've fooled me."

"No, I mean it. She and I were never in love. Not like that anyways."

"You were using her."

Ronny winced. "I like to think we were using each other."

Tom's shoulder tightened, and he strode closer.

"Relax, she and I haven't had sex since Gitmo. Thanks for that by the way."

Squirrel laughed, choking on his dinner. Ronny rolled his eyes at him.

Squirrel nodded toward Tom and spoke with his mouth full. "Tom's going to beat the crap out of you any minute."

"Guess I have it coming." Ronny slumped into his chair and laid his head in his hands. "I love Dawn, I really do. We made a deal at seventeen. Dawn was hot and I was horny. I would've agreed to anything. And her friends competed with each other to get my attention." He glanced at Tom who glowered at him. "Are you going to say you wouldn't have taken that deal? You're a goddamn liar if you are."

Squirrel laughed and waved his fork at Tom. "He has you there. At seventeen I would've given her anything too."

Tom growled and spun away, slamming the door of his room behind him.

"Don't worry about him," Squirrel said, "he's jealous is all. Cameron speaking to you yet?"

"No. I sent her a letter and haven't heard a peep. I'm going to go talk to her mother again Saturday. This can't go on. Angie is really upset too which means Dan is angry with me."

"Try— "

The beepers clipped to their belts went off. Both men stopped speaking and peered at the number. Squirrel grabbed his phone and hit a speed dial. He hung up a second later. "We go in thirty." Both men ran to their rooms.

TWELVE

———— • ◆ • ————

THEY HAD HER FOR A WEEK NOW

Wind whipped through the open door of the helicopter, ruffling the edges of Ronny's ghillie suit. Beside him, Dan checked his pack one last time before putting it on. Ronny sat unmoving, his entire body tense. JT slapped his shoulder.

"Good to go?"

"Hoorah!" Ronny shouted.

Dan reached over and squeezed his knee. "We'll get her back. All in, all the time."

Ronny nodded. Rear Admiral Reeves and his staff had been kidnapped along with the Mexican ambassador and thirty other members of the civil government from a dinner party in Mexico City. Fifty-four men had been killed, including twelve Marine guards.

The kidnappers had disappeared into the hills with their hostages. So far, no demands had been made. No contact with the kidnappers at all. No groups had officially claimed credit, but the first tentative IDs placed those responsible as the Gulf Cartel

CIA intel had a possible lead, and his team was on the way to determine if the hostages were there. Three other teams were checking other leads. Every moment spent in the hands of a cartel lessened her chances.

The Gulf Cartel was in the midst of dealings with Los Zetas, by all accounts the most ruthless of the cartels in Mexico. While the Gulf Cartel was known for taking hostages for ransom, the Los Zetas killed their captives as a statement of power. Not a small organization, the Zetas controlled almost the entire eastern border of Mexico and ruled with an iron fist, going so far as to shooting down military helicopters that passed over their drug fields. He prayed to God the Gulf Cartel had her.

He'd thought the moments had passed with glacial slowness before when she wouldn't answer his calls, now they seemed to stand still, each one an infinity of time.

The helicopter dropped them above a bend of a shallow river within five miles of their goal. A steep, rock-covered hill hid them from view while they dropped from the copter. Cool water soaked his legs to the knees as he scrambled to the bank. The rotors whipped a fine mist of water into the air, which soaked the rest of him. Gray morning light brightened to a pale golden sunrise as the helicopter peeled away.

JT lead them at a swift walk through dense jungle until they reached a barren hillside. Deep gullies from water runoff crisscrossed the hill. Dry now, the ground crumbled under their feet, their passage dislodging an avalanche of dirt and stones.

At the top, they dropped to their stomachs and crawled forward to peer over the edge. Before them, the hills lowered into a deep valley. This one broken up by cultivated fields and roads scattered with houses.

A small town in the center boasted a few two-story buildings and three paved roads. To the right, about twenty miles away, the far-off glimmer of the sea shone in the afternoon sun. Farms, houses, and thick, dense patches of forest lay between them and the sea. To the left, the roads disappeared into deep jungle. The hill before them held short, stout trees and dense shrubbery. Only a few water gullies marred this side of the hill.

Ronny peered through his binoculars at their target. Only the target building's red wooden roof was visible from where he lay. The underbrush and surrounding forest were too dense to see through. "I make it about a mile and a half."

JT gestured to the left. "Cut around the side here; we don't want them to see us coming. When we reach the bottom, we'll take a break for food and rest."

The men squirmed back the way they'd come, not standing until the hill blocked them from view, then cut around the left side. It added a mile to the trek but kept them from observation.

Ronny ate his MRE mechanically and sipped his water. Twenty minutes later, they headed out, jogging along the edge of a coffee plantation before cutting cross country again. Every hour they took a ten-minute break. Each break was a torturous wait for Ronny.

The house was empty when they arrived. Every

room had been recently cleaned and smelled of disinfectant. No paperwork or personal items remained, not even clothing. Lee knelt beside a tripwire on the top step, dismantling it.

Ronny slammed his hand on the Formica countertop. "Fuckers knew we were coming."

JT nodded and gestured his team to the door. "They did, but we have more addresses to check." Ronny stomped from the room and leaned his forehead on the wall beside the front door where he stood taking deep breaths.

Dan paused beside him and laid a hand on his shoulder, saying nothing.

"Head out," JT said and led them off at a jog.

<hr />

The front door rebounded off the wall with a resounding thud. Ronny ducked as he entered, following his gun into the room.

Flies rose from a meal left partially eaten on the table. A wooden chair lay on its side as if the occupant had jumped up and left hurriedly.

Furious fear made his palms sweat. Cameron had been missing a week now. A week with no word or demands. Every house they'd searched had been empty as if the Gulf Cartel knew they were coming.

"We're catching up." JT gestured to the overturned chair. "They left in a hurry this time." JT beckoned to Lee. "Check every scrap of writing personally. The rest of you clear the buildings. Be careful of booby traps and nobody reports a damn thing. We didn't plug our leak with Alfarsi's arrest. Lee, you get a hint of where they're going, we'll get ourselves there."

JT spun away and ran up the stairs two at a time.

Ronny began opening kitchen drawers and riffling the contents. Most contained nothing except kitchen supplies. A small drawer beside the dented refrigerator held mail both opened and unopened. He flicked through the envelopes, tossing them to the floor one-by-one. He stopped and clutched one, then squatted to open his pack.

"Got something," Lee asked and peered over his shoulder.

One finger traced the list of known addresses from Gulf Cartel members the CIA had given him. Ronny stabbed the page. "A match." He handed the letter to Lee.

A frown on his face, Lee examined the paper. "Sorry, Ron, nothing definitive. This could mean shit. These assholes all know each other. It's an invite to a birthday party."

Ronny inadvertently crinkled the paper he held when he clenched his fist. "They've had her a week now, Lee."

Lee nodded and rose. He rotated his neck and wind-milled his arms. "Keep looking. If we don't find a better lead, we go there next. Without reporting."

Ronny yanked the next drawer out. Utensils scattered across the cracked linoleum. After searching the kitchen, he headed upstairs. The mussed beds and cut zip-ties made nausea roil in his stomach.

JT closed the door of a room and took his arm. "It's good we know they were here."

Ronny pulled away from JT and opened the door. Two bare mattresses stained with blood filled the small room. A wooden chair, matching the ones in the kitchen, sat between the mattresses. From the number of broken zip-ties, quite a few people had been held in this room. Hot and cold waves traveled him, and for a moment the room spun. He closed his eyes and clutched the door, breathing deeply until the swirling sensation stopped.

"Tripwire in the next doorway," JT warned.

Ronny straightened his shoulders and continued searching for clues.

Four hours later his team gathered in the side yard.

JT knelt in the grass with a map spread before him. "We're going for a jog straight across country to the house in Ameca. Darmin's going to kick my ass, but I'm reporting we're holing up here for the night. If we're quick enough, we can reach our next target before morning."

JT lead them out across the field at a jog. Every ten minutes he power walked for five. Two hours and thirty-seven minutes later they reached their goal.

"Fuckers didn't know we were coming this time," Ronny murmured with savage satisfaction. His gaze traveled the lighted windows of the small farm house.

Dan laid beside him and peered through his scope. "No sign of hostages. Two men and one woman eating in the kitchen. They seem calm. We can't go busting in there like thugs."

A low growl escaped Ronny.

"We'll check. I'm just saying we can't go breaking down doors of innocent bystanders."

Ronny glared at Dan. "Innocent my fucking ass. Those assholes are cartel. The natives might be scared of them, but I'm not."

Dan rose to his haunches and picked up his rifle. "Cameron's my friend too, and I remember all too well the feeling when Angie was missing. Believe me, we aren't going to let them keep her. You go with JT and Tom and search the outbuildings. Lee will break in and search the house. He gets one inkling their involved, and we'll make the fuckers talk."

Ronny stared into Dan's blue eyes a moment before nodding and crossing the yard in a hunched run. He lifted one hand to cup his ear, the better to hear Lee's mumbled reports.

"I'm in," Lee whispered as Ronny eased through the open door of the barn in the side yard.

The barn appeared abandoned. A tractor with a missing front tire was tipped against a slatted wall. Moldy hay and rotting sacks of grain blocked the back door, filling the air with a damp musty scent. Late afternoon sunlight streamed through the wide cracks in the rough siding illuminating the dirt floor in stripes.

JT held a penlight in one hand, resting the other on his holstered sidearm as he swept the beam across the floor searching for a hidden cellar. Ronny knelt to the right of the doorway covering JT.

"Looks like we've got a winner," Lee whispered. "I found a stack of fancy purses in the closet here."

Ronny straightened. JT glanced at him, then motioned him to leave.

"Confirmed. The first three I checked are matches to our list of missing personnel's personal effects. Statistically improbable that the woman here bought them separately."

JT held a hand to his face to muffle his voice. "Give us five minutes to complete this sweep and take our position outside the house. Keith, cut the phone line on my mark. Dan, make sure our chat remains uninterrupted."

Ronny practically vibrated with eagerness.

"Lee, anyone else upstairs?"

"All clear. They're discussing what to watch on TV. I don't think our hostages are on the property."

"Squirrel, you and Ronny enter from the front. Keith and Tom the back. Dan, cover the back and left side; I got front right," JT said. He continued to sweep the floor with his light as he spoke.

Every muscle in Ronny's body felt tight and he almost groaned aloud as JT paused to nudge a pile of empty wooden crates aside to check the floor beneath them.

The radio in his ear crackled as Lee spoke. "The men are watching a game; the woman is heading upstairs."

"Can you take her quietly?" JT asked.

"Affirmative."

Ronny ran from the building, hearing JT's instructions in his headset.

"Do it. Get in position. Gimme one click when you're set."

Ronny clicked his mic as he crouched to the right of the front door. Squirrel stood to the left with his hand on the door handle.

'Open,' he mouthed.

Ronny jerked his chin in acknowledgment.

"Mark," JT said as the sixth click sounded.

"Cut," Keith said.

Ronny ran through the door Squirrel pushed open.

"Get on the floor," he barked to the shocked men.

One reached to his back while the other jumped to

his feet. Ronny kicked the standing man as a shot sounded beside him. The reaching man screamed and clutched his arm.

"We aren't fucking around here. We don't need all you assholes alive. Face down on the floor right now," Squirrel said in Spanish.

Upstairs, doors banged, and booted feet ran the length of the house.

"Clear," Tom called.

Lee entered the room, dragging a woman bound and gagged with strips of sheet. Her wide, terrified eyes flicked from them to the men now lying face down on the floor.

Ronny hauled the shot man to his feet and frisked him before pushing him to his knees. "You get one chance to answer me before I pull this trigger. "Where are they?"

"Where are who?"

Squirrel knocked Ronny's arm, sending his shot into the wall. The woman screamed, the sound muffled by the gag.

"Fuck, Ron, we need them alive to question."

"We don't need all three."

"True," Squirrel said thoughtfully and stepped back.

"Last chance. Don't think for a fucking second I won't spread your brains all over the fucking wall. One of those hostages you took was my girl. Where the fuck are they!" Ronny cocked his gun and pressed it hard against the man's head. The sincerity of his intent must have come through because the man swallowed hard and licked his lips.

"Jalisco. The boss has a house there. I swear, man,

last I knew that's where they were."

Ronny pulled the trigger sending a bullet into the floor at his feet, and the woman screamed again. Breathing hard, he pulled twice more before letting the gun fall to his side. Lee grabbed his arm and turned him away as if afraid Ronny wouldn't be able to stop himself from shooting the man cowering at his feet.

The man before Ronny cringed, his eyes so wide the whites showed. Ronny's hand clenched on his gun. The impulse to fire again was so strong his hands shook. If he fired again, he'd kill the man, not shoot past his face. A deep scowl on his brow, he holstered his sidearm.

Lee relaxed and released him. "Keith, tie these fuckers up. We'll be coming back if this address is bullshit." Lee leaned down until his nose almost touched the man kneeling on the floor. "I won't stop him next time."

The man nodded so hard his hair covered his eyes. He lifted a bloody hand to brush it back. Lee yanked a curtain from the window and cut it into strips that he used to bind the gunshot in the man's arm.

"We should just waste this trash," Ronny said.

"Hedging our bets. If this is a wild goose chase, we'll come back and make sure we got the truth before we waste them." JT slapped Ronny's shoulder, then grabbed curtain strips to begin tying the man on the floor.

The man's warm blood trickled down Ronny's neck as he threw him over his shoulder. He'd never considered himself bloodthirsty before this, but he wished he'd hurt the man more. Scaring him was satisfying, but not as satisfying as hurting him would be. Images of bloody mattresses danced before his eyes.

Panic threatened to bring him to his knees. The CIA thought all of this was inspired by Al-Jadr, that the terrorists wanted Cameron specifically. It would take a lot to break her, but anyone could be broken. Tears filled his eyes as he imagined what they'd do to make her talk.

He let his captive thump to the dirt floor of the basement, a small twelve-by-twelve room lined with shelves and bins and used as a root cellar.

Keith and Lee tied the captives tight to the heavy metal shelving while Ronny covered them with his rifle.

He was tempted to ask if she were hurt but didn't want to give away her identity. Better to let them think one of the other women was his girlfriend. Besides, he didn't think he could stop himself if the answer were yes.

The captives all avoided his gaze and listened meekly to Lee. Their obvious fear of him almost made him laugh. He wondered if he looked as crazy angry as he felt.

Back in the kitchen, JT leaned over the map spread on the table. "Let's borrow their car, and we can be there in fifteen minutes. We'll decide what to do with these assholes once we know if they told the truth."

Ronny glanced up from the woman's purse he was riffling, searching for car keys. "Fat fucking lot of good it's going to do to turn them into the local authorities."

JT glared at him. "We do our job. Like it or not it's our job to turn them into the local police. We're already in enough trouble for going off grid. I don't know about you, but I still want a job after this mission is finished."

"Fuck," Ronny muttered.

"I got the keys. Let's blow this shit-hole." Tom swung the keys around his finger and slammed the kitchen drawer.

Ronny followed him.

THIRTEEN

———•◆•———

KEEP IT TOGETHER

Nestled between dense trees, the small estate in Jalisco boasted four houses and a falling down barn. A porch wrapped around both levels of the main house. Two armed men wearing camouflage and carrying binoculars patrolled the upper and lower level of the porches.

Ronny's heart pounded.

"It doesn't mean she's in there," Dan warned in a soft voice. "They could be patrolling as a regular thing. The CIA told us this is one of the main residences for the Gulf Cartel and don't think it likely they'd risk this house by using it for criminal activity. The local government leaves them alone and turns a blind eye to what happens here because the crimes commited here are usually non-violent, and the cartel responds harshly to noisy neighbors. Keep it together, man."

Ronny clenched his teeth and nodded.

JT slapped him on the back. "Let's circle and reconnoiter. Dan, you and Ronny stay here. Get us some clear pics."

Dan set his pack on the ground and pulled out a Nikon camera. Ronny sighed and did the same. His telephoto lens brought the guards face into sharp focus. He dutifully snapped a picture, wishing he could blow the man's head off and rush inside. Two hours later, the men gathered again.

"We go in at dusk." JT traced a finger across a sketch of the house. "Tom, take Lee and Squirrel to the back door. The rest of you are with me. Only fire if fired upon. Let's try to sneak in. Tie and gag captives. Stay quiet as long as we can. If this is the place, we call for backup before engaging if we can."

JT spread a map at their feet. "Extraction is here." He stabbed a spot on the map a mile away, three miles outside the town. "If these aren't our guys, and the shit hits the fan, don't head into town. Get to the coast. We have a boat hidden beside this stream here. Get to the sea and radio for a pickup. If the shit hits the fan, and these are the guys, we do our best to secure the hostages and get them to the extraction point.

JT tucked the map back into his pack. "The CIA warns the locals might be hostile; use extreme care when dealing with them." He glanced at his watch. "Get some rest, we go in two hours." JT sat farther back on his haunches and examined Ronny. "I'm sorry for the delay, but a daylight extraction is too dangerous. We'd never get them all out safely, and if we go in during daylight we need backup but I don't trust we can get back up here before they learn we're onto them. Our best option is to watch and learn and attack at a time of our choosing."

"If we hear screams or think she's in danger...." Ronny trailed off as Tom slapped his shoulder.

"Then we kill the fuckers," Squirrel said as Dan said," We get her out. But JT is right, rushing in could get them all killed. We'll rest and go in fresh when they don't expect it."

Ronny settled beside Dan and pretended to sleep. Dusk came late here. The sun wouldn't set until eight p.m. Behind his closed eyes Cameron glared at him, her face flushed with anger, but the hurt betrayed expression haunted him. *Please God, don't let her be dead*, he prayed. The memory of her blinding smile when she took his hands in the restaurant almost made him sob. Visions of her bloody face and grimaces of pain filled his eyes with tears.

Every moment he'd spent with her, he examined in his memory. There weren't enough moments. He wanted years of memories with her. They'd never gotten the chance to jog together or play ball. He wanted to stand with her in his arms on a mountaintop and watch the sunrise. The thought of never seeing her body in the moonlight made him moan softly with despair. The beautiful vibrancy that was Cameron was irreplaceable. He rolled onto his side and curled up, hugging himself.

He rose when JT did and ate and drank with everyone else. He watched his assigned sector and made mental notes on every man who passed his hidden position. He wouldn't forget one of them.

A single click sounded in his headset and Ronny began eeling back through the bush, careful to go slow and remain unseen. The sun was just beginning to set, sinking behind the hills in a spectacular display of brilliant orange. Ronny willed it to sink faster. Every muscle in his body felt tight with anticipation when he rejoined his team.

Dan put an arm around his shoulder and squeezed, his worried gaze examining him. The gesture eased some of his tenseness. Dan understood his loss and had his back. He'd gotten Angie back against the odds and wouldn't give up on Cameron. The thought straightened his spine.

"Get in position." JT gestured Tom to take his men.

Every sense alert, Ronny followed JT.

A guard roamed the yard, occasionally pausing for a cigarette or to lean idly on a tree. JT nodded to Dan.

Dan eased soundlessly through the trees.

"Ready," Tom's voice came through the earpiece clipped to Ronny's ear.

"Next pass, I'll grab him," Dan said.

Ronny strained forward, wanting to rush into the house with all his soul. On his tiptoes, he poised for flight. When Dan engaged, they'd rush the door and the guard on the porch.

As if to frustrate him, the patrolling man paused to light a smoke. A flare from a match illuminated his unshaven cheeks.

Dusk settled into night with startling suddenness, bringing an insect chorus to life in the trees. Loud squawking and soft hoots from birds filled the night air. Somewhere in the distance, an engine ran, the sound fading as they waited for the guard.

Intent on the guard, he didn't notice Dan until he grabbed the man and yanked him backward into the trees. Ronny ran forward, leaping the railing and landing on the porch behind the guard there as the man turned, raising his rifle.

"He— "

Ronny hit him, harder than he intended too, cutting off his word mid-yell. The man's head snapped back, and he slumped. Ronny caught him and eased him to the floor. JT stooped and began tying him. Ronny didn't wait, he poked his head through the open window. Seeing no one, he climbed in as he gazed around. He stood in a small office with an open door. Thick, dark-wood furniture crowded the room. Light shone in the hallway and men spoke in hushed voices in another room. Ronny ran to the door and crouched to peer around the corner.

Unlit, wooden stairs with a faded red runner lay to his left. A brightly lit room lay across the hall from him. The corner of a table and back of a man sitting in a wooden kitchen chair showed in the doorway. He headed to the stairs.

At the top of the stairs, he dropped to his stomach and examined the hallway. Black booted feet and a tipped back chair met his gaze. He jumped up and lunged forward, grabbing the man in the chair right as he sat and reached for the rifle leaning on the wall beside him.

"One guard," he said as he swung and connected, falling with the man to the floor. JT crouched beside him and began tying the man.

"Slow down. You're going to get yourself killed," he hissed.

Below them, a commotion broke out

"Fuck." JT stood and pulled his sidearm.

Two doors opened in the hallway, one right in front of Ronny, the other, three doors down.

Below them, Tom yelled in Spanish for someone to get on the floor. A shot rang out.

Ronny grabbed the man who'd opened the door by the shirt and pulled him close with one hand, reaching up with the other to his throat; he squeezed as he pushed him backward into the room. A bullet hit the door frame beside him. Sharp splinters of wood stung his cheek.

Four tied people stared with wide eyes as Ronny leg swept the man in his grasp to the floor. JT stepped over him and placed his back to the door. Keith took up an identical position across from him.

"This is the spot," JT said.

"Roger that," Dan replied.

Ronny knew Dan would be calling for back up. It was all he could do to hold himself back from rushing into the hallway and busting down doors to find her. His heart cried out for him to hurry.

Glass shattered in the room next to them. The echo of Dan's gun rumbled. Screams and men yelling interspersed a flurry of gunshots below them.

Ronny zip-tied the man's hands and feet, then peeked around the doorframe as JT shot blindly down the hall. Ronny aimed and shot once before running down the hall as his target thumped to the floor clutching at the spirting wound on his chest. Ronny's heart thudded painfully in his chest. Each gunshot made him cringe. He stepped over the dead man in the doorway.

Admiral Reeves was tied to a bed beside the ambassador. Ronny cut him loose.

The admiral grabbed the dead man's gun. Ronny ran from the room

"The admiral is free; don't shoot him," he said as he twisted the door handle of the next room. The door opened with a creak, revealing blackness. Muffled sounds, hard to distinguish over the yelling and ringing in his ears, came to him. Gingerly, standing to the side of the doorway, he felt for a light switch and flipped it. Soft, yellow light illuminated the doorway. He risked a quick glance. Behind him, the admiral and JT spoke in low tones.

His heart thudded so painfully he thought he might pass out. Cameron was tied to the bed. A sheet covered her legs. Bloody handprints stained her khaki T-shirt. Two other women were tied on the neighboring bed, but his gaze locked on hers. Knife in hand, he ran to her and cut the ropes on her wrists, then sliced the gag off and kissed her hard.

She sobbed once, tightening her fists on his shirt. He drew back to see her face.

"I swear to God, it isn't what you think. I love you with all my soul." Without waiting for her reply, he kissed her again so relieved he wanted to cry.

"Are you okay?"

She nodded against his shoulder.

For a moment, he buried his face in her neck, breathing her scent.

"Can I have a gun?"

He laughed as he handed her his pistol. Gun in hand, she hugged him hard.

"My feet are still tied."

He kissed her again before cutting her feet loose. They freed the other two women. "The admiral and ambassador are free. Wait here." He hit the chin switch for his mic.

"I have her, and she's okay. Two other women are with her."

"Copy," Dan said, sounding relieved.

A machine gun chattered outside the house. Dan's gun roared, and the machine gun quieted. "They called in reinforcements. We better get the hell out of here."

Ronny realized he'd heard nothing since he set eyes on Cameron and didn't know if it was because no one had reported or he just hadn't heard. "How many hostages are unaccounted for?"

"Twelve," Squirrel said with laughter in his voice. "Fall back with your three."

Ronny swung his SCAR to the front and cocked it.

"Come out the third window onto the porch. I have it cleared," Dan said.

Ronny glanced behind him. "Follow me and stick close." A quick glimpse in the hallway showed JT kneeling at one end, covering the stairs while the admiral herded a group of half-dressed people into the room Dan had said was clear. Ronny waved his group forward.

Cameron stopped beside him, looking angry, betrayed, sad, and afraid, and he didn't know if the expression was for him or the situation.

"I love you, go," he said.

Tears sprang to her eyes. "You better have a good story." She kissed him and ran after the women.

"Cameron has my pistol and is with the admiral."

"Check the rest of the rooms," JT ordered. "See if you can find a way to the attic and clear that. Tom, what's it looking like down there?"

"One room and the basement left. I need five minutes.

"Two more trucks have joined the first, I make thirteen new hostiles," Dan warned.

"Hold them back for seven minutes," JT said. "Tom, I want you headed out in five."

"Roger that."

While they spoke, Ronny had opened another door in the same manner he'd done the first. An empty room greeted him. He checked under the bed and the closet before moving to the next room.

Someone shot at him when he flicked on the light in the next room. Crouching, he glanced in the doorway. His head jerked back a second before a hail of bullets impacted the wall behind him. A hard grin on his face, he returned fire unaimed. His glance had shown a lone gunman standing on the bed in the corner of the room.

A gurgling scream and breathless profanity met his shots. He waited a moment, then waved his gun before the door. When no gunfire ensued, he peeked again. The gunman now lay on the bed.

"Hostile down, unknown condition."

The man could be pretending, hoping to lure him into range. He could shoot him from the doorway and ensure he was dead or close the door and hope he was. Ronny grimaced and sidled into the room, his rifle resting on his shoulder. As quietly as he could, he eased to the side, staying low before straightening. Dead brown eyes stared back at him. Ronny grabbed the man's gun and felt for a pulse.

"Room's clear. Hostile dead." The next room was empty. The following one held four people.

"Four hostages secured," he reported as he cut them loose.

"Hurry up," Dan said, and his rifle boomed. Three seconds later it boomed again, the sound distinct despite the rattle of gunfire.

Ronny gestured the hostages to the window. Out in the hallway, JT opened fire. Ronny ran back.

"Squirrel?" JT sounded annoyed.

"Tom and I are busy, give us a second." Muffled gunshots traveled through the floor.

"Coming out," Tom hollered.

"Ronny, get out here and help cover," Dan said.

Ronny turned and raced back to the bedroom. He pushed past Keith and the two people waiting to exit. On the porch, he ran to the left corner and opened fire on a pickup truck full of armed men.

"My corner, now!" Dan fired again.

Ronny ran down the porch and shot blindly around the corner. An answering hail of bullets peppered the wall behind his head. He crouched and reloaded. The wall above his head disintegrated. If he's been standing, he'd be dead. He leaped to his feet and peered through the hole, raising his SCAR and aiming before firing. The man with the rocket launcher balanced against the roof of the pickup crumpled.

Ronny ducked. Now on the other edge of the porch, JT opened fire. A minute later Squirrel appeared, leading a group of freed hostages, and joined Ronny. He fired around the corner and laughed at the answering hail of bullets.

Ronny stuffed an earpiece in his ear. Still able to hear his radio, his other ear rang unpleasantly.

Squirrel signed for Ronny to go to Dan.

A glance showed the last of the hostages had disappeared over the rail. Ronny swung himself over and dropped to the ground, rolling and springing to his feet. Behind him, Cameron and a man wearing a blue suit helped the last hostage to the ground. He grabbed her hand and pulled her with him, trusting Dan had kept the house behind them clear.

Lee waited at the tree line, a rifle to his shoulder. His cameoed face split in a grin and he slapped Ronny's shoulder, then gave Cameron a quick one-armed hug. "All the hostages are accounted for. Let's get the hell out of here. The first group is already headed to our rendezvous."

"Go with Lee," Ronny said, releasing Cameron's hand. Without waiting to see what she did, he ran to Dan's position and crouched behind him. He lifted the scope to his eyes and scanned like he'd been trained.

"See the trees fifty yards to the right on the hillside? Go to the midpoint between the trees."

"Got it."

"Drop straight down a hundred yards to the large boulder."

"Got it."

"Go fifty yards from four o'clock to the last small boulder in the field."

"Got it."

"The sniper is twelve yards away at three o'clock, just inside the edge of the brush."

"I see him." Dan pulled the trigger.

Ronny kept searching for threats.

"Fall back and keep us covered," JT ordered.

Dan slung his rifle on his back. Ronny handed him the scope and crouched, rifle at the ready, as Dan retreated. They leapfrogged back the way they came. For the first ten minutes, no one pursued.

"This is mother bird," a man's voice said on their channel. "I see my chicks and will be arriving in four minutes."

"Roger that," Lee said. "Some chicks have flown the nest and are being rounded up."

"Copy that. Daddy bird is behind me."

JT, Tom, and Squirrel joined them.

"Company," Ronny warned as he lifted his gun to fire.

Men yelled in the distance. Gunshots sounded, but none came close. The team kept dropping back.

"Mother bird is fully loaded. See you at the nest."

"Why do I always have to be Daddy Bird?" a man complained. "That's the stupidest handle ever."

"Waiting on you, all chicks accounted for," Lee said.

"We're hurrying," JT snapped as bullets whizzed over his head, shredding the leaves above them.

Squirrel and Ronny crouched at the edge of the clearing where the helicopter hovered, covering the others retreat.

Dan's rifle roared, the distinctive sound unmistakable. Ronny knew he'd be laying aboard the copter covering them now. Squirrel and Ronny turned and ran for the helicopter

"Rocket launchers, hurry your asses up or walk home," JT snapped.

Dan shot again. Tom leaned down to pull Squirrel into the hovering helicopter. Ronny spun and fired at the men firing on him.

"Shit! Get us out of here," JT said. "Ronny, head to the shore. Stop! Grab her."

JT was still speaking when Cameron landed on him, knocking him over. Over his head, six rifles and three machine guns barked. Ronny grabbed her hand and ran for the edge of the woods. She stumbled hard to her knees, yanking him to a halt. He risked a glance backward as he scooped her up. His heart pounded with a mix of adrenaline and fear for Cameron.

"Are you shot?" he gasped as he ran.

Pickup trucks carrying armed men chased the helicopter across the field. Another group of twenty or so men chased them on foot, firing as they ran. In his mind, he yelled and cursed, but he saved his breath for running. He could yell at her later if they survived.

FOURTEEN

———— ◆ ————

I Love You, And Only You

The sound of gunfire dimmed behind him as the helicopter pulled further away.

"I can run," she said.

So relieved he felt like crying, he let her go. "Don't look back." He gripped her hand tighter and pulled her forward. Before them, a dirt lane edged a thick forest. Together, they ran down the road. The crack of rifles and soft wheet of bullets smacking the ground behind them urged him faster. At the first break in the bush, he tugged her into the trees.

"Shouldn't we—"

"Quiet." Ronny yanked her with him. He released her hand to brush foliage from his face. "Follow me as close as you can. Don't speak unless you fall behind. Try not to break any more brush than necessary to pass."

The forest shrouded them in darkness. Ronny

slipped his night vision goggles on, wincing as she tripped and stumbled behind him. He headed straight north. The forest cleared as the ground rose, still thick, but easier to force through. Suddenly, they broke through. The forest abruptly disappeared, leaving a shale covered hillside dotted with a few scraggly pines and low scrub brush.

"Can you climb it?"

"Yes."

Taking her at her word, Ronny started up. Lithe as a mountain goat she followed. He halted and jerked back, cursing under his breath

"Fucking spider the size of a dinner plate. I hate spiders." He shuddered and pulled her past it while she snorted with laughter.

At the top, he laid and peered back the way he'd come. The night goggles flared as his head scanned. He removed them and closed his eyes a moment, letting them adjust. Below them in the trees light glimmered and dimmed erratically. They were being followed.

"We have about one mile on them. We need to break our trail." He gave her the goggles. "Go left over the side of this hill, we'll be hard to track on it. At the bottom, head straight east.

She hesitated, then pointed to lights glimmering in the distance." The town is south."

"Yeah, and they'll have people there and expect us to head that way. We're headed to the sea, but first we need to shake them. I expect they'll give up in a day or so even if we don't lose them if we can just stay ahead and don't telegraph our destination. So, we head away. The sea will still be there next week."

She headed up the slope, avoiding sandy patches and sticking to hard rock as best she could. Ronny stared at her feet and kept his arms up to block branches swinging back. Back in the jungle, the pace slowed until they hit a stream.

"Follow it until you see a good spot to leave. Somewhere nice and rocky or clear enough we don't break branches."

For two hours, they headed downstream. The water was cool, but the footing treacherous.

A sympathetic grimace crossed his face as she stumbled and fell for the third time. Fifteen minutes later, she headed back into the brush, limping now.

"Stop," Ronny murmured. He opened his pack and removed an ace bandage. "Let me see your leg."

He felt along the length of her leg, making her hiss as he gently pressed her knee. The hand that reached down to brush his away was cold.

"Sit and rest a minute."

While she sat, he shrugged out of his ghillie suit and removed his uniform shirt.

"Put this on. I'm sweating in my suit. I forgot the night can be chilly. Wrap your knee. How bad is it? Don't lie; we can't afford to lame you."

"I can keep going."

"Okay, ten minutes here, then continue, but slower. We might have lost them already."

They sat without speaking for ten minutes. She rose, flexed her leg, and turned to face him. The goggles hid her eyes and most of her expression. He was shocked when she hit him. Before he could react, she hit him again, then brushed his arm.

"Turn around," she said as she brushed her hands

over her shoulders and head. She hit him again, this time lighter.

"Okay, let's go." She turned and headed off.

"Spiders?" he asked in a dread-laced voice.

"You don't want to know," she said laughingly. "Most of the bigger spiders are non-lethal if that makes you feel better. It's the small ones you need to worry about."

"Stop. You're grossing me out."

She giggled under her breath.

Ronny smiled and followed.

They walked through the night, taking breaks every hour. The pace grew slower. By dawn, her limp was pronounced. Ronny kept an eye out for a spot to hole up. He settled for a boulder with a tree growing tight against it.

"We rest here a few hours." He sat with his back to the boulder and pulled her into his lap. "Go to sleep. We'll check the maps when we wake."

She was asleep in seconds, a relaxed, warm weight in his arms. He ran a hand through her hair, removing twigs and pieces of brush. Snarled and dirty her hair clung to his fingers. He kissed her temple and closed his eyes, perfectly content.

When he woke, he was alone. He jumped to his feet, but before he had time to panic, she appeared, tucking his shirt in. She'd placed the ace bandage under her pants and tucked her pant legs into her socks.

Overhead the sun beat down, but beneath the trees it was cool and peaceful. The jungle was alive with sound. Birdcalls and insects competed in a soothing melody.

Ronny handed her his canteen and his last candy

bar.

"This is so good," she moaned as she licked the wrapper.

He glanced up from the map and smiled. "I'm going to lead. This time we're headed for the sea."

"You're not eating?" She narrowed her eyes at him.

"On the next stop. How's the knee?"

"Sore."

"If you need me to go slower, say so. If you see or sense anyone, grab my right shoulder or say my name in a low voice if I'm too far. I make us about twenty-eight miles from the shore. We'll walk until dark, then find a place to hole up. Keep an ear out for water. We need to refill the canteen. But don't worry about it, we can collect dew if we have too."

"I'm sorry."

"For what?" he asked surprised and glanced up from the map.

She bit her bottom lip then twisted it between her thumb and finger before speaking.

"For jumping down. I didn't plan it or anything. I just wanted to help you. Instead, I might get you killed."

"Neither of us is getting killed. This is a simple hike. We'll take our time and be careful, and we'll both be fine. In the future though, stay in the helicopter."

She snorted a laugh.

He ruffled her hair and excused himself, stepping behind the boulder and was just doing his fly when she shrieked.

Load thrashing and a keening sob spurred him on. He rounded the boulder gun in hand and stopped, lowering the gun to his side.

"Stop moving, and I'll get it off. Don't you dare shoot it. A gunshot will pinpoint us."

Wide, terrified, blue eyes met his.

"It's a boa constrictor, not poisonous." While he spoke, he lifted the coils from her shoulder. The snake writhed and turned its head back. Ronny grabbed it right beneath the head, pulling it away from her. She scuttled backward on her hands and jumped to her feet.

"How do you feel about snake for lunch?"

"The same way you'd feel about spiders for dinner." Glaring at him now, she rubbed her arms, then rubbed her hands on her pants. Ronny released the snake and took her hand.

"MRE for lunch then; let's go."

Peering over her shoulder, she followed him.

The jungle was both scarier and easier to traverse in the daylight. At night, you didn't notice the bugs and giant spider webs, you also didn't notice the roots and limbs that tripped you. He thought that might be a fair trade as he averted his gaze from another enormous hairy spider.

Six hours later they reached a clearing. A broad field of cultivated plants lay before them bordered by a rough dirt road.

Ronny pulled her back into the brush. "Rest here until dusk, then we'll cross this field." They finished the water and split his last MRE

"Tell me about Dawn," she said.

"I will. Let's get somewhere safe first or at least more water."

She nodded, looking unhappy.

He cradled her skull with one hand and kissed her

lips. "I love you and only you."

A shudder passed over her as she leaned into his shoulder, hugging him tightly. "I'm a terrible person for wanting you when you belong to another."

He groaned and kissed her, tempted to make love to her right there in the brush, but she deserved better. It was hard to pull away.

Both her hands rose and smoothed her hair, then wiped her face. "I'm a wreck. I'd kill for a shower."

"You're beautiful. The most beautiful woman I've ever seen." He licked his thumb and tried to clean a smear of dried grass from her cheek and just made her face dirtier. She gave him one of her beautiful smiles. One hand rose to cup his face, making a dry rasping sound against his stubble.

"I need to shave."

"I like it, it's manly." She rubbed her hand against him, making an aroused sound.

Unable to resist, he kissed her again. The sun set behind them as he kissed her in the brush, savoring every soft sigh she made.

"Time to go," he said regretfully and pulled her up when the sky darkened.

With careful, slow steps they crossed the field, trying to disturb the plants as little as possible. Another smaller field lay beyond, this one full of tomatoes. To the left, a farmhouse sat against a low hill. Warm yellow light lit the windows. A barn hunkered into the trees behind the house with a silo beside it. Two pickup trucks were parked before the house.

"Water. They likely have a dog. Take the rifle and give me the pistol. I'll get us water and meet you on the western edge of the field. If I'm spotted, I'll circle around." He hesitated. "If I don't arrive by morning, head to the shore. Follow the coast until you reach a big town, preferably one with a resort on the beach."

He kissed her as tears filled her eyes.

"You can't come with me. You can't run. I'll be perfectly fine. Don't eat too many tomatoes at once and make yourself sick."

Half laugh, half cry, greeted that and she pulled him closer for another kiss. He broke away before he lost all control, and hurryied through the field.

Dust puffed from his running footsteps. Warm night air enveloped him in quiet, not a soothing hush, but straining in the dark for an unfamiliar noise. A porch light guided him.

FIFTEEN

---◆---

FEAR NOT, FAIR MAIDEN

An open barn door beckoned invitingly. Chickens stirred as he passed a coop, their soft rustling and coos not traveling very far. In the distance, a dog barked but quieted quickly. Ronny made a mental note to check for eggs, but water was the priority.

A tractor sat inside the open door on the dirt floor. Six cows stirred lazily in stanchions to the right of the tractor. Penned to the left, a herd of goats milled about. Water dripped from a faucet beside the door. Ronny rinsed his head, then filled the canteen, dropping a purifying tablet into the water. Back in the yard, he eyed the house thoughtfully.

"I bet they don't lock their doors," he murmured. He could easily silence a dog. The tricycle beside the back door gave him pause. He and Cameron weren't starving. Killing a child's pet to steal food wasn't

157

something he was comfortable with. He headed back to the barn.

The purification tablet gave the water a weird iron aftertaste. He drank it anyway, then refilled the canteen and dropped in another tablet. At the chicken coop, he eased the door open and felt beneath the roosting birds.

The chickens began to squawk and flutter. Muffled barking from the house warned him to hurry. No eggs met his questing fingertips. A light came on inside the house as the chickens squawked louder. Ronny stepped back and eyed the loudest chicken. A hard glint in his eye, he lunged and tightened his grip, quieting the shrill squawk. The porch light over the back door flickered on. Chicken in hand, he raced around the edge the field. On the western edge, he slowed.

"Cameron?" he called softly.

"Here." She emerged from the trees, clutching a bulky bag of woven plant fronds to her chest.

He offered her the canteen. "Drink your fill. I can easily get more. And I brought dinner." With a flourish, he held out the chicken.

She curled her lip.

"Delicious, roasted, fried, or raw." He rubbed his stomach, making her laugh.

"We aren't eating raw chicken."

"Fear not, fair maiden. Let us away to the woods where our feast awaits."

"Loon. Get us more water first."

"Your every wish is my command." He settled on the dirt beside the tomato plants. "By the basket, I assume you found ripe ones?"

"Yep." She handed him a tomato.

"Delicious. Better with salt. There's some in my pack." Warm juice trickled down his chin. It was the best tomato he'd ever eaten. Four tomatoes later, he laid back in the dirt. "Let them go to bed for the night. They might have noticed the chicken theft." Reminded, he sat, and drew his knife. While she watched, he field dressed the bird, skinning it instead of plucking it.

"Gross." She made a face as he cut the head off.

"True, but delicious."

He wrapped the carcass in leaves and set it aside before burying the scraps in the loose soil of the garden. "Wait here. I'll clean dinner and get more water." He gathered the dead bird and headed back.

Night vision goggles over his eyes, he scanned the farmhouse and surroundings. The bright green of a lifeform made him pause before moving on. Either a cow or horse wandered beyond the farmhouse, he couldn't tell which, but it was too big to be a man. No lights shone in the farmhouse. The door to the barn was now closed.

Chickens in the coop stirred and muttered as he passed. When he was sure no one lay in wait, he climbed the ladder on the silo beside the barn and pulled out his scope.

Where Cameron waited, a short swath of forest separated that field from another. Behind him, forested hills rose. Another large field lay to the left with two rows of bunkhouses, one with lights on. Distant lights marked another farm house. To the right, a short hill blocked his view, but he knew what was there. That was the direction he'd come from. He climbed back down and eased the barn door open.

All was quiet inside the barn. The goats began milling when he turned the water on. He filled the canteen, cleaned his knife, then rinsed the chicken and his hands.

A hunched shape and low growl greeted him when he turned. "Good dog," he whispered switching his grasp on his knife. The growl rose in volume. "Who's a hungry puppy?" Ronny offered the skinned chicken. The dog perked its ears forward and rose. "Good boy," Ronny murmured as the dog paced forward, sniffing.

Ronny fed the dog raw chicken and rubbed its ears. "Have any friends in the house?"

The dog stopped eating and licked Ronny's hand.

"Hope you don't get blamed for killing this bird."

Both paws grasped the chicken as the dog lay on the dirt floor and began gnawing the bones.

Ronny eased from the barn and headed toward the house, leaving the door open a crack in case the dog wanted to get out.

Sure enough, the backdoor was unlocked. A television played low in the other room. Ronny closed the door behind himself and stepped into the room, pushing his goggles to the top of his head. A typical kitchen met his gaze, dimly lit from the bright moon outside and television in the other room. A dark hallway led to the left.

"*Quiere otra cerveza,*" a man called from the other room.

A quieter voice mumbled something to faint for Ronny to hear. He headed into the dark hallway and ducked into the first doorway right as the kitchen light came on.

Light from the kitchen illuminated a bathroom

sink. Ronny grinned and snatched up the soap and man's razor. Thoughtfully, he felt the mirror and slowly opened it, ready to push it shut if things began to fall from it. An assortment of pill bottles and ointments lay on the shelves. Labeled in Spanish, he had no idea what was what. He shrugged and took a random assortment, stuffing them into his pants pockets.

The light in the kitchen turned off. He waited a minute and ran back down the hall. A loaf of bread lay on the counter beside two boxes of cereal with a bowl of fruit beside them. He dumped everything into the front of his ghillie suit and hesitated in front of the refrigerator.

"Yes, I do want a beer," he mumbled under his breath.

Regretfully, he turned away, leaving the refrigerator closed, and snuck back outside. Once outside, he ran to the barn, clutching the food tucked into his clothing with one hand. The dog glanced up when he entered, still gnawing the chicken carcass. It wagged its tail and continued eating.

A quick search revealed a half-full grain bag and an empty plastic bucket. The goats began to bleat when he slit the grain open.

"Here yeah go, mates," he said as he tipped the bag into the pen. "I feel like animal Santa Clause."

Back at the faucet, he rinsed the bucket then filled it, transferring his pilfered goods into the empty sack. This time when he left he closed the door behind him and slung the sack of food over his shoulder. He headed back to Cameron, carrying the bucket of water.

"I was getting worried," she murmured when he

appeared.

"Let's get out of here. We can stay on the edge of the field and cut through the woods to the next one. I want to get a few miles away before we stop in case the dog tries to follow us."

He offered her the bucket." But first, a treat. I have soap too."

"I love you," she gasped as she grabbed for the water. The smile fled her face, and she dropped her hand.

"Take the water, sweetheart. I know what you meant."

Ronny handed her the soap and emptied his pockets. She gathered them, frowning at the labels.

"Too dark to see. Can I get a few minutes of privacy to wash?"

"Sure, meet me at the corner when you're ready and bring the bucket. Maybe we'll find more water."

She gave him a sad smile and turned her back.

A heavy sigh escaped him as he rose. He brightened as he waited for her. It was clear she liked him, maybe even loved him. Surely, once he explained, she would understand and forgive him. He bit back a chuckle. At least here she couldn't run from him.

Twenty minutes later she rejoined him, smelling of soap with wet hair and a clean face.

He wished he'd taken the time to wash. He handed her the goggles and let her lead.

After the next long field, they hit a dirt road that curved and dipped to the south. A clear, star-filled night illuminated the road enough to make walking easy. Hand-in-hand, they power-walked, making good time.

"Time for a break," Ronny said three hours later. He gestured at the small brook bordering the road.

"This is good," Ronny said fifteen minutes later.

They'd followed the stream into the forest. A wider pool had eroded the stream bed leaving a dry rocky area exposed. On one side of the stream, a steep, rocky bank led into the forest. On the other, a shallow incline covered with low brush led to a cultivated field. Ronny climbed the steep bank and laid on his stomach to use his scope to check the surroundings. Only woods and peaceful fields met his gaze.

By the time he climbed down, Cameron was already eating the bread. He helped himself to a slice and then a banana followed by an orange.

"Yum, tomato sandwiches for breakfast," she said happily, accepting the orange slices he handed her absently. Her smile faded, and she twined her hands nervously.

"Get some sleep. We can wash again before we go."

She fell asleep quickly, using his pack as a pillow. He spooned her back, stroking her hair until he fell asleep.

This time he woke before her. A rock dug into his side, going from annoying too painful as he tried to ignore it. Too big to remove without waking her, he gave up and rose. He stripped and washed, using his T-shirt, the soap, and the small pool of brackish water. The dull razor nicked his skin five times while shaving off the heavy stubble. He felt much cleaner when his face was smooth again. Hands on his hips, he gazed at the filthy ghillie suit, noticing the stench more now that he was clean.

While the suit would help him blend into the

landscape unnoticed, it was hot and heavy to wear, and she didn't have one. Mind made up, he rolled it into a ball and tied it closed, using the dangling scraps of fabric that adorned it. He debated washing his socks, but dirty socks were better than wet socks. He hung his damp t-shirt over a branch to dry and rummaged in the sack for the last of the bread.

The sun rose as he sliced tomatoes on a rock. Weak sunlight caressed her face. She sighed and stirred, rolling onto her side, then stretching before opening her eyes and sitting.

"Uggg, I'm so stiff." She groaned as she stood and stretched again, hobbling into the nearby woods. When she returned, she sat and pulled off her shoes, groaning again.

Ronny handed her the bucket holding the medicines.

One by one she examined them, opening a bottle and shaking out two tablets. She offered them to Ronny and took two herself. "Tylenol."

He took them and swallowed them dry, making a mental note of the writing on the bottle.

"Antibiotic cream." She wagged the tube at him, then applied it to her bleeding feet. Clear puss oozed from a large blister on the back of her right foot. Blood oozed from the left.

"Damn, I should've stolen bandages." Squatting on his heels, he picked up her foot to examine it.

"I'm okay. Give me a few strips from the suit." She smoothed more cream on the blisters and wrapped them with strips from his ghillie suit before replacing her dirty socks.

He handed her a tomato sandwich, earning a bright

smile.

"Think we shook the pursuit?" she asked around a mouthful of sandwich.

"Yes, but we should still be careful. We don't know who or how many there are. If they realize where we're going, they can just go wait. We're easily recognizable. Robbing that house was a risk. If the wrong person hears, they might realize it was us. What we need to steal is clothing to blend in."

"Do you know where we are?"

"Not exactly, but the sea is that way." Ronny pointed west. "If I had to guess, I'd say twenty or so miles away as the crow flies. If we go far enough south, we'll hit the town of Melaque. I'm sure I could sneak in there for a phone and supplies."

"How far?"

"Thirty— thirty-five miles. We can't miss it; we'll hit the Rio Marabasco if we go too far. We could follow the road at night until we reached a populated area. If I can get to a phone, we'll have help in no time."

"And the sea?"

"Well, there's a raft and radio three miles north of Tenacalita bay, assuming we can find it. It's ten miles or so closer, but across country. Mostly cultivated farmland bordered by stretches of jungle. Figure two days of travel at our current pace."

"Which is safer?"

Ronny held up a hand and rocked it side-to-side "Fifty-fifty. Daylight travel versus night, dangerous fauna versus dangerous men. Easier walking, but we'll be separated when we get—"

"I vote beach."

He smiled and ran a hand over her hair. Her eyes

lit, then saddened.

Ronny took her hand and sat, pulling her down beside him. "Let me tell you about Dawn."

SIXTEEN

◆

DAWN

"To understand Dawn and I, I have to start at the beginning," Ronny said in a thoughtful tone. "I grew up in a home very much like Sam's, including the loving parents. The difference being a little girl lived next door to me. I honestly can't remember not knowing her."

"You love her?"

"Very much, but not like you think. Dawn has been my best friend, and closest confident forever. I knew about every crush, and every girl she didn't like. She told me everything. Most days she stayed at my house. Her mother worked hard, two jobs and taking care of her 'sick' husband. I hated that man." Ronny sighed and rubbed his eyes. "I hated her mother for not kicking his lying, lazy ass to the curb."

"He abused her?"

Ronny shrugged and let out an angry snort. "More like ignored. When we were little, he was never around. By the time we were teenagers, he was sick. Liver failure and mean with it, demanding and angry. Dawn's mother tried. She loves Dawn but didn't have the strength to stand up to or leave him." Eyes on the distance, remembering, Ronny sighed. "Hell, I have no idea why she stayed."

Ronny straightened and ran a hand over his head. "When we were sixteen, Dawn called me crying. I rushed next door, and her father is cursing her in the foulest language you can imagine, blaming her for his shit life as if she forced him to guzzle booze until his liver quit. I took her home with me. She was crying hysterically. My parents went over there, and her mother showed up all apologetic. As far as I know, he never did it again, but I promised her I'd get her out of there as soon as I could."

Ronny took Cameron's hands again and kissed them before setting them back in her lap. "It was a real ugly scene, her crying, me yelling, her father cursing, and our mothers trying to calm everything down. You need to understand how upset Dawn was living there, how unhappy. She loved staying at my house and stayed as often as her mom allowed. Two doors down from me she had her own room and everything."

"Your parents like Dawn?"

"My parents love her like a daughter. My mother practically raised her. My parents were both horrified and happy we married."

"When?"

"I'm getting to that." Ronny took a deep breath. "When we were seventeen, we made a plan. I'd join the service and marry her. She could go to school and get out of her house."

"And you got her?"

"Sort of, but it wasn't cold like your implying. I was seventeen and horny like all seventeen-year-old boys. Dawn told her friends we were friends with benefits, and suddenly I was the most popular boy in school. Her friends all wanted to fuck me, a no strings attached boy toy, and I was more than willing.

"Dawn didn't mind?"

"Dawn encouraged it. We laughed together over her friends. I told her everything, and she told me what girls were an easy score. At eighteen we married. I went to boot camp, and she went to college. Her father died three months after we married. We could've separated then, but she loved school, and I didn't care. It didn't cost me much, so we went on.

"A boy at college broke her heart. Ted Baxter. I swear to God, I want to kill that fucker. Ted led her on, the lying son of a bitch. Over summer break she paid him a surprise visit and found out he had a serious girlfriend. He said a bunch of crap, but the end result was she came crying to me.

"You never had sex with her?"

"Not until then. I'm not proud of this, but by that time I was crazy horny. Months of no girls in boot camp and I knew nobody on base. When I saw her, I realized how beautiful she'd grown. I hadn't seen her for eight months. And here she is telling me she wants to be friends with benefits for real, and I was more than willing. Hell, who wouldn't be? A beautiful girl, who you really like, offers to have sex with you whenever you want? Well, I jumped at it. Over that summer we had sex like we were training for the Olympics.

"When she headed back to school, I didn't miss her though. She'd made my reputation again. There's something about a guy taken by a beautiful girl that inspires others to want them. Or maybe it was my attitude. I didn't care if I scored because Dawn was waiting. Whatever it was, I had more girls than I could handle."

Cameron snorted in disgust.

Ronny grimaced. "I was eighteen... I never lied to anyone or lead them on. And the service kept me busy, so while I was happy, the frequency was probably less than most college students."

"Do I want to know how many?"

Ronny glanced at her and blushed. "Probably not."

Cameron made an unhappy noise.

Ronny sighed. 'Twenty or thirty, I never counted. Most were one-night stands, three at the most."

"Except for Dawn."

"She spent summers at my house with my parents or in an apartment on base. We both enjoyed the benefits. I didn't realize until years later what had inspired her to offer sex. I know that makes me dense, and a shit, but I thought she wanted sex like I did.

"What inspired her?"

"Ted. I mean she never said but in hindsight... I confronted him about three months after we got together. She was so upset about him. I was her teddy bear. She came to me for comfort and affection and cried on my shoulder about him. Well, anyway, when I confronted him, he called her a hypocrite and a gold digger. Made her seem real mercenary. And she wasn't like that at all. But I think that inspired her. She had nothing else to offer me for my help, and I was too stupid and inexperienced to see it."

Ronny rubbed his eyes a minute. "I hate that. That I might have hurt her. Over the next years, she had a few other boyfriends, and we called it quits temporarily, but she met no one she loved until Tom. When she met Tom, that was it for us."

"Tom, your teammate?" Cameron sounded shocked.

"Yeah, almost two years ago now."

"And you didn't divorce?"

"No, she needed me. She's my best friend. As long as she needs me, I'll help her in any way I can."

"You support her?"

"In every way I can. Not so much with money anymore. She has a good job." Ronny leaned forward, bracing his elbows on his knees. "You're thinking she took advantage and that isn't true at all. Everything Dawn and I ever did we agreed upon in advance. We were young, but I knew what I was doing, and so did she. I wasn't hiding our relationship; I truly forgot about it."

Ronny sighed again. "That hurt her feelings. I never forgot her, just that we were married. I don't think of us as married. We were never really married. Not like JT and Charlene or Dan and Angie. Dawn and I had a bargain."

"That sounds so cold."

"I guess, in a way. Now that I'm older, I hope I didn't scar her. That my— ahh— enthusiasm didn't make her think less of herself, that she was in any way unworthy of love."

Cameron nodded slowly. "She knew you didn't love her?"

"I do love her, but the sex was just sex. It was hot

and felt good, but once it was over, I never thought of it until I was horny, and she was there. It wasn't like I pined for her or anyone. Dawn was breakfast cereal."

Cameron pursed her lips and regarded him quizzically. "Meaning?"

"You know, you really like it, and it tastes good, but if you never had it again, you wouldn't miss it. Like when I was a kid, I loved fruity pebbles, but now they do nothing for me. But when I see the box in the store I smile, remembering how much I liked it.

Cameron burst into laughter, then snorted. "And me?"

"Your filet mignon, and ice-cream, salad, potatoes, and candy bars." Both hands on her face now, he searched her eyes. "You're every good, essential thing a man needs to survive." He kissed her frown. "I will never forget or get over you. I'm so sorry I never mentioned Dawn. I should have. Not because we're married, but because she's an important part of my life. We won't be married much longer. I asked for a divorce the day I met you, and she came to drop off divorce papers."

"Will she be okay without you?"

"She won't be without me. I'll support her forever. Not sex or money— she doesn't want either from me, but I'll be there for her."

"I don't understand why you didn't really marry her if you love her."

"Maybe I would have if she really loved me, but she never did. I don't want to say she loves me like a brother, but I was never the man of her dreams." Ronny rubbed his face again. "This is so hard to explain. I always knew she wouldn't choose me if given

172

a choice. Well, for a permanent thing anyway. So, I never considered her for a permanent thing either. I mean, it never crossed my mind. I liked our arrangement. Dawn's great company in bed or out. We spent a lot of time just hanging out. It wasn't like I came from a date and screwed her. If either of us was dating another, we hung out as friends. Sure, I teased her, or she teased me, but she's my friend first before being my lover."

"What did your parents say about all this?"

"They don't really know. It's not like we tell people. Dawn only tells her friends; the ones she thinks I'll like. Most of her friends don't even know she's married. My team knows because Dawn asked me to tell them. She thought the men were hot and didn't want them to think badly of me if she flirted. I think my mom suspects, but even when Dawn and I divorce my mom will still love her. She'll be angry at me though..."

The silence when he stopped speaking thickened to uncomfortable proportions.

Finally, Ronny rose and grabbed his pack." We better get going."

Cameron reached to him, placing a hand on his shoulder.

"It's not like I don't believe you. I do. And I understand, but I have to wonder what you'll do if she changes her mind. What if a year from now she decides she wants you as a permanent thing?"

He dropped the pack at his feet and pulled her close. His voice deep and low he spoke. "It wouldn't change how I feel. I would make her see a psychiatrist or something, or maybe an exorcist because that would be crazy and completely out of character for her. I love you, Cameron. I love everything about you in a way I've never felt for anyone before. Sure, I'd drop everything and run to help her, but I'd do the same for any friend who needed me. There's nothing I wouldn't do for you."

"You're going to break my heart," she said soft and sad.

"Never." He kissed her lightly on the lips.

She sobbed and clutched his shirt, kissing him hard. A groan escaped him when her hands went to his belt. Reluctantly, he broke from the kiss.

"God knows I want you like I want air to breath, but now isn't good timing. I want to take my time and make love to you for hours. Not quick in the dirt."

Eyes sparkling with lust she grinned at him. "How about we do hours later and quick and dirty now?" Without waiting for his reply, she began undoing his belt again. He helped her, removing his damp t-shirt and unbuttoning the shirt she wore, revealing the dirty shirt underneath. She kicked off her shoes and lifted her hands to the button on her pants.

Another groan escaped him as the pants hit the dirt. Lacy pink underwear joined them as he struggled with his boots. She was completely naked before he got his boots off. Laughing she pushed him over on the pile of discarded clothes, tugging his pants down and kneeling beside him.

"Mmm," she made an aroused sound as she drew her hand along his length.

Fingers tangled in her hair, he pulled her down for a kiss. Breathing hard, she drew back and straddled him, using one hand to guide him.

"You'll have to pull out. I've fallen behind in my birth control tablets."

He bucked his hips, seating himself deep, making her moan.

"I'm not going to last more than a few minutes," he half laughed, half complained as she began jerking her hips.

Eyes closed, she tipped her head back, an expression of deep concentration on her face. His hands wandered from her breasts to her hips. He wanted to touch her everywhere, the familiar feel of her body was both arousing and reassuring. Tight and warm she encased him, each movement a burst of pleasure.

"Oh God," she moaned and moved faster, filling him with heat.

"I'm going to come," he warned.

"Not yet, please. I need—"

Straining against him, she stopped speaking, sliding hard and fast on him. Despite what she wanted he was going to come soon. Each thrust brought him to the brink. Sweat popped up on his brow as he clenched his muscles trying desperately to hold back. To distract himself he ran his hands over her breasts, running his thumbs over the hard nipples, concentrating on their shape and feel.

Inner muscles clenched him as she screamed and fell forward on his chest. Hurriedly, he lifted her off and bucked against her, coming in long spurts across her stomach as she gasped and writhed. The release left him panting. It almost hurt it felt so good.

He wished they were somewhere comfortable so he could spread her out and admire her body with his hands and mouth. A glance at his watch showed it had taken six minutes; he was surprised he'd lasted that long and bit back a chuckle.

Unable to resist, he ran his palm over her nipples again, making her groan and jerk against him. He rolled her to the side and knelt in the dirt, taking her nipple into his mouth, sliding two fingers inside her. She cried out, a wordless shout, bucking against his hand. His thumb teased her clit as he rubbed inside her, taking turns licking her nipples and rolling them lightly between his thumb and finger.

"God, you're so beautiful," he murmured and blew lightly across her breast, flicking the erect nipple with his tongue.

She screamed when she came again and grabbed his hand, stilling him. "Enough, God, that was amazing. I don't think Dawn had anything to do with you getting all those women."

"I love you," he said and started to stand.

She drew him closer, holding him tight. "I need a minute."

He lay in the dirt and pulled her on top of him, brushing the sand and pebbles from her skin. Warm breath caressed his cheek and neck. An occasional tremble shook her, small orgasmic aftershocks. He rubbed her back until she was completely relaxed against him.

"Are you asleep?" he murmured an hour later.

"No," she heaved a disappointed sigh and moved off him, letting him stand. Laughing, she drew him down for a kiss. "I'm a mess."

Ronny's gaze traveled her. Dirt coated her stomach stuck to his dried semen. Leaves and sticks were trapped in her dusty hair, and her back was scratched and dirty from the hard ground. Despite the dirt, the sight of her naked body filled him with lust. The scratches and bruises made him wince. Sex in the dirt, no matter how good it felt, was hurting her.

"Wait here." He jumped to his feet, pulling his pants up over his growing erection, but leaving them unbuttoned, and grabbed the bucket. He filled it carefully in the shallow pool not wanting to get any insects or slugs in it. Murky brown water was the best he could manage.

He poured the water over her and retrieved another bucket, this time wetting his shirt and wiping her down before using the water to clean himself.

Back at the pool of water, he rinsed his shirt and wrung it out before putting it back on.

Dressed again, she joined him, carrying his pack and the sack with the food.

"Drink as much as you like from the canteen. The area we're traveling will have farms, and we can get more water. Don't drink from the stream. I have enough tablets for a week and matches and a metal cup so we can boil water if we have to. We'll go straight west. If we hit a road, we'll take a break and watch for a bit to judge the traffic. Fields with workers we'll go around. You set the pace. Go as slow as you need. It doesn't matter if it takes a week to reach the shore."

Ronny hugged her, resting his chin on her head. His entire body felt loose and relaxed. The tight grip she had on him was reassuring in a way he didn't have a name for. Even though she hadn't said it, her every action spoke of a deep love for him. He had to force his mind back to business. It would be easy to pretend this was just a hike in the woods and lose himself in the feel of her body against his.

"Once we hit more populated areas we'll travel at night. At the first hint of people, lay low."

The words had barely left his lips when a gout of dirt exploded from the bank behind him. Instinctively, he dropped, pulling her with him before he heard the gunshot.

SEVENTEEN

◆

FIFTY-FIFTY

Ronny's trained ear noted the shot had come from about four hundred yards with no angle on them. While he was thinking that, he rolled to his knees and grabbed the rifle beside his pack, lifting it to his shoulder. Another shot rang out as a man yelled in Spanish. This shot was closer, the angle better. Ronny's narrow-eyed gaze landed on a man running towards them, holding a gun to his shoulder.

Cameron smacked the rifle down as Ronny fired, sending his shot into the dirt of the embankment.

"No, he's a farmer." She scrabbled to her feet, grabbing the pack. "*Lo siento vamos!*" she yelled as she grabbed Ronny's hand and tugged him.

He snatched the bucket and feed bag, letting her pull him, but peering over his shoulder. The skin between his shoulder blades itched.

Perched on the bank, a man wearing dungarees

and a ball cap stared after them, a gun resting on his shoulder.

"*Traficantes de drogas no*!" she called out as they ran around the bend, splashing water with every step.

He took the lead and at the first opening dragged her up the bank and into the trees.

"You okay?" his anxious gaze scanned her.

She smiled ruefully and hugged him. "Yes, but let's keep moving. I'm not sure he believed me."

"Thinks we're drug dealers?"

"Yeah, your rifle and clothes. Maybe we better hide the gun or leave it."

"We aren't leaving it. I'll wrap the suit around it at the next stop."

Ronny gazed at her. The uniform shirt and pants marked her as military. His camouflage clothing did the same. Anyone looking at them would reach the same conclusion the farmer had unless word was out about two missing American service personnel.

He figured their chances were fifty-fifty of running into someone who would try to hold them for the cartel versus someone who offered to help them reach their base. A glance at the compass in his watch showed they were running south. The sun hung directly overhead, he'd spent much longer than he'd meant to making love and talking. He turned east and took her hand.

Thirty minutes later, they reached another field. He let her take the lead, setting the pace to cross it. Cornstalks over their head blocked the view and trapped the heat. Sweat trickled down his brow. He made a mental note to break into the first barn or house they passed for water.

At least in the cornfield he felt safe from view. At the edge of the field, he sat, pulling her down beside him. A dirt road separated the corn field from another field growing knee-high somethings. Beyond that field, dense shrubs and tall trees blocked the view. No people were in sight although he heard an engine.

"Can you run?"

"For a short distance, yes."

"Across this next field?"

"I think so."

"We need a plan in case we get separated. We'll always discuss our next target when we're crossing. Like here we're aiming for the eastern corner. If we're spotted and separated that's where I'll look for you. If it's not safe to wait there, go six hundred yards as straight east as you can. Leave me a pile of rocks or blaze a tree every six hundred yards. Don't wait more than one hour."

Lips pressed tight together she nodded.

"Do what you have to, to stay alive. If that means stealing food or killing someone who attacks you, do it."

She nodded again and grabbed him.

He rested his cheek on her warm hair and rubbed her back. "If you get caught, don't panic, I'll come for you."

"What do I do if they catch you?"

"Get to a phone and call it in." He pushed away to see her face. "Don't try to save me yourself. Call Dan, JT, or the admiral. If you can't reach a phone safely, then wait until you can. Never put yourself at risk for me."

Her lips thinned, and eyes narrowed.

"Please? Do the smart thing, Cameron. It'll be hard, but to save me you'd need to be smart."

A deep frown on her face, she pulled him to his feet.

"Run along the edge, not straight across. The footing will be too uneven hopping those rows. I'll follow you."

She glanced both directions before sticking her head from the corn and running across the road. He followed.

They spent the rest of the day crossing fields and climbing through thick brush. He made two stops for water, the entire time a nervous wreck leaving her alone. Her tense, pale face showed she hated the separations too, but he couldn't afford to take her. The limp was back and getting worse.

On his return with water, he caught her taking a pill from a different bottle.

"What's that?"

She flushed and clenched her fist around the bottle. "Percocet. My knee really hurts."

"Worse than your feet?"

She nodded guiltily.

"Let's see it."

She sighed hard as she dropped her pants.

With gentle fingers, he unwrapped the ace bandage and made an involuntary sound of dismay. A dark bruise ringed the outside of her knee, leaving the entire knee swollen and hot to the touch. As gently as he could, he rewrapped it, wishing they had ice.

"I'm okay," she said as she stood to pull her pants back up.

His heated gaze traveled her, stopping on her blood-stained underwear. He grabbed her hands.

"Did I hurt you?"

"It's not a sprain, just a bruise."

"No, not the knee." He traced his thumb over the dirty lace of her panties. She glanced down and jerked away. A red flush covered her cheeks as she yanked her pants up.

"I need some clothes or something," she mumbled.

He sat back on his heels and grinned with relief. "Don't be embarrassed. I've been buying Dawn's supplies since she was thirteen. She was horrified and too embarrassed to ask her mom."

Tight hunched shoulders told him he wasn't helping. He glanced around. The barn where he'd gotten the water sat half a mile away, only the red roof visible through the trees. Where they sat seemed private, but farmhands worked in a field about eight hundred yards away. He couldn't imagine a reason for one to venture this far into the brush, but the chance remained one would.

Not a great spot to stop, but she needed rest. He settled on the ground. "Sit for a few minutes. Now is a good time to hide my gun."

Thick padding made up the front of his suit. He used his knife to cut it out and into thin strips, which he handed to her. He began wrapping his gun in the remains of his suit, leaving the end of the barrel unobstructed. Two sticks, crossed and tied with a strip of his suit, made a square frame to hide the shape, hopefully resembling a pack. He left the fabric loose by the trigger so he could slip his hand inside if he needed too, and tied the contraption to his pack. She'd watched him, fiddling with the squares of padding.

He gestured to them. "Bury them when you change

them if you can. How many days?"

"Three to four," she croaked.

A grin lit his face at her embarrassed tone. He kissed her brow. "Girls are silly. You worry about the most ridiculous things. I'm not grossed out or anything. I knew about menstruation before you. You didn't shock me."

"Ha, ha."

He smiled and ruffled her hair. "Stay here. I'm going to see what's in front of us."

Cheeks still dark red from embarrassment, she nodded. He kissed her lightly before leaving.

A twenty-minute trek brought him to the edge of the trees where a wide paved road lay before him. He lay on the jungle floor peering from the brush with the scope to his eyes, wishing he still wore the ghillie suit. The T-shirt he wore was so dirty it couldn't be called white anymore, but it was still brighter than he wished.

Before him, across the street, a barbed wire fence bordered a wide plowed field. A grassy field dotted with cows lay beyond that. The road curved and dipped to the right. A black shingled roof and a white edge of a house showed about half a mile away.

The road headed straight east in the other direction, lining the field as far as he could see. Two trucks passed him while he scoped the scene. No people worked the field. A lone tractor in the distance kicked up dust too far away to hear the engine. He glanced at his watch and eased backward. Cameron would be nervous if he didn't get back soon.

He was half way back when he heard crashing in the brush. He stilled, lowering himself to the ground.

Too slow and loud to be an animal, the sounds continued towards him.

"Cameron?" he called.

"Ron," she answered, sounding as if she'd been crying.

He pushed through the woods towards her. She greeted him with a gasp of relief and a hard hug, trembling in his arms.

"Don't leave me like that again."

"Okay. What happened?"

"You were gone so long. I thought you were giving me a few minutes to... and when you didn't come back, I got worried." A tremble shook her, and she clutched him tighter.

"We're okay. A paved road heading west is ahead. Let's rest here until nightfall and check the traffic." Alarmed by the desperate way she still clutched him, he dropped the pack and lowered her to the ground in his lap.

"Are you okay?"

She shook her head and pressed her lips against his neck. With shocking suddenness, she began to cry deep gasping sobs.

"Shh— we're okay," he murmured as he rubbed her back. "It's okay, cry if you need to." He pressed her head against his chest as she began to draw away. "Lots has happened, and your body needs release from stress. Cry, you'll feel better."

She relaxed against him and cried hard for a minute. The tears slowed until only the occasional hiccupping sob remained. He said nothing just rubbed her back and smoothed her hair.

"Sorry," she mumbled.

He fumbled one-handed with the pack, removing the canteen and offering it to her. She sat and wiped her face with her sleeve before accepting it.

While she sipped the water, he settled the pack behind them and leaned back. Above him, a curtain of dense foliage filtered the sunlit, leaving the air dim and cool. Birds flitted through the trees, their soft calls relaxing. The whir of insects was slow in the day. Seeing no giant spider webs, or snakes in the trees, he relaxed.

"Let's sleep for a while. This is nice," he said as she lay beside him, resting her sore knee over his legs, half laying on top of him. Soft and warm, her body curled against his. "Let's go camping when we get home. We can bring a cooler of food and beer and air-mattresses."

The soft sound of contentment she made went right to his groin.

"I want to spend the rest of my life with you."

The hand idly rubbing his shoulder stilled.

"I realize my timing sucks, and I shouldn't ask you to marry me when I'm technically still married, but the minute I'm single again I plan to beg you to marry me. No pressure or anything. We can do whatever you like I just wanted you to know how serious I am about you."

She leaned over him on an elbow. Red rimmed eyes wide in her dirty face, she bit her bottom lip.

"Please don't break my heart. I want to let myself love you, but I'm so afraid."

His heart leaped. "Afraid of what?"

"Dawn. You love her too. And you have history, something I can never compete with." A sob escaped her, and she lowered her head, resting her forehead against his chest. "Dawn is so beautiful, if she wants you again, you'll go to her."

"Dawn is beautiful but not as beautiful as you."

She snorted.

"I can't quantify it, the attraction you have for me, but everything about you turns me on. Never think I find her more attractive— I don't. But it wouldn't matter if you lost your beautiful blue eyes, or your face and body were scarred because I love you, the inner you. The woman who loves to run and bikes and plays ball with a four-year-old for hours. The strength and kindness you showed bringing Juan into the world... I knew then, Cam. When I saw you at the firing range, I fell in love. A woman who shoots like that... I had to meet you."

She giggled.

"Dawn, on a trip like this would be a nightmare. With you, I'm happy despite the lack of food and worry."

"I love you," she murmured.

Ronny's body tensed. "Yeah?" Deep and low his voice cracked, and he cleared his throat.

"Don't change your mind," she whispered.

Elated, he hugged her hard. "Never. Trust me. We're going to be so happy together."

She started crying again. He rubbed her back until she relaxed, sinking into sleep.

He woke in the pitch black when a bird screeched. No light filtered through the dense plants overhead. Still asleep across his chest, Cameron's limp weight pinned his arm, making his hand tingle. With his free hand, he lifted the scope attached to his belt.

"Son of a bitch," he muttered as he spied the giant snake curled around a tree beside them. The scope made visible what daylight couldn't.

"Cam, wake up, sweetheart, time to go." He sat, bringing her with him. She stretched and rubbed her face as he flexed his arm trying to restore circulation.

"I need a bathroom break." She rubbed her knee hard, trying to scratch it beneath the thick bandage.

"Do it right here. I won't look." He stood and peed against the tree opposite the snake while she fumbled with the sack. "Do you want the flashlight?"

"No, I'm good; give me a minute."

Three minutes later they were crashing through the brush. Night goggles covered her face. He used the scope with the night vision attachment and was relieved when they reached the road. Taillights in the distance disappeared as he scanned the area.

"Keep the glasses on. You should notice the flare right away of an approaching vehicle. Say my name, but don't wait for me, head into the bush and lay down. Set the pace. Hurry, but don't hurt yourself." He handed her the last banana and began peeling the last orange. "Finish the cereal and tuck the bag in the pack." At ten forty-three they started out, half jogging, half walking down the road.

EIGHTEEN

— ◆ —

LET'S STAY TOGETHER

Ronny paused beside the roadside, risking using the flashlight and making a mental note of the street names before continuing on. The road before them curved to the south. About half a mile away, a closed gas station sat beside a brightly lit bar. Blue and red neon signs blinked and a bare bulb hung from a pole over a half-full parking lot. Almost all the vehicles that had passed them in the last mile filled the lot.

"We're further north than I thought, on the outskirts of *Agua Caliente Nueva.* I could go steal us a phone, or we could hike about four or five more miles to the boat. If we head for the boat, we might have to wait a day hidden on shore. We only have about six hours of darkness left, and I don't want to launch a raft during the daytime. That's assuming it's still there, and we can find it."

"The raft," she said instantly. "If it isn't there, we

can try to steal a phone."

"Okay, we'll skirt the edge of the forested hills. You set the pace. Go nice and easy. Don't let our proximity make you careless. Route two hundred will be too busy to walk along so will *Manzanillo*, the road leading to *Tenacatita*. There's an arroyo boarding the road we can stay in that should be deserted and dark." He gave her an apologetic grimace. "Watch out for snakes though. The smaller ones can be hard to see with night vision."

"Right," she said and sighed hard.

He ran a hand through her dirty hair, tucking a loose curl behind her ear. "I can go steal a phone instead."

"No, let's stay together."

He nodded and took her hand. They set out along the side of the road headed for the bush.

"It's funny how the smallest thing can change your life," Cameron mused as she walked along the rocky edge of a muddy river.

"How so?"

"If you hadn't seen me on the course that morning and dropped that gift off at just that moment, you might never have noticed C. Howard's name tag." She turned to glance at him, the goggles hiding her expression. "We might never have met."

"We would've met," he disagreed. "I saw you running the day before and planned to go back again until I met you. I should've followed you that day, but I had a meeting. I was almost late anyways because I stopped to help Mrs. Reeves with her picnic basket."

"I'm glad we met," she said shyly.

"Me too." They continued silently for another fifteen

minutes.

"Did Mrs. Reeves have a friend with her?"

"Not that I saw. Why do you ask?"

"It's odd, isn't it? To picnic alone."

"Maybe she was meeting someone."

"That's what I was thinking." Cameron pulled the glasses from her head and ran a hand through her hair. "I hate to say this, but what if she were meeting a man?"

"None of our business." Ronny shrugged.

"Well— I was thinking. Let's say she was meeting a man; someone she's having an affair with. That would explain how Mitchell knew when the office would be empty. It would also explain how he got the codes and how we still have a leak despite Alfarsi's arrest."

"You think she gave them to him? Why would she do that?"

"Not on purpose, but people makes codes easy to remember, they use important dates and names, all things she would know. Hell, sometimes they write them down and keep them somewhere to remind themselves. Like you; your password is taped to the inside of your gun case. The admiral's wife would know where he keeps his."

Ronny frowned. "If that's true..." absently he took her hand and began walking again deep in thought, remembering the clink of glass, not at all what you would expect for a casual picnic among friends. June had brought wine glasses and been nervous when he mentioned her husband. "We can't just accuse her. I mean, she's the admiral's wife. If we're wrong, our careers are ruined."

"If we're right, she's in serious danger, never mind

the risk a security leak like that poses to the fleet."

"Oh, jeez."

They walked in silence a few more minutes. Ronny carried the flashlight but kept it off. Cameron still wore the night goggles.

"I have no idea what to do," he admitted.

"Me either." She shrugged. "It's not like we can do anything now, so no use worrying about it."

For an hour they hiked, both quiet. The river bed narrowed. Only a thin trickle of fast-moving water ran down the center of the narrow channel, leaving thick, smelly muck ten feet along each side. Clouds covered the stars, the air smelling of rain and the sea. The wind picked up. He was sure it would rain before morning. This river would likely overflow its banks with the runoff.

"I'll have to report this," Ronny finally said, tapping the flashlight against his hand absently. "We could just ask her, but she could lie. I could follow her, but your right, she could be in real danger. My career isn't worth her life."

"Maybe we could— " She shrieked and jumped backward, grabbing at her leg. "Snake. A snake just bit me." The goggles tumbled to the ground as she wiped her eyes, hopping backward on one foot, then falling forward and landing on her knees hard. She screamed again and fell to the side, rolling into a ball and grabbing her legs.

"Stay still," Ronny barked, flicking the light on and searching the ground. A three-foot black snake slithered away from them into the water. A quick scan of the ground showed another curled on a rock about four paces away. Behind him, Cameron cried.

"Were there antihistamines in the medicine?"

"It bit me," she sobbed.

"Okay, sweetheart," Ronny said trying to sound calm and reassuring instead of panicked and scared to death. "You're going to be fine. Take an antihistamine and a Tylenol." Ronny grabbed his knife and approached the sleeping snake.

"What are you doing?"

"Take the medicine." He tucked the flashlight between his shoulder and chin and grabbed the snake with his free hand, slashing with his knife to sever the head. His heart pounded in his chest. If this was a viper, she'd be dead before he could get her to help. The snake jerked and went limp. With a shaking hand, he played the beam across it's back and sagged in relief. A long straight line went from head to tail along the snake's spine. To confirm his observation, he grabbed the snake's head and examined its mouth.

"Just a garter. A big one, but harmless. Let's see the foot. You must have stepped right on it."

Two small punctures right above her ankle oozed blood. He smeared antibiotic cream on them. Still taking hitching breaths, she peered around wildly.

"Look, another one." She pointed to the edge of the water where another black snake looped around a fallen tree limb.

He snatched up the goggles. "Can you walk?"

Her yes sounded like a moan. He laughed and swung her into his arms, carrying her up the bank. A plowed field bordered the river. He carried her down the row of plants.

"I can walk," she murmured.

"When I get tired. This is nice. A moonlit stroll with

my girl. I can smell the sea air. We're almost there."

"How will we find the boat?"

"It's between this river outlet and the rock outcropping two miles north. It'll be buried in the sand against the low dunes, maybe with a camo net over it. I know where to look. We'll find it if it's there."

"I can walk," she repeated as the field gave way to sand.

He set her down, stopping to kiss her thoroughly, then knelt and examined the snake bite. No longer bleeding it appeared puffy and sore with dark blue edges. The surrounding skin felt normal, not swollen or warm, which relieved him. Her forehead felt hot and clammy. She hissed as he felt her lower leg and batted his hand away.

"Take two more Tylenol. A few more hours and we'll be on a helicopter out of here." He glanced at his watch. In less than two hours the sun would rise. If he couldn't find the boat in one, he'd wait until the next day. He found it eighteen minutes later.

She picked at the MRE he handed her from the emergency food supply as he fiddled with the radio.

"Lost chick calling mother bird, over." He waited a moment and continued, "Pan-pan pan pan pan-pan this is lost chick calling mother bird.

"Lost chick, this is the nest; we read you loud and clear. Confirm identity and location."

"This is Zero-Foer-Six-One-Niner-Six-Five-Two-Two, Actual. Location, one-nine degrees one-eight-zero-foer, point niner-seven north by one-zero-foer, degrees five-five-zero-zero, point-zero-eight west."

"Confirmed, lost chick. Do you have the egg?"

"Roger that. Awaiting instructions."

"Proceed to sea heading sixty degrees north, and don't dawdle, a storm is brewing in the area; winds at forty-five and heavy rain expected."

Tempted to say they would wait out the storm ashore in the brush, Ronny glanced at Cameron, who rubbed her ankle with a pained expression on her face. He reached over and felt her forehead again, sure now she had a fever, whether from the snake, poor food, or insect bites, he didn't know. Despite the approaching storm, she needed a doctor and medicine.

"Roger that. Out."

He dragged the rubber raft into the sea, waving her back when she stood to help. Warm waves lapped against his thighs as he braced the boat with his body.

"Would now be a good time to mention I can't swim all that well?" she said as she awkwardly climbed aboard the boat, hissing with pain as she swung her legs over the side.

He threw her his pack, tossed the bucket into the boat, and clamored over the side. "Seriously? You're in the Navy and play every sport I've ever heard of." He took a moment to activate the transponder and secure the radio with the Velcro strap. To his relief, the small engine started on the first pull.

"I can swim, just not really good," she said defensively. "I failed my lifeguard examine."

He grinned at her. Wind dried the sweat on his face as he steered with one hand, heading out to sea at sixty degrees. "Don't worry about it; I passed mine." He nodded towards the life vests tied to the side of the boat. "Put one on and hand me one. And see if there's any candy or water in the supplies."

She slid on her ass across the floor of the boat to

hand him the jacket, water, and a chocolate bar, then sat leaning on his legs. "I don't feel so good."

"Sick?"

She nodded.

"Sea sick?" he asked hopefully

"I don't think so, it started before we boarded."

Ronny said nothing just smoothed her hair back from her sweaty forehead. A few minutes later she moaned and struggled to the side of the boat where she vomited.

She didn't return to him, instead leaning over the side, splashing water on her face. He stopped the engine and crawled to her side where he checked the snake bite again. It hadn't changed.

"I don't think it's the bite," he said as reassuringly as he could as she vomited again.

She nodded miserably.

"Do you hurt anywhere else?"

"Just my leg, I'm hot and sweaty though, and my heart feels like it's going to beat out of my chest."

He took his shirt off and wet it, applying the cold compress to her face and neck, then felt for the pulse in her wrist. "Probably from being sick. Try to relax. I'm ninety-nine percent certain that was a garter snake."

"Am I going to die?"

"No!" His heart began to beat as fast as hers. "No," he repeated in a calmer voice. He gestured over the ocean. "Look, we're almost home. Just another hour or so."

Faint light from the transponder caught in the glitter of tears on her cheeks. His heart thudded so painfully he thought he might vomit too. The wind picked up, a cooling breeze caressing his bare skin, and whipping a light spray over them. Waves rocked the boat harder, the prow rising and slamming down before rising again.

She moaned piteously.

"The ride will be smoother with the motor on."

She waved him away, laying her face against the side of the boat.

NINETEEN

———— ◆ ————

I GOT YOU

Ronny restarted the motor, this time going slower, trying to make the ride as smooth as possible for her. In the distance, lightning flickered, so far away he couldn't hear thunder. A bare lightening of the sky announced the coming day. Overhead, thick, black clouds scuttled across the sky and yet the promised rain didn't arrive although the air felt heavy and thick.

"How you doing, sweetheart?"

"Better," she said weakly.

"Good. That's good." He wanted to get on the radio and check the ETA but didn't want to release the tiller. There was nothing he could do about the arrival time, so he kept driving. Overhead, a clap of thunder heralded the rain. Hard pellets of rain chilled his skin in moments. The rain was so thick he could barely see her through it. In moments, water lapped against his ankles.

She crawled to his pack and the bucket that lay in

the prow, and began bailing.

"Don't bother," he shouted above the rain. "This boat can float full of water."

Without turning to face him, she dropped the bucket and sat, stretching both legs out and leaning over them. The next wave lifted the prow, making her slid down the boat towards him.

"Grab the side!"

On her hands and one knee, she crawled to the side, dragging her other leg behind her, and leaned over, vomiting again.

"Cam?" he called concerned when she remained in that position.

She turned towards him, lifting both hands to push back her soaked hair. A wave caught the lee of the ship and lifted it on edge.

"Cameron!" he screamed as she tumbled over the side.

Immediately, he released the throttle and leaned over the side where she'd went over. Dark-blue water met his searching gaze.

"Cameron!" he shrieked, staring wildly over the waves.

One-foot waves continuously rocked the boat. A curtain of rain slanted across him, limiting visibility. A flicker caught his eye, the small strobe attached to her life jacket. She was already thirty feet away from him. He scrambled back to the tiller and grasped the throttle hard. The engine coughed and died.

"Mother fucker," he screamed as he yanked the cord and got no response.

He'd flooded the engine. He grabbed the knife from his hip and slashed the transponder loose. Working as fast as he could, he tied it around his waist, then dove over the side of the boat. Warm water closed over his head. He stroked hard in the direction he'd last seen her. The waves teased him, revealing glimpses of light and her bright-orange jacket, lost to sight for minutes at a time as the water turned her.

"Cameron," he screamed again. Within five feet of her now, she floated with her eyes closed and arms outspread, making no attempt to swim, only the lifejacket keeping her head above water. His breath came in short, hard pants, not from exertion— from fear. He sobbed when she opened her eyes and paddled weakly toward him.

"I got you," he repeated over and over, more to reassure himself than her. He forced himself to stop babbling and took a deep shuddering breath. "Can you see the boat?" A hand held over his brow to block the sleeting rain, he peered through the downpour.

She shook her head.

"Don't let go of me." He shook her when she didn't respond. "Cam, don't let go of me."

Dull blue eyes met his. Two red patches set on her pale cheeks.

"I'm tired, and my leg really hurts. It feels like it's burning."

"Don't go to sleep." Ronny swam in a small circle, shading his eyes with his hands, hoping to spot the boat.

"There," she said and pointed.

He followed her pointing finger to the boat, which bobbed about three hundred feet away.

"Just hold onto me, Cam. We're fine." The waves tried to push him back, but they also brought the boat closer.

"Almost there— "

Cameron screamed and released him, yanking his gun from his holster as something rammed into his side, rolling him through the water. *Shark*, he thought as he reached for the knife on his hip while kicking to the surface. His head surfaced as Cameron fired his gun. Inky red water surrounded him.

"I'm bleeding," Cameron sobbed as she squeezed the trigger again.

A shark floated on its side to the surface in a spreading pool of blood, a ragged hole torn behind its dorsal fin. She fired again at another circling fin.

"How bad?" Dread laced Ronny's voice.

"We need to get out of the water." She fired again, and the fin disappeared.

He tugged her through the bloody water. A large shape brushed by his feet. Another leaped through the air and submerged. The dead fish began to bob erratically as the others fed. Again, the gun went off, and blood filled the water around the dead shark.

"Save your bullets," Ronny gasped. The boat tantalized him, floating just out of reach. He put everything he had into reaching it. Behind him, the water roiled. Another fin approached, and Cameron fired again.

"I'm out," she said on a gasping moan.

Teeth settled into his foot and tugged, pulling him under. He slashed with his knife, making contact, but having no idea where. A gray-white belly inches away from him filled his vision. He stabbed. Thick skin punctured and blood oozed from the wound when he withdrew his knife to stab again. The skin was too tough to slash. The shark released him. He stroked hard for the surface a foot away.

The boat smacked into his head when he emerged.

Cameron reached to him, a panicked expression on her face. He yanked her through the water and grasped her waist, lifting as she grasped the side and pulled. He shifted his grip to her legs and shoved hard, pushing himself underwater as her torso slid over the side of the boat. She screamed shrilly and rolled over the side.

He had no time to ask if she were okay. The shark pulled him under again. One had him by the foot, pulling him down. Another swam at him, jaws gaping. He thrust downward at the bullet shaped head of the approaching shark, grasping it with both hands as it reared back and thrusting his knife into the side of its neck as it rolled him through the water. The shark grasping his foot released it again.

Rough skin under his hands jerked and twitched as he stabbed again, not able to get much leverage for fear of losing his grip on the gaping maw.

The other shark hit the injured one, pushing him deeper underwater. Ronny's lungs began to burn. He released the shark and swam hard for the surface as the two sharks fought. The boat was now ten feet from him.

"Cam," he called, worried she wasn't peering over the side with his rifle.

A gasping moan answered him, constricting his heart. In the distance, the sound of rotors approached. He glanced behind him where two fins circled the pool of spreading blood he floated in. *How ironic,* he thought, *my team will get here just in time to see me eaten by a fish.*

A shark brushed his side, smacking him with its tail. Another fin headed to the shark he'd just killed.

"Fight it out, buggers." Ronny gasped as he stroked towards the boat, keeping his knife in his fist.

A bright light passed over him and swung back. He laughed as the unmistakable sound of Dan's gun sounded. A rappelling line lowered from the hovering Seahawk. A man dressed in camouflage, including a face mask, slid down the line, letting go halfway and landing in the boat. A hand reached for him as Dan's gun sounded again.

Squirrel pushed up the face mask and grinned at him. "Thought you were dead for sure. What the hell took you so long?"

Ronny didn't answer, letting Squirrel pull him aboard. Water half-filled the boat. Cameron leaned against the side, grabbing the strap to hold herself up and keep her face out of the water. He scrambled to her side. She screamed shrilly when he grabbed her.

"My leg." A grimace covered her white, pale face.

She screamed again when he slit the leg of her pants, his eyes scanning the snake bite.

"Where are you bleeding?"

"God, my leg; don't touch it," she moaned.

He ignored her and slit the pants further as she grasped for her leg. Swollen to twice its size, red streaks traveled from beneath the ace bandage on her knee, up her leg, towards her groin. With hands that shook he removed the bandage, making her scream again.

"Sorry, sorry," he mumbled as he examined the dark-blue flesh of her knee. He realized Squirrel was speaking to him but made no effort to answer. There was no blood.

"Where are you bleeding?" Frantic now, he slit the other leg of her pants. The only blood in the water appeared to be coming from his foot. Hopefully, that meant her injury wasn't severe. He grasped her cold hand and felt for her pulse. Irregular but strong beats met his searching fingers. He dropped her wrist and framed her face with his hands.

"Cam, where are you bleeding?"

A red flush climbed her cheeks. He sat back on his heels and laughed, then gathered her in his arms.

"You scared me to death," he murmured.

A hand grabbed his shoulder, and he reluctantly released her.

"Thought it was a good day for a swim?" Tom asked as he knelt in the water beside Cameron. Not waiting for an answer, he keyed his mic with his chin. "Send down the board. Sorry, Cam, this is going to sting a bit." Tom reached into his bag and brought out a splint and a roll of ace bandage.

A deep moan became a scream as Tom straightened her leg, tying it to the splint with the ace bandage. She began to dry heave, writhing with every gasping groan. Ronny lifted her, trying to support her body.

"Relax, sweetheart, don't fight it."

"You two made up, I see," Tom said happily as he checked her pulse and eyes. "I have to say, I'm relieved. I was starting to feel guilty about Dawn."

Cameron laughed, a small breath of sound. "He's all mine."

"Good to hear," Ronny said as he smoothed her hair back.

"Let me see the foot." Tom reached for Ronny's boot. Reminded, his foot began to throb.

"It'll keep. Let's get her aboard."

Tom shrugged and waved his arm. A body board lowered from the Seahawk. The three men loaded Cameron aboard it. Tom strapped her leg down, immobilizing it as Ronny leaned over her head, trying to block the rain from her face. Above them, the helicopter dipped and bobbed. Squirrel laid a light plastic poncho over her face and shoulders and tucked it in.

Tom keyed his mic again. "Good to go."

Black lines released from the helicopter. In moments, they had her connected and lifting into the sky. A harness swung down. Ronny stepped into it and gave a thumbs up.

Dan released him and sent the harness back. Ronny crawled to Cameron's side and took her hand.

"How you doing?"

"I'm okay."

"Liar. You should've told me how bad it was."

"It wasn't that bad till the snake." Tears filled her eyes. "I can't believe a snake bit me. And a shark.

"Did you get bit?" he asked alarmed, searching her body again for signs of injury.

"One hit my leg, I thought he tore it off." She lowered her voice. "My blood attracted them."

"Maybe, but it's not like you jumped overboard. Don't worry about it. We're both okay."

"Your bleeding.

"Just a nip, I'm fine."

"I hate Mexico."

"I hear that," Dan said. He kissed her forehead and

brushed her hair back. "Hang in there; we're on our way to the *USS Truman*. They have first rate medics. My wife will be happy we found you. She wanted to call Isabela Pedro, but I made her promise to wait a week. I'm relieved we didn't need to go that route. I'm sure Isabela's help wouldn't be free or even cheap."

While Dan spoke, he was removing Ronny's boot and used the knife on his hip to split Ronny's pant leg.

"We counted three dead sharks when we came in. How many were there?" Dan asked as he cleaned and wrapped the bite on Ronny's ankle. Ronny's left boot was shredded. The thick leather had protected his foot from the teeth of the shark. Two deep puncture wounds and six superficial scratches were all he had to show for the encounter.

The bite on his ankle was worse. Now that he saw it, it began to hurt. A ring of teeth marks encircled his left ankle going partway up his left calf.

Squirrel squatted beside him, handing Dan bandages. "Good thing the fucker released you or you'd have one less foot. It'll be a cool scar though."

Cameron snorted, and Tom laughed.

"I counted seven fins," Cameron said. "I shot two for sure and maybe injured another. Ronny killed one with his knife."

"Kid thinks he's a badass, jumping into shark infested waters," Dan said as he straightened from Ronny and laid his hand on Cameron's brow. "That's some fever you got there. When did that start?"

"Right after the snake bit me." A shudder racked her, making her moan softly.

"I'm pretty sure it wasn't a poisonous snake." Ronny took her hand. "I think when you fell you hurt

206

your knee more. It looks like there might be some blood poisoning too."

She tried to sit up to see her knee better, and he pushed her back down. "Some antibiotics and rest and you'll be good as new."

Tom had hit his chin mic again and spoke with the pilot asking him to have a snake kit ready when they landed.

She closed her eyes and laid back down. Dan and Ronny exchanged worried glances over her head.

TWENTY

---◆---

KNOWLEDGE IS POWER

Medics met them on the deck of the Truman and whisked Cameron away before the rotors stilled. Ronny limped after them.

"Where's JT?"

"Sickbay, waiting on you," Tom said. "We all thought you got killed or captured when you didn't show on the second day. After seeing her knee, I'm surprised you got to the boat as quick as you did. Did you steal a ride?"

"Nope, we walked, but her knee wasn't that bad. She had a slight limp, no infection."

"It sure as shit is bad now. Are you positive it was a garter snake?"

"I'm positive the snake I killed was a garter, and it looked like the one that bit her, but that fucker slithered away before I could catch it."

"I can't wait to hear all about it. You're bunking

with me, Lee, and Squirrel. Meet us in the cafeteria when you're done in sickbay." Tom slapped him on the shoulder and ducked through a bulkhead door that faced a narrow corridor.

The *Truman* was familiar to Ronny; he'd served aboard her for eight months when he'd first joined the service.

JT greeted him with a slap on the back when he entered the medical bay. While a medic stitched his leg and cleaned the bites, Ronny told JT about their trip cross-country.

"Any word on Cameron's condition?"

"She's being prepped for surgery to fix her dislocated kneecap. The doctor is sure the snake wasn't poisonous. She has an infected spider bite causing a bit of blood poisoning. When she fell, she burst open a pocket of pus under the skin, spreading the infection rapidly."

"Will she lose the leg?"

JT laid a reassuring hand on his shoulder. "Not if the antibiotics work."

"I need to speak to my commander privately," Ronny said to the medic.

The medic nodded and gathered the discarded medical supplies. "Stay off the foot as much as you can. Keep it elevated and get the stitches checked in five days. I'm giving you a script for antibiotics. If you notice any redness or swelling, report too medical. Use the rubbing alcohol on the bug bites."

He handed Ronny two small plastic containers and began taking a blood sample. "I need urine and feces. Leave them with the seaman on the desk." Blood samples in hand, he nodded to JT and left the room.

Ronny absently rubbed the arm the medic had taken blood from. "Cameron and I were talking, and we had a thought you're not going to like."

JT rose an eyebrow and pursed his lips.

"I ran into June Reeves at Balboa Park. She was alone, carrying a large picnic basket containing glass, and seemed a bit nervous of me. At the time, I chalked it up to a stranger approaching her and offering help, but now..."

Ronny lifted his foot, examining the bandaging, avoiding JT's eyes. "Cam thought she might've been meeting a man. Glass dinnerware is too fancy for a meal with girlfriends. She pointed out it would explain how Mitchell knew the office would be empty and might explain how he'd breezed through the office security. If June let someone into her home, that someone could search it for passwords."

JT heaved a deep, unhappy sigh. "Well, fuck. The bearer of that scenario is going to be roasted alive even if it's correct."

Ronny nodded unhappily.

"Shit. I'll handle this. Who else have you told?"

"No one except you. Sorry, sir, I don't like implying that without proof, but Cam is right. If June is having an affair with a spy, she's in danger. Not to mention the danger to the fleet."

"You did the right thing. I'll report to Darmin. Go write up your action reports. Squirrel has your kit. Get cleaned up and eat before checking on Cameron. That's an order."

Aye, aye, sir." Ronny saluted and stood.

———————◆———————

Ronny had spent the last five hours writing reports while waiting impatiently for word on Cameron's condition. Lee had dragged him away from the tiny waiting room, and Keith sat in his chair in the waiting room when he returned.

"Relax before you get arrested for conduct unbecoming. You're a married man, remember?" Keith turned to peer over his shoulder, but they remained alone in the room.

Ronny stilled his limping pacing and rubbed his neck hard, glaring at Lee. "Fuck. This is such bullshit. I totally forgot about Dawn again. Don't you dare tell Tom. Is all I need is him on my ass too."

Lee held up both hands in a placating gesture.

"And don't say it. I know it's my own fault. Jesus, you must think I'm a real asshole treating my wife this way."

"No, I think you were young and stupid like the rest of us. Hell, I would've done the same at eighteen."

"Dawn will always be my best friend, but Cameron..."

Lee slapped his shoulder. "I get it, man." He glanced at his watch, then gestured to the door. "We have a meeting. I can make excuses for you if you like. I'm sure JT won't mind if you want to catch some shut eye."

"No, I need to know what's going on."

Lee poked his head inside the open door where a woman sat before a computer screen.

"Can you tell me the condition of Petty Officer Cameron Howard?"

The woman taped keys a moment. "Out of surgery and expected to be in recovery for five hours. No visitors until o-six-hundred. She's listed as stable with no complications." The woman leaned forward and lowered her voice. "I heard the doctor say she was responding well to the antibiotics. I think your friend is going to be fine."

"Thanks." Lee rapped his knuckles on her desk. In the waiting room, he slapped Ronny's shoulder. "Time to get back to work."

Ronny squeezed his shoulder gratefully and followed Lee from the room.

"How's Cameron?" Dan asked when Ronny entered the conference room.

"Responding to the antibiotics, thank God. She'll be off her feet awhile longer, but I think she'll be okay." Ronny sat at the dented metal table and rotated his shoulders, trying to ease the soreness. The metal table and chairs around it practically filled the small space, leaving a narrow aisle around the table.

"Good to hear. Angie will be relieved. Pass on our invitation to recuperate at our house. Angie said to tell her she can stay as long as she likes in the downstairs bedroom. She's already having a wheelchair ramp installed in the back and the doors to that room enlarged."

"You don't need to go to all that trouble. I can take care of Cameron."

"Sure, while your home, but I assume this meeting is a briefing for a call out. Angie can take care of Cameron while we're gone. I'm sure Charlene will offer too, but our house will be easier for her to navigate. Charlene's guest room is on the second floor."

"Thanks, I'll tell her. Any word on where we're headed?"

"CIA is coming to brief us, so back to Mexico, I guess," Tom said.

"You up for it?" Lee gestured towards Ronny's bandaged leg.

"Yeah, the stitches come out in a few days."

A short, stocky man with shoulder-length brown hair slicked back from a tan face, carrying a beat-up black briefcase, entered the room.

"Dai!" Lee exclaimed as he jumped up and hugged the man. "Why didn't you tell me you were coming? Good to see yeah, bro."

Dai grinned and pounded Lee on the back for a moment before stepping back and examining him critically. "You look good. I have a message from Mom. She told me to tell you that defending our nation is a good and honorable profession but neglecting one's family duties makes one a savage."

Tom laughed. "Call your mother, man." He held out his hand to Dai. "Tom Moran one of your brother's roommates and teammates."

"David Rubinstein-Wong but call me Dai." He shook Tom's hand then went down the row, shaking their hands as he spoke. "I'm the agent in charge of this operation." He placed his briefcase on the table and opened it, removing a map, which he unfolded.

"Our intel links the Golf Cartel with Al-Jadr." Dai unrolled another large paper covered with portraits connected by various colored lines and taped it to the wall. "Diego Ruiz, the current head of the Gulf Cartel was seen meeting with Mahir Alfarsi last week in Puerto Vallarta along with these three men."

He passed around blown up candid portraits. "We have no identity on the other three attendees. One was found dead in the house in Jalisco where the hostages were held." Dai sat on the edge of the table and swung one leg, using a laser pointer to point to the men's pictures.

"We believe this wasn't a kidnapping for profit, but information. The admiral reports interrogation on a wide range of subjects, but most disturbingly he was questioned on a top-secret surveillance and communications technique just now being tested in the field. A technique that shouldn't be known of. His assistant, Petty Officer Howard was also questioned forcefully."

"They tortured her?" Ronny said in alarm, leaning forward, and clenching the edge of the table with both hands. He wanted to smack himself for never asking her about her time in captivity. His hold on the table tightened when he remembered the bloody handprints on her shirt.

Dai nodded briskly. "By all accounts she gave as good as she got. She killed two men when they broke into the reception and injured one severely during the, ah, questioning. The admiral was in the room and was most impressed with her.

"Is she privy to this technique?"

"She designed it. I'm sorry, I'm not at liberty to give details. Suffice it to say, we don't want this technology falling into the wrong hands. Doctor Howard is a relatively new recruit and expected to rise fast in the ranks." He placed the red dot of his pointer on the picture of Joshua Greer.

"She attended school with him, graduated two years before him, but worked with him in his freshman year. Doctor Howard assures me he can reverse engineer her work as easily as she can his."

"Doctor Howard?" Ronny sat back in his seat and crossed his arms, realizing he knew nothing about Cameron. Everything he knew about her was surface interests with no real depth. He frowned, staring at Dai.

"The Navy recruited Cameron in her sophomore year, and they're very glad they did. Her work has been phenomenal. Because of this attack, we're convinced we haven't ended the threat of the spy with the capture of Komar Alfarsi."

JT rapped the tabletop with his knuckles. "Have you spoken to Commander Darmin?"

"Yes, we have agents following June Reeves now. The admiral remains unaware, but I'm afraid that will change." Dai highlighted another picture of one of the men who'd met with Diego Ruiz. "This man escorted June to a restaurant in San Diego. His name and ID's have proven to be forgeries, and he isn't in our database, so we're using the alias he uses with June as an identifier. He goes by the name Michael Wilson. June and Michael met at Balboa Park and afterward disappeared into a hotel for two hours followed by dinner at a nearby restaurant. Our agents confirm a sexual relationship. It can't be a coincidence. "

Dai turned to Dan. "The agency would like to put a few agents in your home. Petty Officer Howard will need a safe place to recuperate and work. A Marine guard will be stationed outside your home while she's in residence."

Dan nodded slowly. "How much danger and for how long?"

Dai tipped his hand side-to-side. "We don't expect a

group of armed men to storm your home to take her, but we could be wrong. As far as we know, Al-Jadr remains unaware we're onto them. I expect they'll let her return to work unhindered in the hopes of stealing her research.

"False information has been fed to June on the severity of Cameron's injuries and the status of her projects. Cameron should be able to return to work very soon while they think she's recuperating. We plan to ask the admiral to visit her with his wife at your home to shore up our lies."

Dai held up three fingers, tucking one down as he spoke. "The first thing we hope to accomplish is the admiral's assistance. Our profilers say he'll cooperate but hiding the degree of anger I'm sure he'll feel will be difficult." Dai waved his other two fingers at Dan. "Assuming the admiral cooperates, and June remains unaware, we hope to show her a convincingly sick Cameron and very tight security."

"You think June's a willing accomplice?" JT asked.

"Not at all, but my agents report Michael is a very smooth interrogator. Over dinner, she revealed not only the condition and whereabouts of her husband but of Cameron and SEAL Team Nine."

Ronny winced.

JT nodded thoughtfully. "I assume we're being assigned guard duty?"

"For a short time." Dai gestured with his chin to Dan. "Cameron's work can be completed from your home. When she's finished, a bogus copy will be left available for June. SEAL Team Nine will be sent to retrieve the copy and arrest or eliminate the men who take it. I don't expect it to take her very long to finish.

The prototype works. What she's doing now is programming to notify when the device is tampered with."

Dai stood and stretched before resuming a seat. "Clearance should be forthcoming to brief you fully on what she's working on, but let me assure you, it isn't inherently dangerous."

Dan laughed. "We get it; she's making a super spy computer. One small enough to place and use almost anywhere. None of us have the math skill to understand more than that anyways.

Dai laughed. "Those mathematicians speak another language, that's for sure. I have two in my family, and when they speak, I can't understand a word.

"Eso es porque eres un ignorante salvaje aspenas major que un hombre de las cavernas," Lee said.

Tom and Squirrel laughed.

"Ignorant savage, pfft; I speak four languages." Dai pretended to buff his nails and examined them. "Maybe not up to Denali's class, but more than you anyway.

"Barely literate for our family, and I speak five," Lee added in Arabic.

JT cleared his throat, and Lee sat back in his chair, grinning at his brother.

Dai straightened his suit jacket and winked at Lee. "Speaking of my sister Denali, she'll be in touch with Cameron and might need to visit. She was helping on the project," He sighed and ran a hand through his hair, retightening the elastic that kept it off his face. "The admiral will come by as well, working with Cameron. SEAL Team Nine is the only team informed of his wife's involvement, which is bound to make things awkward for everyone. I suggest you all act as if you didn't know."

JT snorted.

Dai winced sympathetically. "If it helps, he reaches mandatory retirement age in one year two months.

JT snorted again.

"Is there a guard on Denali?" Lee asked.

"No, but she's keeping a low profile working at Olympia's school. There would be no reason to connect her to Cameron's work."

"Not true. Greer will know Cameron and Denali were friends and roommates for a time."

"She was sixteen then, and while he'll know she was a genius, there's nothing to connect them currently. As far as the world knows, Denali is a student and part-time teacher. Her two published works are coauthored by Anya on autism, and she's working with Olympia; everyone should assume her focus is on mathematics in education with her family. Relax, Lee, she's in no more danger than every other mathematician in that class."

Lee nodded.

"Your sister is welcome to stay with us too," Dan offered.

"She's perfectly safe," Dai said.

"God help you if she does," Lee muttered.

Dai snorted with laughter as he gathered his papers. "That's true; you don't want the Rubinstein-Wong clan to descend on you. I'll be in touch again on shore. I'm glad we finally got to meet. Thank you for letting us use your home." He offered his hand to Dan, then grinned at Lee again. "The admiral will be unhappy with you guys for a while, sometimes ignorance is bliss.

"But knowledge is power," Lee said, and the two men bumped fists.

"How many sisters do you have?" Ronny asked as the door closed behind Dai.

"Eight sisters, and seven brothers." Lee smirked at Dan. "Careful offering hospitality or they might all descend."

Ronny leaned back in his chair, staring thoughtfully at Lee. They'd been roommates almost a year, and he had no idea. He realized his relationships were pretty shallow with most of his team except for Dan. Besides knowing their favorite beers and sports teams or what they liked to eat, he didn't know much about them.

His gaze landed on Tom. Dawn was serious about him, and Ronny had made no effort to get to know him better, too wrapped up in his own life to even notice he didn't know.

"Ignorance is bliss, but knowledge is power," he repeated thoughtfully under his breath.

TWENTY-ONE

---◆---

SHE FELT THIS ALL THE TIME

Dark circles ringed Cameron's eyes and her cheeks appeared pale and drawn. Her hand rose weakly to his face, and she grimaced. Ronny grabbed her hand and squeezed, wanting to kiss her, but the doctor's presence inhibited him. Behind him, Dan cleared his throat and pushed by to kiss Cameron's forehead.

Ronny leaned down and kissed her forehead too. One hand fisted in her hair and he breathed deep, but she didn't smell like herself. She smelled of antiseptic and plastic.

Dan drew him back and positioned himself between Ronny and the medic. "My wife will want a report on Cameron's condition. Will she make a full recovery?"

The doctor closed the folder he held and placed it in a plastic file holder on the foot of the bed. "If she follows our instructions. The antibiotics are already doing their job. We've seen improvement, but she needs to stay off the leg at least two weeks." As he spoke, he felt the pulse in Cameron's wrist.

Ronny bit his lip on the words he wanted to say. Tears filled Cameron's eyes, and she squeezed them closed.

"The pain bad?" The doctor asked in concern.

A hollow, empty feeling grew in Ronny's stomach. Cameron needed him. She needed comfort and reassurance, and even though he stood right there, he wasn't free to offer either. While he might not consider himself married, the world did and in his world having an affair would get him court-martialed and maybe Cameron too. For the first time, he considered how he risked her career. A career she loved.

Cameron cleared her throat and tried to straighten. "No, I'm okay."

Dan pressed her shoulders to the bed. "Stay down and listen to the doctors. A helicopter will be returning you to San Diego base tomorrow." Dan turned to the doctor. "How long until I can take her home?"

"At least one day. The doctor on shore will want to rerun all our blood work and make sure the fever is under control before they release her. She'll need full time care though." He smiled at Cameron. "Sorry, but you'll need to spend a week or so –"

"No, she won't. My wife will look after her at our house," Dan said

Cameron shook her head. "I can't ask— "

"Don't be silly. We insist. Ang and I think of you as family. And think of the fun Sam will have helping."

A soft snort of laughter escaped her. "Your son does love to help."

"Soon as they release you, you're coming home. We

can get a nurse or therapists, whatever you need. Besides, it'll be easier to guard you there."

"Sorry to be such a bother."

Dan kissed her forehead again. "Never think it. I owe you my family. It's a debt I can never repay."

The doctor gazed at Dan thoughtfully.

"Rest now. We can talk more later." Ronny's voice cracked, and he had to clear his throat.

Her sad eyes hurt. The hollow ache inside him grew. She felt this all the time, this distance and barrier between them. While he went blithely about his day enjoying her company with no thought of Dawn, she felt it. He was an idiot who needed his face slammed into realities before he saw them.

"I'm so sorry— about everything. I swear to God I'll do much better. Get well, Cam." He reluctantly released her hand and stepped back.

"Nurse, give Petty Officer Howard two ccs of Lidocaine. There's no need to suffer," the doctor said to Cameron.

Ronny winced and headed to the door. Dan followed him. The doctor thought her tears were from pain and they were, but not physical pain. Lidocaine wouldn't help the hurt he'd caused.

"I'm an ass," he murmured to Dan as they left the room.

"I sort of agree, but it isn't something you can't fix." Dan clapped him on the shoulder and chuckled ruefully. "My advice is don't try to keep the parts of your life separate. It'll be hard and awkward as hell but the two women in your life need to meet, and the three of you need to work out what's best for everyone."

"The four of us you mean." Ronny gestured with his chin to Tom.

"Like I said— awkward."

Ronny snorted.

Dan snickered.

———◆———

The Marines guarding the door of Cameron's hospital room in San Diego let him pass without challenge. Ronny halted inside the doorway, a red blush climbing his cheeks. Admiral Reeves sat beside Cameron's bed.

"Excuse me, sir," he stammered and turned to go.

"That's quite alright. No need to run off." The admiral gestured vaguely around the hospital room. "For all intents and purposes this is her home. No need to be formal." The admiral stood and offered his hand. "Thank you for releasing us. My inattention to my personal life put her in danger, and for that, I'm truly sorry. Learn from my mistakes, son. Don't get caught up in war games and forget what's really important in life."

"Yes, sir," Ronny said, the flush burning hotter on his cheeks.

The admiral headed to the door, turning back to speak to Cameron. "I'll see you tomorrow, and I apologize if the part I play insults your work. Your work has been exemplary."

"Thank you, sir."

The admiral left, closing the door quietly behind himself.

Ronny kissed her cheek and handed her the bouquet he carried. "How you feeling?"

"Really good. I'm dying to get out of this bed. The knee itches like crazy. The doctors say that's good."

"Don't rush it. Give the leg time to heal."

Yes, sir, Doctor Mitland." She saluted, grinning at him.

He sat beside her on the bed and took her hand, rubbing her fingers absently. "Why didn't you ever tell me you had a doctorate?"

"My work is classified. If I go around telling people I have a doctorate, they'll wonder why I'm a secretary."

"Why are you a secretary?"

"I'm not. I work in the admiral's office on his computer. I do occasionally work as an interrupter for him at public functions to cement my cover, but mostly I work alone in his office."

"That must be awkward. I mean when he's there."

"Not really, he isn't there a whole lot, and when he is, I work in the outer office or take a break. My work requires an active office with as real a scenario as I can manage, so they stuck me with him." She glanced at the door and lowered her voice. "If I can crack his security, then I'll know it really works. It's much too dangerous to remotely access the computer. Someone could piggyback on my signal."

"What you're making will work remotely?"

She tightened her lips and sighed, looking unhappy.

"Right, sorry. Forget I asked. We can skip the work details, but I want to know about you."

She laughed and drew him down for a kiss. "I really love when you kiss behind my right ear, and if you massage my itchy thigh, I might swoon."

His eyes lit. "Not those types of details although you're killing me... I want to know about your life before all this. I was shocked when I found out you were a doctor and then your roommate in college was Lee's sister. I didn't even know you knew him."

"I didn't know him. I knew his oldest brother Tianzi and his mom and dad and her little brothers and sisters. There was a whole passel of Rubinstein-Wong's I never met. Denali taught me to shoot. She and Tianzi took me to the range with them."

Cameron paused, a thoughtful expression crossing her face. "Learning to shoot got me interested in being in the military. I hadn't considered it before then. Military life suits me. I love the order— no more having to worry about what to wear or how to greet my superiors. In school, it was awkward. Some professors get insulted if you skip their full title and some get insulted if you use it. Here, I know exactly what to do, and the job itself is interesting, and I even like being an interpreter; it's a nice break. Everyone is on time and polite and my requests for supplies or lab space don't pass through the who do you know— what's in it for me— line.

Ronny sighed unhappily. "I didn't even know Lee had siblings, never mind that staggering amount." He smiled suddenly. "Dan has got to be nervous Angie hears and wants that many."

"All Lee's siblings are adopted."

"Even better, they already have Sam. I have to call Angie; this is too great an opportunity to pass up."

Cameron snickered. "Your evil. No sane person has sixteen children. Even doctor Rubinstein's colleagues thought she was nuts. I still have the articles on my laptop if you want to read them. It's a fascinating experiment."

"They adopted the kids as an experiment? That

sounds so cold. Poor Lee."

"A parenting experiment, and don't feel sorry for him; they're a close family. I was jealous actually. My mom is great, but I always wished I had brothers and sisters.

"Me too. I had Dawn but..." he trailed off, flushing again.

Cameron sighed, bringing his hand to her lips and kissing it. "We all have a past. I'm not angry about Dawn. I do want to speak to her though and make sure she's really okay with us."

"Is there an us?" Ronny leaned forward, smoothing her hair back with his free hand, and staring into her eyes.

"Yes, if you're sure—"

He kissed her for a minute, pulling back when they were both breathless. "I've never been more certain about anything. I want you to meet my family."

"After you divorce. Being a homewrecker makes me really uncomfortable."

"You aren't."

She held up a hand to stop him. "Seriously, Ronny, I love you, but let's not talk about meeting parents or anything until your free to do so."

"Fair enough. Was your mom upset you're staying at Dan's and not with her?"

No, she's glad I have friends willing to take care of me. She doesn't know about any of this, that Dan was ordered to do it."

He offered before being asked." Ronny hesitated then blurted. "Are you mad at them for not telling you about Dawn?"

A red flush climbed Cameron's cheeks. "I'm

embarrassed. Angie's reaction made it clear she thought I knew. They're all going to know we didn't spend our time talking." She gazed down at her fingers twining in her lap. "We rushed. I don't know much about you either."

"You know the important stuff," Ronny disagreed as he traced one finger along the edge of the hospital gown she wore. The gown crisscrossed her body, tieing in the front on the left side. He halted his slow movement and placed his hand over her breast, feeling the nipple harden beneath the thin material.

Eyes on hers, he rubbed the stiffening peak with his thumb. Her lips parted, and she leaned towards him, sliding her hand over the growing bulge in his pants.

"See, you know exactly what I like," he murmured as she stroked him lightly through his pants with her fingertips.

She giggled and pulled him down for a kiss. He jumped off her bed as the guard at the door spoke. A second later the door swung open, and Angie entered, carrying a small suitcase in one hand and Juan with the other. Sam held the handle of the suitcase with her.

"We brought you the clothes you requested." The baby fussed, and Angie jiggled him absently.

Ronny took the suitcase from her and set it on the bed.

"Sam drew you a get-well picture. He was worried and wanted to see you." Angie knelt beside the boy and put an arm around him. "See; Cameron is fine. She has a hurt leg, so you'll have to do all her running around until she recovers, but she'll get better."

Sam nodded and hugged Angie hard, hiding his face in her shoulder.

Ronny exchanged a dismayed glance with Cameron. Sam thought you came to a hospital to die. "Hey, sport, let's say you and me take Juan and show him around while Mommy helps Cameron get ready to go?" Ronny took Juan who yawned and scrunched his face up before settling back to sleep.

Angie murmured something too low to hear to Sam, then wiped his face with the clean diaper resting on her shoulder.

Sam grimaced and batted it away. "I'm not a baby like my brother."

"No, you're not," Ronny agreed, taking the boy's hand. "Uncle Lee has seven brothers and eight sisters, wouldn't that be fun?" he asked as he led the boy from the room.

Cameron laughed.

"Really?" Angie said, sounding interested as he closed the door.

Ronny snickered.

TWENTY-TWO

---◆---

SQUIRREL

Squirrel tapped the send button on his cell phone as he straightened from his slouched position against the wall.

A wave a *deja-vu* passed over him, and he smiled grimly. Once before he'd guarded a teammates wife and caught an intruder in a hospital corridor. That time he'd taken pictures; this time he turned away and spoke loudly on his cell phone, complaining about missing the tide.

Cameron was armed and waiting, and Al-Jadr didn't want her dead, they wanted to be sure of her condition.

Keith approached wearing Bermuda shorts, ray-bans, and a wig with long snarled brown hair. His flip-flops slapped against the tile floor. A T-shirt, three sizes too big, hung over the pistol holstered on his waist.

"Our guy?" he murmured as he handed Squirrel a soda.

"Yep."

Squirrel's curly hair peeked from a ball cap he wore backward. Mirrored sunglasses hung from his dirty T-shirt. Naturally darker skinned from his Latino heritage, he appeared tanner than Keith. He wore a hint of red makeup across his nose and cheekbones to give the effect of sunburn.

"Dude shaved his beard and probably thinks his makeup is hiding the color difference, but these fluorescent lights make the mismatched skin tones glaring. Ahh— he's heading into her room now."

Both men waited tensely until the man reappeared two minutes later. The cell phone on Squirrel's waist vibrated, and his shoulders lowered.

Cameron was fine.

The two men followed Cameron's visitor, arguing over the best place to catch good waves in midafternoon. They stepped into the elevator beside their quarry.

"Call Jas, he'll tell you." Keith snatched at Squirrel's phone, jostling the man in the elevator.

Squirrel laughed and shoved him away, slipping a disk the size of a penny into the man's back pocket. They left the elevator at the cafeteria level still arguing, letting their quarry continue without them.

"He's marked," Squirrel said on his cell, then slipped it back into his pocket.

He headed back upstairs. Lee lay in the room adjoining Cameron's with a fake cast and his leg in traction. Squirrel leaned against the wall outside his door and pretended to speak on his cell every time a new person appeared on the floor.

Dan would get a picture of the man who'd entered Cameron's room as he exited the elevator. He sat in the lobby beside the front desk pretending to read the paper and beeped Squirrel every time someone hit the button for the fourth-floor elevator. In an hour, they would trade places.

An hour and a half later, Benson passed him in the lobby wearing his uniform and carrying an M-15 over his shoulder with his sidearm openly on his hip. Squirrel rose and folded his paper.

JT had called and warned him they were going to guard Cameron openly now that their target had gotten the information they wished him too. Paper tucked under his arm, he headed to his bike in time to see Tom's truck pull into the lot. Squirrel didn't acknowledge Ronny in any way. The men passed each other as if they were strangers.

TWENTY-THREE

---◆---

FUCKER PLANNED THIS

A shrill shriek of an alarm jolted Ronny from a sound sleep. His feet hit the floor before he identified the sound as a level-one intruder alert. Lights flicked on outside his bedroom window, lighting the room with a cool, white glow.

"Get in the safe room," he yelled as he grabbed for the pistol in the nightstand.

Cameron sat and reached for the gun in the drawer beside her.

Ronny took the time to pull on the sweatpants crumpled in a ball beside the bed. Overhead, the muffled sound of a baby's cries abruptly cut off. *Angie must have put the kids in their safe room,* he thought as he eased his bedroom door open.

Clad in bright blue boxers, Dan ran down the stairs shirtless, buckling a holster around his hips.

Men outside yelled questions and directions. Dan

pulled his sidearm from the holster and signed for Ronny to follow.

A CIA agent on guard inside the house glanced over from his position beside the front door. "Section six alarm tripped. Two men approached the rear wall, but we have no visual. They ran off when the alarm sounded." His gaze passed Ronny and he frowned. "Get to the safe room, Petty Officer Howard."

Ronny turned and glared. "Go! What the hell do you think you're doing? You can't even walk." Aggravated, he grabbed Cameron's wheelchair handles and pulled her into the bedroom, ignoring her protests. "I get it, Cam, you're a good shot and able to take care of yourself, but you put us all in danger if we have to worry about you. Stay in the room until the all clear sounds." He pushed her into the custom-made closet and hit the red button beside the door before he closed it.

"This isn't necessary," she hollered as the door sealed shut.

The metal door cut off all sound with its airtight seal. Six titanium rods sank into place with a grinding thunk. She could live locked in the closet for three days on the canned air and water. It would take power tools and more than one man to break her out of that room. Specially reinforced concrete surrounded the room on all sides. Even a house fire should be survivable in the safe room.

Upstairs, in the master bedroom, another identical room lay above this one. Each bedroom closet on the second floor became a smaller, less elaborate version of this safe room. The pantry in the kitchen could also be locked from the inside and contained a radio, cell phone, and weapons. Dan had made his home as safe as he could for his family.

Outside of the house, cameras and sensors monitored the fence and yard using state-of-the-art technology. Panels inside the safe rooms displayed footage of the entire house and yard. An alarm triggered not only the police but JT. The information shown on Dan's security system was sent to JT, leaving it to JT's discretion whether the team was needed or not.

Ronny ran back to the living room where Dan and the CIA agent spoke in low voices as they examined the security footage. Dan had holstered his gun and now carried a fluffy white cat.

"Can you take Seraphim to Angie, please? She'll be worried about her. Tell her nobody crossed the wall and I'll be up soon."

"Can they come out?"

"Not yet," the agent said before Dan could reply. "Let my team make sure nothing was placed, and the area is clear.

Ronny took the cat from Dan, glad it was Seraphim and not Demon. A grin crossed his face as he ran up the stairs two at a time. Dan wouldn't have picked up Demon. That cat didn't take to being manhandled by anyone except Sam and Angie.

Outside the closet door in Dan's bedroom, Ronny hit the speaker. A camera in the corner of the room swiveled to point at him. The door opened with a click and whir of hidden machinery.

Ronny handed Seraphim to Angie. Behind her, Sam sat on the floor clutching Demon. The cat's eyes narrowed at Ronny and a menacing growl issued from his snarling face.

"Dan says he'll be up in a minute. Nothing to worry about; everyone is just being cautious. The baby okay?"

"Sound asleep again." Angie glanced at the drawer pulled out from the built-in shelving along the back wall. Juan lay on his back inside the drawer, sound asleep. Clothes hung in neat lines along the walls. To the casual observer, the safety features wouldn't be apparent, the complex machinery the room housed was hidden from sight with only the screen beside the door visible.

Ronny crouched and ruffled Sam's hair. "How you doing, sport?"

The cat's growl kicked up a notch. Sam squeezed the cat tighter, bringing the cat's face to his and kissing the top of his head. An odd coughing snort replaced the growl.

Ronny glanced dubiously at the cat. "Should he be doing that?'

"Demon won't hurt me. Will you, boy?" Sam rubbed between the cat's eyes, and the sound grew louder.

Ronny realized the cat was purring and laughed.

"Be careful with him, Sam. Don't try to make him stay with you," Angie warned. She shrugged at Ronny, a half-smile on her lips. "Demon loves him. Thanks for bringing us Seraphim. How's Cameron?"

"Annoyed to be locked in the closet. Sorry we're disrupting your peace."

Angie gave him a sympathetic smile. "Don't worry about it. This might have nothing to do with you. Last month the alarm sounded when two kids tried to cross the wall. They thought our backyard would be a nice, private spot to make-out. Dan scared ten years off their life chasing them down the street."

The deep thwap of an approaching helicopter interrupted her.

Ronny ran from the room. Behind him, the closet door closed with a grinding thud. He jumped over the rail, heading to the back door, landing lightly on the balls of his feet.

"Ours," Dan called.

Ronny peered from the window above the backdoor into the yard. A squad of Marines carrying M-16's, gestured to each other, fanning out to cover the perimeter. Overhead, a police helicopter hovered, the downdraft flattening the grass on the lawn. A spotlight played over the men and house. In the distance, another helicopter approached.

"Holy crap," Dan said, and the CIA agent laughed.

Ronny ran back and stared from the front window. Red and blue lights flashed through the trees before Dan's house. The camera on the front gate showed four cop cars all with sirens blaring and lights whirling. An unmarked black car pulled up, and two men in black suits exited the car.

"FBI," the CIA agent said. He winked at Dan and headed upstairs. "I was never here," he called over his shoulder.

Dan stared after him thoughtfully. "Fucker planned this."

"Yeah?"

"What are the chances we got this much response for a simple house alarm with no warning?"

Ronny narrowed his eyes and nodded. "They could have told us. We went along with all their plans so far."

Dan shrugged and glanced at his boxers. "I better go change and talk to Ang. Let Cameron out." He snickered. "You better take the gun from her first thing. She looked pissed."

"Ha ha," Ronny called after Dan's retreating back.

She was going to be pissed, but she needed to understand that if bad man came here they would be looking for her. It would be beyond foolish to give them a shot at her. Resigned to her anger, he rapped on the door, then pressed the intercom button.

"You can come out now."

"Told you it was unnecessary." The speaker made her voice sound tinny and cold.

"No, retreating to a safe room was completely necessary for the team."

He helped her stand and hop to the bed where she flopped down and used both hands to move the leg with the cast onto the bed, then grabbed the pillows, smacking them hard before settling them behind her back.

He sat beside her and took her hand, clenching it when she tried to pull away. "Cam, I'm not arguing your skill or even how tough you are. This is about training." He frowned thoughtfully. "How'd you like to take some classes? It takes more than skill with a gun to handle armed men."

"I don't think I need them."

Ronny took a deep breath and ran a hand through his hair. "That's fine too, but you're going to get us killed if you keep rushing in." He held up a hand when she started to speak. "I know you mean well, and want to help, but you don't know how. If bad men had been on the property, you might be dead right now because you don't know not to stand in doorways. Especially doorways in line with windows. Any man with a rifle could've killed you easily without even coming inside. You have to trust your teammates and do what they say. If Dan says duck, I duck, I don't look around or wonder why— I just do it."

She nodded slowly.

"When we send you to the safe room, it isn't because you can't fight, or you're a girl or anything; it's because you're the target. Without training your chances of being hurt are very high. I don't mean weapons training but fighting."

"I can fight."

"Not the physical act of fighting, the advantages training can teach. Like where to stand when looking through doors, or what untrained men are likely to do versus trained men. We learn to distinguish weapons by the sounds they make and count shots. We learn to note patterns in shooting and movement to time our moves across rooms. One of the first things they teach us is to never silhouette ourselves. There's a lot more to winning a fight than being good with a gun."

"Okay, I'll get some training."

He tweaked one of the soft, black strands standing on end. Absently he smoothed her hair while he spoke. "I'll see if JT can set it up. If not, there are private classes, but, Cam, until then, do what we say. We all want to keep you alive."

She hugged him, resting her cheek against his. Warm breath caressed his neck. He closed his eyes and savored the contact. A type A personality, she liked games with rules, order, knowing exactly what to do and doing it, to be in control. Sitting on the sidelines was hard for her. One of the things he liked best about her was her willingness to consider another's point despite how much she disliked it.

———————◆———————

June Reeves visited the next day without her husband. Angie escorted her to Cameron's room. Cameron lay in the bed covered by a light blanket with her eyes closed. Sam sat cross-legged beside her coloring.

"Shh— we have to be quiet so Cam can rest." The little boy held up a picture of an orange cat. "I made this for her."

Cam opened her eyes and smiled at Sam. "Can you get me more apple juice, please?"

Angie followed her son from the room.

Ronny stayed, sitting quietly in the corner. The newspaper over his lap hid a pistol.

"My husband asked me to visit and deliver a gift from the Mexican ambassador. I hope you're recovering." June placed a gift bag on the nightstand beside the array of pill bottles that littered the top.

Cameron straightened, winced, and groaned softly as she reached for the bag.

Ronny hid a smile behind his hand.

"Thank you, it was very kind of you to deliver it personally." Cameron removed a blue, metal tin from the bag and smiled. "Oh, coffee. That's perfect. I'm so tired all the time. I can't keep my eyes open for more than ten minutes at a stretch."

"You need rest, sweetheart."

June glanced at him without a trace of recognition. "How long will you be off your feet?"

"At least three months, but the doctor says I can

resume work in another month."

"If the infection clears," Ronny added.

June glanced at him again.

"She's in a hurry to return to work, but the infection in her blood tires her too much." He nodded to the pile of pill bottles. "Let the medicine do its work while you rest." He laughed lightly and rose, placing the paper wrapped pistol on the seat and offered his hand to June. "She's asleep already. I'll remind her you were here. Sometimes she doesn't remember."

June shook his hand with absent minded politeness as she walked to the doorway. "The doctors think she'll be okay though?" June glanced back at the doorway.

"Yes, in time.

Sam approached, carrying a glass of juice.

"Cam fell asleep again," Ronny said.

The little boy nodded and tip-toed into the room with exaggerated steps.

Ronny laughed.

Angie grinned at him. "He loves to help. I'll sit with her a while; take a break."

"She needs constant care?" June asked in dismay.

"She can't get out of bed at all so someone is usually with her. As you saw, it's Sam's favorite pastime." Ronny escorted June to her car and returned to the house grinning. Back in his bedroom Cameron sat in the chair with Sam in her lap.

"She bought it hook, line, and sinker," Ronny said

"Bought what?" Sam asked.

"Coffee," Cameron said and ruffled his hair.

Ronny took the box and placed it back in the bag. "Just to be safe, no one drinks this."

Angie sighed. "That's too bad, I really love coffee."

"Me too," Sam said, making Angie and Cameron laugh.

"Come on, sport, let's go make lunch." Angie led Sam from the room.

Ronny left hurriedly with the coffee can. For all he knew it could be a bomb.

TWENTY-FOUR

THIS PLACE IS CURSED

Stationed by the front door of the medical building
where Cameron's knee doctor kept his office, Squirrel
eyed the men and woman entering. He didn't expect
trouble. Balanced on one leg, he leaned against the
wall with the other, smoking a cigarette. Two FBI
teams waited outside the building. Both clearly
noticeable for what they were to an informed observer.

Squirrel's eye's widened as a man approached the
building. Clean shaven, with his dark hair neatly
combed, the man wore jeans, a blue oxford shirt, and
a Nike windbreaker. All perfectly normal.

Without conscious thought, Squirrel ducked and
kicked out, connecting solidly to his target's knee. The
man he'd seen in the hospital, who'd entered
Cameron's room and took pictures, snarled an oath in
Urdu and hit back. His hand reached behind his back
under his light windbreaker.

"Fucker," Squirrel snapped as he grabbed the man's arm and kneed him hard in the groin, twisting the arm he held as the man gasped and jack-knifed. Squirrel hit him again with his fist this time, snapping his head back. Still twisting the arm in his grasp, he forced the man to the ground.

Two FBI agents ran up.

"Saw his gun," Squirrel lied as he released his captive, letting the agents take over.

"He attacked me," the man shouted in barely accented English. "I was walking down the street minding my own business."

The agents ignored his yelling and hustled him to a nearby black sedan. Men working nearby with a laser level stopped and stared. Jackhammers and saws competed with the sounds of trucks and backhoes as work continued on the demolished garage. The men resumed their work as the sedan drove away.

"Saw his gun huh? Neat trick behind a windbreaker." Dai grinned at Squirrel.

"Recognized him from the hospital. The missing beard blends better now, but I'm sure it's the same guy. Shit, I hope I didn't break our cover."

Dai slapped his shoulder. "Nope, it's all good. The fucker was up to no good. He had no reason to be here except a hit. We better leak a little more progress to June. Seems our terrorists are getting antsy. Keep Cameron inside from now on. Don't give anyone access to her."

Squirrel followed Dai as he spoke. The two men entered the six-story medical building together.

Dai lifted his hand to his mouth and spoke into the mic taped to his sleeve. "Search the perimeter. Let's make sure he didn't think he could her force her away at gunpoint. Check the license of every car within six hundred yards."

Squirrel drew his gun and pushed the door to the stairway open. Dai continued to the elevator. Cameron's doctor was on the fourth floor.

———◆———

Ronny straightened in alarm as Squirrel entered the waiting room. His face white, he pushed into the exam room, surprising the doctor and Cameron.

"Sorry." He gestured lamely and left the room, leaning on the closed door. "What?"

"Intruder. Dai is on it."

Ronny closed his eyes and swallowed hard. "This place is cursed."

Squirrel snickered.

"I swear, I got the heeby-jeebies just walking in. Why couldn't Cameron just be a regular secretary? This is nerve-wracking."

"What would be the fun of that?"

"Fun?" Ronny glared as he paced to the window and peered out over the construction site. "When it's your girl in danger, let's see if you think it's fun."

"That's your problem— settling down like this. Too many fish in the sea to choose just one."

Ronny rolled his eyes and snorted.

Squirrel flopped onto a padded waiting room chair, put his arms behind his head and kicked his feet up on the coffee table. "So many women; so little time."

"I used to think like that too— until I meet Cameron."

"She's pretty awesome, but they're all awesome. I like Dawn too, and Charlene, and Angie, and Keith's

Mary. What's the point of picking one though?"

Ronny shrugged and perched on the corner of the couch. "No point per say. When you meet the right one that's the only one you'll want. And before you ask, I can't explain what makes her the right one; she just is. Cameron is everything I ever wanted and more than I dreamed possible."

"Aww, that so sappy..." Squirrel snickered, then stood as Cameron exited the doctor's office.

Ronny grabbed the handles of the wheelchair.

"See you again in two weeks." The doctor nodded politely at Ronny and Squirrel and returned to his exam room.

"All good?" Ronny asked.

"Yep. I'll have another scar but should get full mobility back with some therapy."

"Great."

Squirrel held up a hand and motioned them to wait as he opened the door. He glanced both ways, then gestured them forward. Dai stood beside the open elevator doorway.

"My team caught another three men. My partner is making sure the elevator hasn't been tampered with. It wasn't a hit attempt, but a kidnap attempt. They had an ambulance waiting half a block away."

"What?" Cameron said, sounding scared and confused.

"Squirrel caught an intruder." Ronny smoothed back her hair, offering her a sickly smile. "It's nothing to worry about. You're safe with us."

"Miss Howard, we'd like you to remain inside the walls of Dan's property and stay armed," Dai said.

Cameron nodded, her wide-eyed gaze flitting over

them. "Maybe I should stay somewhere else. God, what if they attack Dan's house?"

"They won't, and they can't attack from outside it either. Anyone goes within three feet of the walls an alarm will sound. The closest building with line of sight into the backyard is over two miles away. Very few men can make a shot from that distance. The front yard is a little less secure, but the chances of a sniper being in position while you cross the yard are slim. As long as you stay on the driveway or walkways there's no line of sight. Mr. Barstow considered carefully when he had his house built. It's a very defendable position tucked into the hill like that."

Ronny smiled tightly. "It wasn't an accident. The site work alone cost him half a million dollars."

Dai rose an eyebrow.

"Dan's wife has security issues."

"I'm aware. Lee told us. I'm wondering how he afforded that though."

"Don Pedro's reward." Squirrel grinned at Cameron. "Ask Dan to tell you how they got Seraphim sometime. It's a hair-raising story."

Ronny snickered. "Then ask him how he got Demon."

"That story I heard, and Char showed me pictures." Laughing now, Cameron grinned at Squirrel.

Ronny pasted a fake smile on his face and pushed her to the car. Terrorist were hunting her and likely would keep doing so until they had her or the plans she was working on. He didn't have a million dollars to build her a fortress to live in. His gaze flew to Squirrel, and his shoulders relaxed. What he did have though was a team of trained professionals to keep her safe.

Squirrel slapped his shoulder when Ronny sighed in relief on seeing Lee waiting in the van. "All in, all the time." He reached through the window to bump fists with Lee.

Money couldn't buy what he had, Ronny thought gratefully. "Hoorah," he said softly and tapped Lee's fist with his.

TWENTY-FIVE

---◆---

A FAVOR TO ASK

Dan entered the room from the kitchen carrying two cups of coffee with a folder tucked under his arm. Angie trailed him, holding a glass of milk and a plate that held slices of coffee cake. She handed the milk to Sam who sat with Cameron as she read a story and offered cake to everyone before setting it down on the coffee table.

"Shall I take him?" she asked, indicating the baby sleeping on Ronny's chest.

"No, he's fine." Ronny accepted the coffee Dan handed him with a smile of thanks.

Dan handed the other to Cameron, placed the folder on the coffee table and returned to the kitchen.

"None for me thanks," Angie called after him.

She sat in the chair opposite them, smiling slightly as Cameron continued to read to Sam. Dan returned and leaned against the doorjamb with a grin on his face, sipping his coffee.

Cameron finished the book and slapped it closed.

"Nope," Dan said before Sam could ask for another story. "It's bedtime, and Cam needs her rest too."

"Aww." Sam sighed then smiled, squirming around in Cameron's lap until he could hug her.

Ronny received a kiss on the cheek and the coffee cake crumbs from Sam's shirt.

Angie rose and took the baby. "Good night, everyone. Come on, Sam."

Sam ran over and gave his father a kiss, then climbed the stairs behind Angie on his hands and knees.

Dan grinned after them, then sat in the chair Angie had vacated. "Thanks for them."

Ronny shrugged uncomfortably. Beside him, Cameron hunched into his side. He knew it made her uncomfortable when Dan thanked them. She felt guilty for bringing Komar Alfarsi into their lives.

"Ang and I have a favor to ask, and it's a dozy. I don't want you guys to answer right now, but really take some time to think about it."

Ronny quirked an eyebrow. By Dan's serious tone this favor wouldn't be easy.

"Our job is dangerous, and while I believe the hit has been canceled on Angie, I could be wrong. Our children need a guardian. Angie and I would like it to be you and Cameron." Dan held up his hand when Ronny opened his mouth. "This house and everything else we own is in a trust earmarked for our children. There should be more than enough money to pay for their educations and the cost of raising them, but they'll need a caretaker. The trust can fund a nanny and housekeeper, but they'll need someone to oversee that and make sure they're being taken care of properly. Angie and I trust you."

Dan's gaze traveled them, and he smiled. "You two aren't married, and this would put you in contact for the rest of your lives. So, there's that on top of this huge responsibility. And keep in mind, Ang and I want more children."

Ronny laughed.

Dan grinned. "I promise no more than twelve though."

"Twelve? "Ronny asked incredulously.

Beside him, Cameron began to chuckle.

Dan leaned back and pursed his lips, his eyes on the distance. "Probably more like six, and maybe as few as four, but definitely no more than twelve...I think." He turned his gaze to Ronny and laughed. "So, you can see, this is a big favor. A huge favor, and we won't hold it against you if you say no."

"I don't need to consider it, I say yes, but if you're killed, it's likely I will be too," Ronny said.

"That's why we have Cameron. And Angie wants to ask Lee as a backup."

"Lee? I would've thought Charlene," Cameron said.

"Lee is just as likely to be killed in action with us..." Ronny sat back in the chair and eyed Dan. He'd been honored when Dan asked, thinking he considered him a good friend, but as far as he knew, Dan and Lee weren't that close. Now he wondered why Dan had asked him.

"Angie pointed out that Lee has a big family. Even if he died one of them would likely accept the children on his behalf or at the very least see to their care and that they stayed together. His family is well-to-do and will have the contacts necessary to manage a trust and the children. Lee is a practical choice. We haven't asked him yet. You two our favorite choice, an emotional choice, because you love them already."

Dan rose and handed Ronny the folder. "Take some time and talk this over together. I trust you with my life, Ron, and you're my best friend. Trusting you with my children is easy. Someday, when you have children, I'd be honored to become their guardian."

Dan turned to Cameron. "We don't mean to pressure you or put you on the spot, and it really is okay to say no with no change in how we feel for you. I hope you say yes; you'd make an excellent surrogate mother."

Ronny had to agree. Cameron was patient and kind to the children. Add in her intelligence and management skills and the choice was obvious. He wanted her to be the mother of his children. The thought aroused him, and he shifted in the seat.

"Look through the paperwork. And take your time. See you tomorrow."

Dan gave them a hopeful smile and went upstairs.

Ronny turned to Cameron. "I didn't expect that."

"Me either, but it makes sense, that they asked, I mean. I'm not sure I'm a great choice. We haven't known each other all that long, and my life isn't exactly calm."

"Neither is mine, but all their friends will have the same issue. They picked you because you've proved you can care for the children. I would pick you too. You're the perfect choice." Ronny's voice deepened, and he leaned closer to kiss her lips. "I want you to choose me too."

Ronny's heart sank when she pulled away, resting her face on his shoulder. Tense in his arms, she didn't want to hear him talk about their future. It hurt. Dawn stood between them. At least he hoped it was just Dawn.

"I love you, Cam."

"I love you too. Let's go to bed and sleep on this." She rose, taking the folder from him.

In their bedroom, he began removing his clothes. "We should pay rent we stay here so much."

"You have very good friends. None of mine would put me up like this."

"That's because you haven't been here long enough to make any. Wouldn't your friends from home put you up?"

"My roommates from college would." She snorted and flopped on the bed to kick her pants off. "I would've said a few of my classmates would, but frankly, I wouldn't trust any of them except Denali. I'm wondering how I missed Greer and Mitchel being so extreme and who else I missed. It's not like they're just a little discontent with our government, they're full-fledged crazy radical." She folded her clothes and placed them on the chair beside the bed.

Ronny's heated gaze traveled her body. Every time it was the same. Seeing her skin, feeling it, instantly aroused him. It was almost embarrassing how easily she excited him. He turned away to better concentrate on her words.

"Did they hang out together?"

"Yeah, but as far as I knew not more than they hung out with the rest of us. They didn't seem like real close friends. Greer's roommates seemed like regular guys too. They never spouted any crazy talk or acted like they hated women."

"I'm sure the FBI is watching his roommates."

"And if they're innocent that must suck."

"What did his roommates study? Computers like you guys?"

"No, Terry Wheaton studied aerospace engineering, and Ralph Mauldin studied engineering systems. Both seemed like really nice guys."

Ronny sat on the edge of the bed and sighed heavily. "How common do you suppose the name Mauldin is?"

"Why do you ask?"

"I know a Mauldin. Met him in basic. Henry Mauldin and the reason I ask is I just met an old friend from basic working in the same building as you."

Cameron inhaled sharply.

"Todd Baily seems normal. We used to go drinking together. He, Henry, me, and about sixteen other guys. I usually left right away with a girl, so I can't really say what they got up to, but it seems like a hell of a coincidence."

"Wouldn't the FBI have investigated Todd?"

"Why? They have no connection. Didn't even share a bunkhouse. It could be a coincidence. It isn't like Todd could request to work with the admiral."

"True but..." Cameron rose and grabbed his T-shirt, pulling it on as she headed for the closet and her computers.

Ronny followed her and leaned over her shoulder as she sat and began typing.

"What are you looking for?"

"When he started working with the admiral.

"He got married two years ago, and they just had a baby... he doesn't really seem like the terrorist type."

Cameron glanced at him and typed some more, flicking through screens before Ronny got a chance to really read them. After ten minutes, she turned to him and winced, pointing at the screen.

"He married Seaman Wanda Gryth and asked for a transfer here where she's stationed. Not proof, but... I wonder how they met."

"I could find out, meet him for drinks and ask." Ronny straightened and ran his hands over his head. "Jesus, I hate even thinking this."

Cameron rose and hugged him. "Could be nothing."

"Neither of us believes that."

"Will you report it?"

"Yeah, and I feel like a heel for doing so. Todd was a friend, granted not a close one, but still... And I'm going to sic the FBI on him."

"Well, if he's innocent, it's no big deal. You and I've both been investigated and it didn't hurt us."

Ronny said nothing just breathed in the scent of her skin. She flicked off her computer and led him back to the bed.

In the dark room, he held her close, his mind spinning. He fell asleep thinking of Dan's request.

The next morning, he called JT and reported.

"Cameron's right it could be nothing," JT said. "I'll report to Darmin, but meanwhile give Todd a call and go out for a drink— and be careful. In fact, take Keith with you and have Squirrel be in the bar. Don't bring Lee, he might recognize him.

Ronny felt like Judas when he made the call.

"I'm glad you called," Todd said. "I was just thinking of calling you. I heard about your brush with the sharks. It'll be nice to get out of the house." Todd chuckled. "I love my daughter, but she has a set of lungs on her."

Ronny wondered how Todd had heard about the sharks. As far as he knew that mission was classified.

As if reading his mind, Todd said, "I probably shouldn't mention anything about the sharks on an open line, I only know because I pass on the reports to the big guy. I'm sure you have some great stories. I'm kind of jealous. You're living the dream, and I'm a secretary..."

Ronny laughed. "I worked on the *Truman* chopping vegetables for six months, and it inspired me. You can always apply for SEAL training."

"As if... No way would I make it. I can barely swim, and besides, my wife would kill me."

Ronny laughed. "I'll bring my teammate Keith. He's been a SEAL longer than me and has some great stories. See ya tonight."

"Later."

Todd hung up, and Ronny turned to Cameron.

"I admit the shark thing sent a tingle down my spine. But if he were a spy why admit he peeks at the files?"

Cameron shrugged. "Cover? Admitting it makes him seem innocent."

Ronny turned away and went to the window, speaking with his back turned. "I really hate this."

She put her arms around him, resting against his back. "I'm sorry."

Her warmth comforted him. "Not your fault," he said as he clasped her hands in his, pulling her closer. He turned and lifted his shirt off her. "Much better."

She giggled and kissed him, twining her leg around his. That's all it took to fully arouse him. He lifted her, balancing her with one hand as she put her legs around his waist and grasped his shoulders. He used the other hand to guide himself into her.

Warm and wet, she welcomed him with a deep moan.

"You make everything better. I feel like I was only half living before I met you." His words made her moan again. "Make love to me, Cam." He lowered them to the floor with her on top.

Her blue eyes stared into his as she began to sway her hips slowly. His soul responded to her. She filled him with a deep need, a sensation he'd never experienced before with anyone except her. The touch of her skin on his excited him and made him want more. Not sex, but her. He wanted all of her— to belong to her completely.

His hands wandered her body, memorizing the shape and feel of her, lingering on her breasts and thighs before returning to her face and twining his fingers in her hair to press her close for a kiss. Lost in her taste, he let himself go, coming in long spurts. She jerked against him and groaned as she came, hips bucking in short spasms.

Collapsed on his chest, her relaxed weight felt exactly right. "I could hold you forever." He stroked his hands across the muscled planes of her back, resting them on her ass and pressing her against him. Her soft sound of contentment brought tears to his eyes.

He loved her so much. The thought of Dawn coming between them terrified him. It took all his courage to mention her.

"Will you speak with Dawn if I call her? I don't want to make you uncomfortable. There's no rush. You can meet her and talk in person if you'd rather." He heard himself babbling and couldn't stop. With all his soul, he wanted to make things right between them. "She graduates soon, and I planned to attend. I'd love it if you came too. You'll see she and I aren't in love. We never were, not like this."

"This is so awkward— being the other woman. I believe you, but I'm afraid you're wrong."

"No—"

"Not about how you feel, but about how she does." Cameron pushed away to see his face. "What if she wants you? What kind of person steals another woman's husband? I really hate that you belong to her." Tears filled Cameron's eyes, and she laid her head on his chest again.

"I'm so sorry. I wouldn't hurt you for the world." Ronny winced; he'd more than hate it if Cameron were married to another. Jealousy tightened his shoulders just imagining it. God, it would kill him if she wanted to remain in contact with her ex, but how could he abandon Dawn? He loved her too.

"If you never want me to see Dawn again, I won't, but let me tell her goodbye and explain. I really don't want to hurt her feelings."

"No, I can't do that. How could I take her family from her?"

The quick hard breath she took told Ronny she fought tears.

"Your family loves her; they're going to hate me. And I don't blame them, I am tearing your family apart."

"No! That isn't true at all. Dawn and I were going to divorce before you. That was always the plan. Please, Cam, trust me. My parent's will love you. Dawn will love you. If you give her a chance, you'd like her. I know she'll be a fiercely loyal friend to you, at first for my sake, but once you get to know her, she'd be a friend for your sake."

Ronny groaned and pulled her even tighter against him, making her squeak. "I hear myself saying this, and I realize how unfair it is to you. I would hate it if the tables were turned— if you wanted me to be friendly to a man you loved; an ex-lover. God, even thinking of it kills me. I wish Dawn and I had never had sex. If I could take it back, I would. At the time, it seemed so uncomplicated..."

Cameron snorted lightly. She rose and headed to the bathroom, speaking over her shoulder. Ronny sat to watch her.

"For you, I'm sure it was uncomplicated, but Dawn is a woman, and for her, I'm sure it meant more. Call her, see if she wants to meet me. If not, that's okay." She paused at the door and turned back. "I love you. We'll work something out."

Ronny laid back on the floor and threw an arm over his eyes. "Damn it." He laid there thinking a few minutes before joining Cameron in the shower.

TWENTY-SIX

---◆---

IMPRESSIVE WORK

"You're finished then?" Ronny asked as he picked up the cardboard box.

"Yep. The decoy took longer. It needs to work but also be uncopiable. If they pry it open, it will surge, destroying the interior. After one hundred uses the memory will wipe. I debated making the number of uses much smaller, but I figure every time they hand it off they'll show how it works."

"You're sure they won't be able to reverse engineer it?"

"Not from this." She tapped the box, then shrugged. "But Greer is brilliant, and if he stole my notes— then maybe... I'm working on a jammer now." She sighed and swiveled in the chair. "I hate to do it. All my work negated, but we need one in case Greer passed his work to someone else. Make sure you keep in mind it *will* work. Any radio or cell phone you use can be hacked into. Traditional jammers won't work. Nothing I know of will work. Is all they have to do is point this at you to hear what you're saying." She held up the black rectangular box and waved it. One finger tapped the screen built into the side. "They can turn it on and scan the area for signals, so it'll work even if they can't see you. Be careful. Don't even turn your radios on."

"That's impressive work, Cam."

"I had help. Denali designed the computer code and the software which decrypts. Even talking in code won't help you, the program works really well. The more you speak, the more accurate the results are."

She tapped the smaller screen above the larger one. "This screen will show where you are. Right now, it has a range of eight hundred yards. Too many radio signals will confuse it, but they need to be on different channels. I tested this in an apartment complex with over two hundred people and was able to pinpoint the senders I tracked despite televisions, radios, internet, and cells. Granted they weren't trying to confuse me and it took me a while to manually enter which signals to ignore, but I did it."

"We'll be fine, Cam."

Cameron bit her lip and looked worried. "I wish they'd send someone else. I'll never get over it if I get you guys killed. From the notebooks you recovered, I know Greer was working on this same idea, but I don't know how far he got. He stole Denali's code and for all I know her decryption program." Her eyes narrowed, and she pinched her bottom lip. "I think he was working on a way to not only locate but intercept the signal."

"Like hijack it?"

She nodded. "Nothing in his books make me thinks he succeeded, but he had notes on ideas." She threw her hands up and rose. "I still can't believe I missed his hatred towards women. His notebook is just vile. It must've killed him to hide it. Losing his grant to an eighteen-year-old girl pushed him over the edge."

So many young minds corrupted there makes me think a teacher is involved."

"Me too. I'm sure the FBI is looking into it."

Ronny glanced at his watch and rose. "I've got to run. Stay inside until I come back." He kissed her cheek and took the box she handed him containing the real scanner. Her troubled gaze followed him out.

JT met him at Admiral Reeve's office. The admiral's secretary waved them inside.

"He's expecting you."

The admiral stood at the picture window behind his desk, viewing the harbor. "Sit," he said without turning. "Agent Vargas will be joining us." He turned and opened the box, removing the scanner and setting it on his desk. "I've read Petty Officer Howard's report, and I'm impressed. The applications for this are staggering."

His secretary ushered in a man wearing a dark-blue suit. In his mid-forties, he wore his brown hair short and his chin clean shaven. Ronny thought he looked average, a faceless businessman no one would look at twice. His appearance probably suited him very well for his work.

"Hello, I'm Agent Vargas, call me John." He extended his hand to each of them as they exchanged introductions.

Ronny thought even John's voice was non-descript. He shook his hand surprised at the strong grip. John didn't appear muscular.

"Please, sit." The admiral waved at the chairs before his desk.

"Thank you, we've received the report on Todd Baily and would like to pursue that angle for two reasons. First, our profiler is concerned that if June reports the completion of the work, Michael might kill her to cover his tracks." John took a deep breath and released it on a heavy sigh. "I'm sorry. I know this is awkward. We don't wish your wife to be harmed. We'd like for you to tell your wife this afternoon that Cameron is feeling better and back at work. Maybe ask her to invite Cameron to a working dinner at your home in a few days. Then tell her you'll be occupied this evening. Give her time to meet and pass on the news. She should be perfectly safe as long as they think Cameron isn't finished."

The admiral nodded, rubbing the bridge of his nose.

John smiled briefly in acknowledgment. "What we'd really like is concrete proof of Mr. Baily's involvement. Tonight, when you meet for drinks, we want you to mention you brought this here." John tapped the box the decoy rested in. "Give a vague hint, with vague reassurance on Cameron's health and work. Find out how he met his wife if you can. So far, they both check clean. We'll give him a few days to act before we mention anything to June.

John winced and glanced at the admiral. "If you could keep June occupied for the next two days..."

"Yes, I can keep her at home for a few days. More if needed." Admiral Reeves leaned forward and tented his hands on his desk. "I want assurances if we do send my wife to meet Michael every precaution is put in place to assure her safety. My neglect left her open to this sort of manipulation. I don't want her risked."

John leaned back in his chair. "We won't use her at all if we don't have to. I'll speak to the agents guarding her, and we'll interrupt her meeting with Michael right after she mentions Cameron sent a package to your office. You can be standing by and call with an excuse that will get her home right away."

Admiral Reeves tightened his lips. "I'm not sure anything I say could get to her to leave or if she'd even answer her phone."

John held up his hands in a what can you do gesture. "We can send an operative into the room dressed as a maid. He's unlikely to kill your wife right that minute if he believes they've been seen together. But there is risk. Every time she meets him, there's risk."

The admiral spun his chair to face the window. "Every time I let her go I betray our vows as much as she. To risk her like that... My position brought this man into our lives. My neglect made it possible for him to seduce her. What chance did she have against a trained manipulator? If harm comes to her from this..."

Ronny bit his lip. He'd never considered that, thinking only June was a woman of low morals but now... Now, he felt sorry for her and the admiral. They had both betrayed the other.

John stood. "We'll do our very best to see no more harm comes to her. Your right, a lonely woman would be easy prey. I'll be in touch as soon as we learn anything." He turned to Ronny and JT. "Gentlemen, if you'll accompany me, I'll get you outfitted with recorders."

Ronny rose with JT. The admiral didn't turn from the window.

He waved a hand in the air. "Dismissed," he said softly.

TWENTY-SEVEN

OVER HIS HEAD

Todd held a beer and sat across from Ronny at a round table in the corner of the bar. A little overweight but still good-looking Todd appeared relaxed and at ease.

Keith scanned the bar and frowned. "Not many women here and most are already taken. Ahh, that one isn't, wish me luck." Keith stood and sauntered to the bar, heading to a short, blond holding a bright blue drink.

Ronny snorted, and Todd laughed as Keith slid onto the seat beside her.

"I sort of miss that." Ronny nodded towards Keith.

"Dawn never stopped you in the past."

"Dawn and I are getting a divorce. I met someone new, and she wouldn't put up with it."

"Holy crap, really?"

"Yeah. You might know her, actually. She works in

the same office."

Todd rose an eyebrow.

Ronny couldn't tell if he was faking not knowing or not.

"Petty Officer Cameron Howard."

"Really?" Todd sat back in his seat and took a big swig of beer, then leaned forward and lowered his voice. "I read the file of your last mission. I'm not supposed to, and I hardly ever peek, but I saw your name. She was with you. Were you together then?"

"That's when we got together." Ronny grinned. "We didn't talk much, but she's amazing."

"I heard she was injured."

"Yeah, but she's getting better. She's a work-a-holic." Ronny frowned and took a sip of his beer. "Actually, I'm not sure how long this will last."

"You two not hitting it off?"

Ronny grinned again. "When she can spare me the time. It's finding time that's hard. She tires easy, still some infection in her blood, and would rather work than..." Ronny took a big sip of beer before setting the almost empty glass before him and spinning it on the table idly as he spoke. "And she doesn't talk about her work. I'm starting to wonder if she's brushing me off."

"Don't see her much then?"

"I see her every day. We're staying at a buddy's house while she recovers 'cause she can't stay alone, but..." Ronny took another drink. "Meh. There's more women. Cameron is hot, and I like her and all, but sometimes I think I'm a bother for her, she's always on her laptop. Or I'm a convenience, dropping things off for the admiral as if a secretaries' files need special protection."

"She had you bring her work to the office?"

"Actually, I'm not sure. She had me bring him something in a box. Said it was important, and to give it to him, but it could've been a birthday present. Oh look, Keith struck out."

Ronny laughed as Keith returned to the table with another pitcher of beer.

"So, how'd you meet your wife?" Ronny asked, trying to act casual.

Todd blushed slightly. "The internet. Not all of us grew up next to a beautiful woman and had to search for ours."

"The internet huh?" Keith asked, sounding interested. "A dating site? I was tempted to try one but was worried they'd all be ugly, horrid, or desperate to marry."

Todd laughed. "Not a site, a chat room. A photography chat room. We had so much in common we hit it off right away."

"Weren't you worried she'd be ugly in real life? Or crazy or something?"

"Not really. If I didn't like her, I didn't have to see her again, and she lived far away so it wasn't like I'd have to go out of my way to avoid her." Todd turned the drink on the table before him. "She's a good wife."

Ronny exchanged tense glances with Keith. Todd had said it sadly.

"Well, I'll give the internet a try." Keith chuckled and stretched, his gaze scanning the room. "But honestly, the uniform works wonders. The trick is wearing it to a place with lots of single women. I accept every wedding invitation I get."

Ronny laughed. "Enrique"— he turned to Todd— "is

a teammate. He goes to dance halls, the kind that gives lessons. He swears by it."

Todd eyed him doubtfully. "Aren't the women in those places all old?"

"Most, but he says more single woman than you'd think go, and they all need partners and almost always say yes when asked to go on a date to a dance club."

"Wipe the interested look off your face," Keith said and grinned as he refilled their glasses. "What would your wife think? Besides, Enrique goes to really learn how to dance. We went to this club once..."

Ronny tuned Keith out as he told a long involved story, concentrating on Todd's reactions, but he seemed perfectly normal. He joked and laughed and never mentioned Cameron again. He brought up a few of the other guys they used to hang out with and made small talk, seemingly at ease the entire time.

Todd squinted at his watch and leaned forward as if to say something, then glanced around the room and straightened. "Well, I gotta get home." He rose and offered his hand to Keith, then slapped Ronny on the back. "Promised the wife I wouldn't stay out late. This was fun though. We should do it more often."

Ronny and Keith watched him leave. Keith meet Ronny's eyes and shrugged, then ordered another round. The two drank a while longer than split up. Neither glanced at Squirrel who sat at the bar wearing a fake beard, ball cap, and jacket with a trucker logo.

———— ◆ ————

"Well? How'd it go?" Dan asked when he entered.

Cameron glanced up from the table where she waited, an untouched coffee in front of her.

"No idea. He seemed perfectly normal."

"How'd he meet his wife?" Cameron asked.

"Chat room." Ronny sighed when she winced. "Yeah, I thought it was suspicious too. I really hope I'm wrong."

"We were invited to the admiral's for dinner in three days."

Ronny thumped into a chair. "Now I hope I'm right. I really don't want to go there and pretend all night."

Dan snickered.

The next day Todd intercepted Ronny as he headed to the range. Dark circles ringed his eyes, which darted over the parking lot. Ronny tensed, scanning him for weapons.

A sickly, fake smile on his face, Todd said a cheery, "Hello."

"Hey, man. What's up?" Without thinking about it, Ronny had taken a defensive stance. He made himself step forward and offer his hand. Something wasn't right with Todd. Tension radiated from him in waves. He appeared to be on edge, scared to death, about to do something that terrified him.

Todd winced and licked his lips. "Just wanted to see if you'd like to meet the wife, maybe come for dinner?" he said loudly. His gaze darted around, but he didn't turn his head. As he drew closer, he lowered his voice to a whisper. "We need to talk— alone— and not obvious."

"Hey, wanna see Dan shoot?" Ronny gestured with his chin towards the range.

"Yeah, that would be good." Todd sounded relieved.

The two men spoke of guns as they walked to the booth where Dan waited. Todd's gaze continued to dart about and sweat trickled down the side of his face.

"Dan, this is my friend Todd. Todd, my partner Dan.

Todd shook Dan's hand weakly and sagged against the table that held Dan's gear.

"Ron, I'm over my head here and sinking fast." He straightened and gestured at the range with one hand. "Keep shooting, I'm sure I'm being watched, and it could be anyone."

"What's going on?" Ronny handed the logbook to Todd who opened it and stared unseeing at the first page.

Dan laid on the ground before his rifle and took a shot. Ronny turned and gestured as if speaking to Dan.

"We can't help unless you tell us. Who's following you?"

"I don't know. Jesus, this is a mess. My wife and kid are in danger, and I don't know who to trust." Todd shifted and laid the book on the table, stepping closer and lowering his voice. "I did a bad thing, and now they want me to tell them what you and your girlfriend are up to. I'm not stupid. It must be linked to the attempts on her life and the admiral. God, someone shot the fucking admiral and I'm involved with that."

Ronny handed Todd the binoculars and lifted his scope to his eyes. Dan shot again.

"What did you do and who are they?" Ronny asked.

His pulse pounded, and he used the scope to scan the area, gesturing with one hand as if he described the scope's mechanisms. Of the five people in sight from where he stood no one appeared at all interested in them.

"I borrowed money and got in over my head." Fuck, this is such a fucking mess. You remember back when we were in basic my mom got sick and they let me go home a week? I thought she was going to fucking die. Well, anyway, she had cancer and dad couldn't pay the bills. Henry had a friend, a loan shark, I guess, who lent me money and my fucking dad took it to Atlantic City. He thought he could double it and pay the guy back."

Todd ran a hand through his hair and squatted behind Dan as if he were watching the shot.

Dan fired again.

"He fucking lost it all. I had no choice but to borrow more." Todd sighed hard and lowered the binoculars. "I was stupid. I knew I couldn't pay it back." He stood and placed the binoculars on the table, avoiding Ronny's eyes. "A guy came to me and offered me a way out. In return for canceling the debt, and paying Mom's bills, I would do him a favor. And it didn't seem so bad. He just wanted to know the comings and goings on base here."

"How'd you get yourself stationed here?"

"He gave me a list of names and websites. Told me to get one of them to marry me." He glanced up at Ronny and winced. "Yeah, it was a shitty thing to do, but... anyway, it doesn't matter. I did it. At first, Wanda was just business, but I fell in love with her. The guy paid for my mom's care, she's in remission now, and is all I had to do was pass on stupid information."

"Like?"

"Who came in and out of the admiral's office, schedules, Cameron's hours. What was delivered there. Nothing really classified. I knew I was fucked when I got a call right after you called me. He not only knew what we said but wanted me to go and find out everything I could. He was waiting in my living room when I got home last night. In my fucking living room with my wife and kid asleep upstairs."

Todd clenched his hands then relaxed them, rubbing them on his pants. "He's going to kill them or worse..." Tears filled Todd's eyes, and his hands began to tremble. "What do I do here, Ron? If I go to the police, they're dead. My phone is obviously tapped."

Dan squatted and gestured for Todd to kneel beside him. He pretended to show him the SR-25 he held. "Who is he?"

"I don't know. I call him Mr. Smith." Todd snorted. "My wife doesn't know I'm a lying asshole. She's a real nice girl. This is going to kill her." Todd sobbed and placed his hands over his face, then dropped them. "Fuck, I'm really going to get her killed."

"What's Mr. Smith want you to do now?"

"Steal whatever it is you brought the admiral." Todd drew in a deep shuddering breath. "They got me, and I know it. First, I spy, now steal, then what? murder? I didn't know until you called me I was involved with the attempts on Cameron's life— I swear it. All last night I tried to pretend everything was normal as if I could wish it away by not acknowledging it. But then Mr. Smith was in my fucking house..."

Ronny squatted beside them and gestured to the range. Dan laid down again and took another shot. Ronny continued to point as if he were explaining his job as he spoke. "Not that I don't want to help, but why come to me?"

"You're obviously involved in this, and a SEAL, and I hoped our friendship would matter. But please, help my wife. Get her and my daughter to safety somewhere. I'll take what I got coming, just save them."

"Okay, keep it together, man," Dan said and stood. "We'll help her— and you. The CIA is already onto you. You're right, we are involved. Mr. Smith is an Al-Jadr operative."

"Oh fuck." Todd stumbled backward into the table.

Ronny thought Todd might vomit. He swallowed convulsively. One trembling hand reached up to wipe his sweating brow while the other clutched the table.

Ronny grasped his shoulder, then threw an arm around it, pointing out at the range. Todd's face was bone white and his entire body shook.

Ronny slapped him on the back and laughed as though Todd had said something funny. "Relax, take a deep breath. We're having a nice, friendly conversation. Go to work like usual. An agent will be in touch."

"I swear to God, I had no fucking idea. I thought he was a mobster or something."

Ronny slapped his shoulder again, squeezing it hard. "Pull yourself together," he hissed through his fake smile.

Todd swallowed hard again and nodded woodenly. "How will I know your agent isn't from Mr. Smith?"

Ronny released him and began packing up the supplies on the table. "Code word little chick. Do whatever he says. Men are watching you, but they might be FBI or CIA not be from Mr. Smith."

Dan began packing his gun away. "This is almost

over. Hang tough a few more days. I wish I could think of an excuse to send your family to stay with mine, but I can't. The best I can offer is a few of my teammates watching your house."

Todd squeezed his eyes closed. "Please— Do what you can to make her safe. Mr. Smith warned me if I try to send her away, I'll never see her again."

Ronny slung the black duffle bag containing their gear over his shoulder. The three men walked back to the parking lot together. Men passed them heading to and from the range. To Ronny's eyes, all appeared normal. No one seemed to stare or take undue interest in them. "Call me later with dinner plans," Ronny said as they paused beside a group of men gathered around a coffee cart.

"If your wife wants a break from cooking, come to my house. We can cook on the grill to give the ladies a break and a chance to become acquainted," Dan offered in a loud voice. "My wife doesn't know too many people here and would love the opportunity to make more friends."

"Thanks. My wife's lived here her entire life. I'm sure she'd be happy to show yours around." Todd shook Dan's hand and offered him a sickly smile. "Call ya later, Ron."

Dan and Ronny watched him leave, then got in Dan's truck.

Ronny rotated his stiff shoulders. "Wow, didn't see that coming."

"Me either. We better report this ASAP."

TWENTY-EIGHT

— ◆ —

WHY HIS DEATH IN PARTICULAR

Dai joined Dan and Ronny in Darmin's office.

Darmin gestured them to seats before his metal desk.

Dai turned to Ronny. "You think he was on the up-and-up?"

"He convinced me. If he was faking scared and horrified, he should win an Oscar."

Darmin leaned back in his chair and cracked his knuckles. "Dan?"

"I agree. I thought the guy would faint when he realized he was working for terrorists. He's scared as shit his family is going to be killed."

A slight smile tilted Darmin's lips. "And let me guess, you offered to guard them, discreetly."

Dan shrugged sheepishly.

Dai handed Ronny a grainy color photo of two men speaking. One sat in a dark-blue ford Taurus, the other leaned in the open window. "My men are on it already. Todd's family is as safe as we can make them. We followed Mr. Smith last night. The driver is Mr. Smith. We have no ID yet on his acquaintance.

"It's Henry Mauldin's brother Tim. I met him once, six years ago, now. He's fatter and balder, but that's him," Ronny said.

Dai opened his briefcase and flipped through a folder, then frowned. "We have no record of another brother."

"I'm pretty sure he wasn't a biological brother like Ralph. This would be Henry's stepbrother from his mom's first marriage or for all I know it was utter bullshit, and he didn't really have a stepbrother." Ronny stabbed the picture on the desk with his finger. "Is all I know for sure is that this man was introduced to me as 'my brother Tim' from Henry. The guys droopy right eye is unmistakable."

Dai nodded and made a note. "We're really cleaning house with this. Mr. Smith led us to twelve new suspects already. His real name is Nadir Rafiq a Pakistan native, and he's in this country illegally." Dai glanced at his watch. "My partner, Michele, is following him as we speak. Well, her and a slew of FBI agents."

"What about Todd?"

Dai rubbed the bridge of his nose. "We're going to meet with him in an hour to go over the plan."

"What *is* the plan?" Darmin asked.

"To let him steal the decoy. The hand-off will be dangerous. More dangerous than Todd imagines, I'm sure. We're pretty sure they plan to kill him and plug that potential leak."

"Jesus," Ronny whispered.

Dai waved his hand in a placating gesture. "We'll do our best to not let that happen."

Darmin leaned forward across his desk, resting his elbows on the metal surface and tenting his fingers.

Dai winced slightly and cleared his throat. "To cement Todd's value to Mr. Smith, he needs new information they'll wish to pursue. To make Mr. Smith think they have Todd firmly in their pocket, he must commit a crime so heinous he's sure to go to prison for it if caught."

Darmin nodded as if he'd been expecting this and leaned back. "Murder."

"Yeah, we'll set up Todd to 'kill' someone during the theft. Along with the planted information, we believe that will be enough to save his life at the drop."

"And afterward?" Dan asked.

"Witness protection for him and his family. That's assuming he cooperates fully. If he doesn't cooperate, he'll be charged with treason. His wife will be still be offered witness protection though."

"Um—" Ronny ran two fingers under his collar, loosening it. "His wife is sure to be pissed when she finds out he married her for money and to spy, or are you not telling her the truth?"

"That, we haven't decided. If Todd cooperates, we could tell her he was working with us and is now in too much danger." Dai shrugged. "Frankly, it doesn't matter to me if she leaves him; he deserves it. Don't forget he was a spy. Whether he knew he was working for Al-Jadr or not, he knew he was spying. What he did to his wife was beyond shitty. He's lucky to have any way out at all."

Darmin rapped the desk with his knuckles, the

tinny sound echoing in the small room. "Which one of my men is your sacrificial goat?"

A slight smile on his face, Dai jerked his chin at Ronny. "If Mr. Smith thinks Todd is willing to kill a friend to complete his assignment it will help. Also, in their eyes, there's the added benefit of disrupting Petty Officer Howard."

Darmin's eyes narrowed." Now, why would his death in particular disrupt her?"

Sweat sprang up on Ronny's palms. Dan shifted in the seat beside him. Dai gave him an apologetic glance.

Ronny gathered his courage and spoke. "Cameron and I plan to marry once my divorce is final. Over the last two years, I've seen my wife less than thirty days. We've grown apart. We both agree we married too young and have parted amicably." He wanted to wipe his brow but didn't want to appear to be lying.

"I see," Darmin said thoughtfully. He tapped the desk with his fingertips a moment before leaning back in his chair. "Cameron is a beautiful woman and danger can be an aphrodisiac; don't let it ruin your judgment. Marriage is nothing to take lightly or discard on a whim. I expect you to behave in a manner befitting your rank."

Ronny swallowed hard.

Darmin leaned forward, his eyes intent on Ronny. "One hint of impropriety and I'll throw the book at you. Not only your career, but Petty Officer Howard's is riding on your good judgment. This is an extremely serious situation; one which your romantic urges can screw up with deadly consequences to the civilians we have sworn to protect. Tell me right now if this assignment is going to be a problem for you."

"Good to go, sir." Ronny stood rigidly at attention.

"I swear to God," Darmin said in a more relaxed tone, "if your wife comes complaining to me, you're going to be in a world of shit. Dismissed."

Dai winced sympathetically as he gestured him out the door.

TWENTY-NINE

———◆———

NOT FOR SELF, BUT FOR COUNTRY

Dai tucked the blood bag against Ronny's chest and slapped a piece of tape over it. His partner, Michele, knelt beside Ronny with her hand in his pocket, adjusting the bulb that when squeezed would burst the bag, sending an electrical charge to the small, shaped-charge to force a rubber pellet through his shirt, mimicking a bullet hole.

"One short, sharp squeeze," Michele said as she straightened. She carefully placed the wires against his chest and taped them down. "Let Todd grab your gun. Keep both hands raised and act as if you think he's joking. Stay in line of sight of the left-hand windows."

Dai handed him his shirt as Michele stepped back. "Todd shouldn't reach for the gun until you place the package on the desk, but if he goes for it early, let him take it. Make no resistance until he shoots you. Make sure you touch him with your bloody hand. We aren't sure if they'll watch, bug him, or just question him after, and we want them to see evidence of his dedication."

Michele straightened his collar and ran her hand lightly over his chest. "Looks good. No bulge or wrinkles, but don't bump it with the package. Remember to lay motionless on the floor. I'll be one of the paramedics sent in. It can be claustrophobic as hell constrained in a body-bag but hang tight, and as soon as we're in the ambulance I'll release you. It might take longer than you'd like because we'll be going slow enough to give everyone a good view."

"Sounds... awful." Ronny picked up the cardboard box containing the sabotaged listening device.

"Todd's already reported the box you delivered earlier was retrieved and returned to Cameron. He'll greet you right inside the door and call you to his office on a pretext. Remember your friends with no suspicion he's anything else. Give him a realistic greeting. And don't get him so bloody it'll be noticed on his way out. We need Mr. Smith to think he got away clean."

"Right, mention Cameron's new work, be friendly, die quietly, got it."

Dai stifled a laugh. Michele smiled, transforming her businesslike expression into a thing of beauty. Ronny gazed after her as she began packing up her supplies. A knowing grin on his face, Dai put an arm around Ronny's shoulder and led him from the room.

"She doesn't even know she does it," he whispered, chuckling when Ronny flushed. "Good thing she seldom smiles like that on the job. Her hard as nails expression doesn't have quite the same devastating effect."

"You just don't expect it..."

Dai glanced back at the closed door. "Michele has hidden depths alright. You never met a more competent woman in your life." His glance flitted to Cameron who waited beside the front door. "Or maybe you have," he finished softly.

Ronny met Cameron's eyes and smiled, aiming for reassuring, but coming off lustful. She did nothing except return his smile, but it felt like she yelled I love you. Her eyes continued to yell warnings at him; be careful, come back to me. He hoped his answered in a similar manner. More than anything, he wanted to hug her and feel her warm lips on his, but Darmin stood five feet away, and he was still married to Dawn.

"Loud and clear, but not obvious," Dai said as he stepped away from the front door.

Ronny handed Cameron the package, opened the front door, and stepped out into the grass one foot to the right of the doorway.

"Will you be here when I get back?" He tried to project his voice without seeming too. The FBI had arrested a loiterer with a parabolic mic yesterday. Dai had told him they knew the house was being watched from the upstairs windows of a house half a mile away. The only clear angle they would have on the front door was exactly where Ronny stood in the grass.

Sweat beaded his brow. A sniper could take him out with ease from half a mile. He forced himself to continue in a calm, light voice. "You're working too hard." He took the box from her and tucked it carefully under his arm. "I'll drop this off and bring us something back."

"Something quick, I really want to get started on my next project."

"Cam... your work is important and all, but what about me?" Without waiting for her reply, he strode to his borrowed truck and drove away.

This was the tricky part. Mr. Smith might've decided to take the box in transit, not relying on Todd's ability to steal it. The gun on his waist contained blanks. The twenty-two on his ankle held a full clip though, and agents surrounded him in unmarked cars. His shoulders remained tense the entire drive across the bridge to San Diego Base. He didn't have to fake his glower as he entered the admiral's building.

"Hey, Ron, got a sec," Todd called as he entered.

"Not really. My girl's got me running errands again." He headed to Todd instead of the stairs still complaining. "I thought she'd have more time now that's she's finished, but she has less. Some new brilliant idea she just has to work on before she forgets it. Maybe when she moves into her new office upstairs things will calm down."

Ronny ran a hand through his hair and plopped the package on the desk. He perched on the edge, swinging one leg, staring directly out the left-hand windows. "I keep giving her all these chances, and she keeps putting me off. I get it, her work is important. She's designing some kind of radio interceptor now that this is finished"— he flicked the package beside him with his finger— "but what about me?"

Todd leaned forward as if he were going to open a desk drawer and instead grabbed the forty-five on Ronny's waist.

"What the hell are you doing?" Ronny straightened and held his hands out.

"Sorry, Ron." Todd grabbed his jacket off the seat back and shot through it. The gun still made a thunderous noise in the confined space.

Ronny squeezed the bulb in his pocket and clutched his chest. He staggered forward two steps and placed his bloody hand on Todd's chest before sliding to his knees and letting himself flop to his face on the floor. Todd dropped the gun and ran into the adjoining office.

Ronny waited. A man stuck his head in the office and exclaimed. Dai ran in wearing a uniform and crouched beside him. He made a show of feeling for his pulse.

"Call a medic and the police, he's been shot. Dai flipped him over and pretend to give him CPR while keeping the growing spectators back.

A few minutes passed with Ronny laying unmoving on the floor before he heard sirens.

MP's arrived and began taking pictures. Ronny assumed they were fakes as none touched him or performed any sort of measurements. They shooed the crowd back, allowing the paramedics in. He did his best to act like a corpse as Michele and another man loaded him into the body bag and onto the stretcher.

It felt like forever until Michele released him from the bag.

"Good job. Our teams on Todd report he got away clean. We picked up two cars following him that followed you here. I almost hate to remove Todd; he's bringing the rats out of the woodwork so well for us."

She handed Ronny a t-shirt, jeans, and a blue

zippered sweatshirt with the word Yankee's emblazoned across the back. From a medical bag, she removed a blond wig and a blue ball cap. Last, she handed him a windbreaker with the word 'paramedic' on it. He kicked off his boots and stripped, using his ruined shirt to wipe the fake blood from his hand. Once he had the jeans on, he ripped the tapped blood bag off his chest.

"Put the windbreaker on. Step out after the hospital crew takes the stretcher. Remove the jacket and put the sweatshirt on, wave and head to employee parking. Dai will pick you up and take you to your team. And good luck."

Ronny shook her hand.

Her partner climbed into the body bag and they zipped it up. The siren stopped as they entered the hospital zone. Michele opened the rear doors and stepped out. Two men wearing hospital scrubs helped her remove the stretcher.

Ronny did as he was told, stepped out, took off his jacket, and put on his sweatshirt. He waved to Michele as she entered the hospital and headed to employee parking.

Nothing and no one seemed the least bit suspicious. Dai, disguised as a balding old man greeted him with a mumbled complaint on missing Judge Judy to pick up his sorry ass. He continued to mutter complaints in a whiny tone until they were in the car.

Once on the highway, he resumed speaking normally.

"Todd has made contact. Mr. Smith seems pleased with the information he passed on. He told Todd to sit tight, and they'd get him out if it looked like he was going to be charged with murder."

"Disappear him, you mean," Ronny said sourly.

"Actually, they might try to smuggle him away. A man who will kill for a cause might be useful to them and not in a way he'd like. Todd's proven he isn't above murder and will do anything to save his family. He'd make a great suicide bomber, wouldn't he?"

"I really hate these people."

"Me and you both. Luckily, they're really aren't that many people willing to kill innocent strangers. Of course, the few nuts that do cause a lot of harm."

"That's why we get the big bucks."

Dai laughed until tears ran from the corners of his eyes.

Ronny grinned at him.

"Not for self but for country," Dai said softly when he finally stopped laughing.

The two men bumped fists.

THIRTY

---◆---

MAKE YOUR ISLAND DREAMS COME TRUE

Ronny peered over Cameron's shoulder at the computer before her. An aerial view of the city shifted and spun before steadying and centering on a glowing, green dot.

"They have the decoy, and it's moving." Cameron tapped the screen with a fingertip. "Not headed to an airport on this route. If I had to guess, I'd say they're headed to Harbor Island unless they have a safe house nearby and an expert waiting."

Ronny glanced down at his fatigues and grimaced. He hated fighting wet. On his right, Lee stretched, first his arms then his legs before rotating his neck. Squirrel sat on his left, leaning over to see the screen too. Across from him, JT and Dan spoke quietly. Reminded, Ronny doublechecked his headset.

Cameron peered over her shoulder. "Remember, they can hear you on that." She nodded towards the radio.

"Yep, we're good." He wanted to kiss her, but he was working now.

She smiled and laid two fingers against her lips for a moment before turning away. The small gesture made Ronny's heart beat faster. Not that she wanted to kiss him too, but that she understood him so well. He made a silent promise to himself that he'd be to her what she was to him— everything.

"They're testing it again," she said as she tapped on her computer screen.

Her intent tone turned his attention to the screen before her.

Agent Vargas glanced up from his cell phone. "Are you keeping track?"

Cameron tapped the screen again, and another window opened. "I'm sending the info to Admiral Reeves and your office. So far, they've tested twelve times, and it appears random, but I sent the frequencies and cell numbers on." She turned to face John. "Get it back intact if you can. I have it recording them but can't transmit that data without them maybe finding the frequency." She turned back to her screen, then leaned forward to speak to Keith who drove the van. "Can you get a bit closer? I'm cutting in and out here."

Cameron was using her real scanner to follow the thieves and copy their transmissions. The device needed to be close though. A screen clipped to the dashboard showed Cameron's screen to Keith so he could follow. Cameron's stolen device was a block over and half a block down.

"I think they're headed for the highway, Keith,"

Cameron said. "Can you get in front of them? John, do your agents have them in sight if we lose them?"

"Yes, we're tracking by satellite and have a helicopter ready to go."

Cameron nodded and returned to staring intently at her screen.

"Cam, what if they find your transmission?" Ronny asked.

"It won't tell them much, just that a radio signal is near. I'm not sending; I'm receiving. They could backtrack to me, but why would they? Besides, I'll see my frequency come up on their display and can just turn mine off."

Ronny nodded and settled back into his seat. Two benches lined the interior of the van. Cameron sat at a small desk bolted to the floor in the center of the van. Mirrored windows on the sides, front, and back of the van provided privacy but allowed her scanner an unobstructed path.

Dan glanced at him, then Cameron, and gave him a reassuring nod. Ronny's shoulders relaxed a fraction; his team had his back. He closed his eyes and leaned on the wall behind him. This could take a while.

He dozed off. When he woke, the van wasn't moving, and John stood behind Cameron, leaning over her shoulder, speaking in a soft voice.

"Yes, then just enter the frequency here," Cameron said.

"I got this. Go take a break," John slid into her seat as she stood.

Ronny glanced at his watch. Two hours had passed. Half his teammates slept against the walls. Cameron stretched as much as she could in the low-ceilinged van, bending side-to-side and rotating her hips before heading to the cooler beside the back door of the van. She took a soda and offered one to John who absently shook his head. Keith accepted one. Ronny declined, taking a sip from her can and handing it back.

"I couldn't do surveillance. This cramped room would get to me. I've been here less than five hours, and I feel like the walls are closing in," Cameron said.

Ronny rose and rubbed her shoulders, having to stoop to avoid hitting his head on the ceiling.

"Hear anything good?"

"Nope, they're still targeting random frequencies. They're up to thirty-nine uses. At this rate, they'll hit a hundred within eight hours."

John turned to her. "How about if we scan them? Will we lose them if we change the channel?"

"No. I can input it manually." Cameron returned to her chair and put on a headset. "We take a chance they notice what I'm doing, but the chance is small if I check frequently instead of leaving it on their channel."

"Do it," John said and leaned closer to watch her work.

She spoke in a low voice explaining what she was doing, pointing to the numbers and graphs that appeared on her screen as she spoke. John nodded comprehension. Ronny followed along but was soon lost. He understood the mechanics but not the science. John appeared to understand both.

Deep wrinkles appeared on Ronny's brow. Cameron was way smarter than he. Before he could get too upset, she turned to him, grinned and hit a switch making her headphones audible.

"Meet us at the dock. We'll wait at sea. Bring the money, and you can take it with you. Otherwise, your 'expert' will have to tag along." The words had a robotic quality but were perfectly understandable.

"Spoken in Urdu," Cameron said and pointed at the screen. I can't prove it's our guys, but it seems—"

She cut off as a man spoke again to someone else, this time in English.

"Meet us at the ship. It's going down in a few hours."

"Want me to bring the crew?"

"Yeah, the scanner works. This shit is awesome. We're going to make a fucking fortune."

"And Greer's notes?"

Agent Vargas leaned forward.

"No, we keep them. No one knows we got 'um. Give us some time, and we'll figure out a way to contact him."

"Good luck with that," Agent Vargas muttered.

JT stifled a laugh with his fist.

"Did you call everyone?" the man on the radio asked.

"Everyone that's got the dough. Ralph can make us copies while we line up other buyers. He isn't comfortable with us, so let him meet with Mr. Smith. Keep him happy, money, drugs, girls— whatever he wants. Nothing radical near him; we don't want to scare him away."

"Easier to chain his ass to a wall and make him work."

"If we have to, but let's do it this way first and get his best efforts. It's not like the kind of skilled people we need are growing on trees."

"Speaking of that, how's recruitment coming?"

"Slow. The feds are all over the fucking place, and I have to lay low. It'll die down, and they'll move on. Next semester there's a few possibilities entering as freshman. I'll get myself assigned as their advisor. Get me some younger girls. The ones I've got are getting too old. I can keep Jenya to break them in. Move the rest up. They did a great job. Make sure the others see we reward them good. Maybe Rafiq can use them out west as perks there."

"You're going to Hell," the other man said and chuckled.

"Neither of us believe in that bullshit. I'm fucking going to the Cayman Islands and retiring with a drink in my hand and a girl on each arm."

"I hear that. See ya tonight."

The line went dead

Cameron replaced the headphones. The screen before her flickered as she sampled frequencies, listening to small tidbits of conversation before going on to the next one.

JT peered over Cameron's shoulder. "What's the legal status of this? Do we need a warrant to use it?"

She rocked her hand side-to-side "It's a gray area. We aren't entering properties just gathering airwaves right out in public. A case could be made we're violating civil rights, but a case could be made it's in the public domain. Because this scanner is secret and under development, we have more— ah— leeway."

"Leeway," JT repeated and snickered.

"Movement," Cameron warned.

Keith placed his soda can in the cup holder and started the engine.

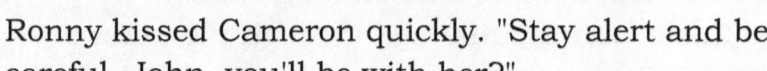

"I lost them, but we know where they're going. Head to the marina," Cameron said.

Ronny kissed Cameron quickly. "Stay alert and be careful. John, you'll be with her?"

"Yes, and I have back-up coming."

Cameron grabbed his bullet-proof vest by the neck band and shook it. "You be careful too."

He hesitated at the door. He wanted to really kiss her, to feel her lithe curves against him, to smell her skin and feel her breath on his cheek.

She lifted two fingers and rested them on her lips, brilliant blue eyes shining with love. He touched his pointer finger to his lips, gave her a jerky nod, and ran after his team.

A Coast Guard boat waited. Already aboard, Schrowder's team had two black rafts inflated and ready to go. While JT and Schrowder spoke, Benson joined Dan and Ronny and bumped fists. Camo paint covered his face, making his crooked teeth very visible as he grinned.

"Neilson and Pritchard have their groups standing by. Darmin has two Coast Guard cutters on the way too." Benson leaned closer and lowered his voice. "The kids on this boat look like they should be in school."

Ronny glanced around and grinned. Benson wasn't wrong. The Coast Guard crew stared at them with wide eyes.

Dan shrugged. "Maybe we got a training ship. JT asked for the closest one." He hefted his rifle and sighed unhappily, then shrugged again. "Makes me all antsy when no one has my team's back."

Benson slapped his shoulder and laughed. "Our

sniper says the same thing. He hates leaving the big gun behind too." He nodded towards the SCAR in Dan's hands. "You can shoot that thing, right?"

Dan snorted, making Benson laugh again.

The Coast Guard cutter slid through the water at forty knots. Cool sea air caressed Ronny's cheeks. Rubber rafts tied to the aft rail flapped in the breeze. Ronny wondered how the captain even knew where they were going. Without radio communications, they traveled the sea blind.

A red and white flicker in the sky drew his eyes. A helicopter approached. Soon the deep thwap of the rotors could be heard over the boat engines. The cutter coasted to stop, rolling along the gentle swell of the ocean. The helicopter circled, sending up a light spray of seawater. It hovered above them, and a man wearing black armor rappelled to the boat, dropping the last five feet and landing easily on the swaying deck. The helicopter peeled away.

"Dai," JT greeted him with a smile.

Lee grasped his brother's shoulder and squeezed.

"Brought you the intel. Coordinates for your skipper and pictures for you." As Dai spoke, he handed a plastic folder to JT.

The men crowded close and passed around the pictures.

"Sync your watch with mine. We'll be transmitting any new information we receive in thirty-second bursts every twelve minutes. Cycle the channels, starting at twenty-two. Once you engage, your free to use the radio, but keep in mind they could hear it." Dai shrugged one shoulder. "It isn't likely they'll leave an active listener at that point as all men aboard will be trying to repel you."

"Do we have a count?" Schrowder asked.

"Six confirmed men on board. The pictures there." He tapped the folder in JT's hand. "But there might be more below deck."

Schrowder rose a bushy eyebrow. "Two SEAL teams for six men?"

"We want them alive if possible, and we expect another ship to be arriving with an unknown number of assailants. Our profiler assures us they won't surrender. If we want them, we got to take them hard and fast." Dai turned to JT. "Your team's priority is the retrieval of the box and any notes they have regarding it or anything else they might be working on. If the box or notes can't be retrieved, then ensure its complete destruction. If at all possible, get us pics of the notes at least, but we really want them."

"Yes, sir," JT said.

Dai slapped Lee's shoulder. "Watch your back, bro." He ran over to the captain who waited, and the two men headed to the bridge.

Ronny's gaze trailed them, noting the dried blood on the sleeve of Dai's black clothing.

"I bet he has interesting stories to tell," he mused.

Lee stepped forward, peering after his brother. "We never hear the good stuff, just office stories. Dai was a SEAL before he retired to work for the CIA."

"You plan on doing that too?" Keith asked.

Lee shrugged. "Maybe, but not for years. Dai says this job is great training for his, but he misses his team. He mostly works alone or with a partner."

"You ever meet his partner?" Ronny asked, thinking of Michele's blinding smile.

"Once." Lee laughed. "She scared the crap out of me."

Ronny rose a questioning eyebrow. Beside him, Keith snickered.

Lee gave a barely perceptible shrug. "It's a long story. Keep in mind, Dai is thirteen years older than me. I met her when I was seventeen."

"I'm intrigued," Ronny said, meaning it. "After this, we're going for drinks and you're telling all."

"I'm in," Keith said as Lee nodded agreement.

———————◆———————

The raft ran on a quiet motor, but they weren't using it. They used the oars and rowed toward the ship, a barely discernable darker spot on the horizon. Occasionally, a flicker of light gave the position of the boat away more clearly. Schrowder's team would be entering from the other side in the same manner. At half a mile out, SEAL Team Nine stopped rowing and put their flippers on.

Cool water closed over Ronny's head as he slid over the side of the boat. His rifle rested between the air tanks on his back. A black bag clipped to his belt held his tools and a tracker. Dan carried one too. They'd place the tracker on the boat before engaging to ensure the boat wouldn't be lost from sight.

The swim to the boat was accomplished in minutes. Ronny placed his tracker on the hull. Inert, the small box wouldn't activate until Dai triggered it. If the men aboard were messing with the stolen scanner, there was too much chance it would pick up an active signal.

Short strokes from his flippered feet brought him to the anchor chain where he attached his air tank, keeping the regulator in his mouth and treading water to remain in place while the rest of his team arrived and took position. Too dark and murky to see far, Ronny peered hard through his goggles trying to determine if everyone had arrived. Keith tapped his shoulder and pointed to himself then upward and held up three fingers.

Ronny tapped the man beneath him and repeated the gestures holding up four fingers. A minute later, the man beneath him signaled with ten fingers. Ronny tensed. All were here and ready to go. He waited until Keith released his regulator and swam away before doing the same. The men beneath him would take their positions around the boat after he left.

He joined Keith and Lee at his assigned spot at the prow. A narrow ledge edged with a metal railing surrounded the ship. The rail didn't cover the stern of the boat, which set lower in the water. A small deck floated off the back of the boat, intended to be used for fishing or launching smaller rafts or ease of swimming. Beneath it, four SEALS waited to board.

He and Keith boosted Lee to the bottom rail at the prow of the ship. Once aboard, Lee attached a rope, the small click of the carabiner sounding like a gunshot to Ronny, and disappeared from sight.

Keith swarmed up the rope. Ronny followed. His heart beat fast until he was aboard with his gun in hand. Boarding was the tricky part. If one of their targets happened to be standing in the pilothouse looking out, they would lose the element of surprise.

Already atop the pilothouse, Lee signaled he saw four men. He disappeared for a moment, then reappeared signaling one man approached, carrying a rifle.

Ronny crouched as low as he could get against the pilothouse wall and laid his gun on the decking at his feet.

Behind him, Keith stood with his weapon pointed.

As the man rounded the corner, Ronny surged upward, knocking the man's gun to the side and using his momentum to push him into the side of the boat hard. Before he could yell, Ronny had him in a headlock, braced with his arm across the man's throat, using his weight to keep him pressed against the side of the boat and silent, trusting Keith would get the gun away from him before he could be shot.

The man jerked and gagged, his movement cutting of his air. He clawed at Ronny, doing no damage to the thick neoprene of Ronny's diving suit. In seconds, Keith had him gagged and tied to the rail with zip-ties. The man continued to struggle, making a deep grunting noise behind the gag.

Lee signaled two men coming, one on each side. Keith and Ronny placed their backs to the wall and waited.

Ronny's guy arrived first. He smacked him hard in the face with the butt of his rifle. His target groaned and rose his hand as bone crunched and blood spurted.

Ronny continued the movement forward, using the rifle to slap the rising hand away, then dropping his gun and grabbing the man by the arm holding the rifle and yanking hard.

"Fuck," the man muttered, slurring the word through blood and broken teeth.

Behind Ronny, the sound of a struggle finished

with a gurgling scream.

The boat rocked as the four SEALS at the stern boarded.

"Intruders!" an accented voice cried out.

Gunfire ripped the still, night air.

Ronny concentrated on his target, forcing him to the floor and twisting his arm hard and high behind his back, falling forward to land on his knees on his target's back.

"Me," Keith said and reached past him to tie the man's hands.

"Got it, thanks," Ronny said and leaned on his target's neck with his knee before fumbling for the zip-ties in the bag hanging at his waist. Keith slapped his shoulder and ran around the corner. Ronny tied his captive to the rail, hands, elbows, knees, and feet. He didn't bother to gag him. Between the yelling and gunshots, it would be a waste of time. He grabbed up the gun he'd dropped and ran after Keith.

Tom and Squirrel had two men pinned on the ground and were tieing them with Keith's help.

"Go." Tom gestured to the cabin where sounds of a struggle emerged.

Ronny ran down the four stairs with his gun in his hands. JT rolled on the ground with a fat black man. Dan was patting down a skinny middle-eastern man he held against the wall.

"Company inc," Lee called." Move your asses.

Ronny smacked JT's assailant on the head with his rifle, not hard enough to kill, but hard enough to bounce his head from the deck. He grabbed the man's feet and tied them using three zip-ties, one around each ankle, then one holding them together; he did the same at his knees. By the time he reached the man's elbows, JT had him gagged and went to help Dan.

"My guy isn't gagged," Ronny called.

"On it," Tom called back. Squirrel entered with a captive slung over his shoulder and dropped him on the bound man at Ronny's feet. Keith followed with another.

"ETA four minutes," Lee warned as he brought another tied man in and dropped him.

Ronny ran from the room and dropped over the side of the boat. He grabbed his air tank and shrugged it on. Keith appeared and slipped his tank on his back. Lee would be doing the same.

On deck above them, Squirrel would be dressing in one of their captives clothing. Ronny swam to the north and waited. Beside him, Keith and Lee tread water. He could barely make out the bigger group of seven SEALs fifteen feet away, treading water three feet below the surface, waiting for the ship to arrive.

The sea darkened. Above Ronny, a boat slid through the water, blocking the weak starlight.

Ronny glanced at his watch and flicked his radio up seven channels, then started counting down the seconds to turn it on.

"Proceed," JT said over the radio.

Ronny flicked the channel three up to their usual channel and began swimming for the prow of the ship. This time, he and Keith held Lee up while Lee attached a rope for them to climb. This boat was much smaller. As soon as they showed themselves, they'd be seen and might be felt as they boarded. Neither a wheel house nor interior space blocked men from view. Only thin glass and a flimsy cloth-covered roof separated the driver from the elements.

From the corner of his eye, Ronny saw Benson holding a teammate up to attach a rope.

Over his head, a man shouted. "Toss a rope, asshole, and where the hell is everyone?"

"Below," Squirrel called back. "Playing with the scanner. You bring the cash?"

"Who the fuck are you, anyway? I don't remember you?"

"Engage," JT ordered.

Before he finished speaking, Lee surged over the side with a boost from Ronny and Keith. Keith grasped the rope and pulled himself up.

"Fuck, it's a trap!" someone yelled, then screamed as a shot rang out. Another single shot sounded followed by a short riff of automatic gunfire ending in a shrill scream.

By the time Ronny got on deck, it was all over.

"Clear," Dan said over his headset.

Ronny glanced at the other boat and spotted Dan laying on the roof.

"Dai, we have both boats secured and have retrieved the box intact. Only two casualties, the rest are ready for you," JT said.

"Copy that. Good work, guys," Dai said. "John and Petty Officer Howard are in route to your position and will likely arrive before me. Prepare our prisoners for transport; I'll be arriving in thirty minutes."

Ronny helped pat the men down and secure them for transport, letting the swears and threats slip by unheeded.

His attention sharpened when one of the men mentioned Cameron by name.

"Say that again." Ronny squatted before the bound man and glared.

"We won't fucking miss next time." Michael glared at him through an eye rapidly swelling shut.

"By next time do you mean the fifth times the charm, or do you need like a hundred, and how they hell can you manage even one from Gitmo?"

"Fuck you, asshole! Gitmo? For fucking what? Taking a boat out at night?"

"Has it occurred to you the scanner works?"

Michael pursed his lips, then whitened.

"Not fucking admissible—"

"I said Gitmo, not court. You're a fucking terrorist, and we're going to make your island dream come true." Ronny glanced around with exaggerated motions. "This here is still America. In America, terrorists who blow up buildings get sent away— forever." He sat back on his heels and grinned. "But maybe if you tell everything you know quick enough they'll let you go before your old and gray." Ronny shrugged and rose, kicking Michael lightly in the foot. "Although in your case— an admiral's wife an all...The boys at Gitmo are sure to treat you with special care and attention." He laughed when Michael flinched.

The rumble of an approaching helicopter interrupted him. He lifted his his hands to shade his eyes from the spray and watched Dan help Cameron from a harness. John slid down the line and dropped to the deck. He and Cameron disappeared inside the cabin.

The small boat rocked as the helicopter dipped and turned above them before heading back to shore.

Ronny turned back to Michael. "I don't see any way

out of this for you. For any of you. While you're here with no way to warn them, agents are following up on all the leads the scanner provided. I expected them to have everyone arrested within the month. We'll fucking have to add on to Gitmo to make room for all Rafiq's men never mind Jenya and the girls."

The tied men exchanged uneasy glances. Michael clamped his lips so hard they whitened. Ronny shrugged. "Deals will likely be offered for the first to cooperate, the rest of you can look forward to a lifetime of island living." He grinned and waved as he turned to the rail of the boat.

THIRTY-ONE

GRADUATION

"Dawn Mitland," the announcer called.

Ronny winced and clutched Cameron's hand tighter as Dawn walked across the stage to accept her diploma.

Cameron turned to him. "It's okay that you love her. I see how she looks at Tom."

On stage, Dawn waved her diploma at them, her eyes on Tom.

"I like her." Cameron kissed him, her lips soft and warm. "We can be a family," she whispered. "I trust you, and I always wanted a sister."

Ronny's heart jumped.

"Let's go visit your parents after this and tell them we're getting married."

"Yeah?" he sounded breathless to his own ears as if the happiness that filled him at her words left no room for air.

"Yeah. I'll be the second Mrs. Ronald Mitland."

"You'll be the only one who ever mattered." Ronny closed his eyes and kissed her.

The crowd cheering and clapping for the graduates as they stood and threw their caps in the air brought him out of the daze her kiss induced. It felt like the world celebrated with him.

"We're going to be so happy together," he promised her. "I'm so glad you decided to trust me."

"Sometimes you just gotta take the shot."

He kissed her again, his soul cheering with the crowd.

THE END

About the Author

C. M. Conney lives and works on the family farm in New England alongside her husband and two grown children. She loves animals and owns more than she'd like to admit. Most days, when she isn't baking or planting, she spends her time writing. An avid reader since childhood, she appreciates work in all genres and likes to mix it up a bit in her own work.

UPCOMING BOOK BY
C. M. CONNEY

Al-Jadr isn't finished yet. Alfarsi might be captured, but that doesn't stop the terrorists from hatching a plan to get him back and finish the work Cameron started. With Greer's stolen notes and a ruthless attitude, they get schooled in:

Ms. DENALI
Not Your Typical Teacher

When Al-Jadr attacks Olympus, the private school where language expert Denali works, she knows they're lying when they say no one will be hurt.

Determined to save the children in her care, she attacks with the only weapon she has— her bare hands.

Joined by Ryan Graham, the first police officer on the scene, the two give the terrorists more than they bargained for.

You can find out more about
C. M. Conney's books on her
Amazon Author Page
Or at Acelyonbooks.com